Though she knew it was completely selfish, she half hoped they would, too. It would make her life so much easier if Jack would just go back to Kansas City.

It wasn't just that his arrival had set all the old emotions bubbling. She was a strong woman, and she could handle a little leftover yearning and angst. She had an old scar on her knee that hurt sometimes, too. She took an aspirin and went on with her life.

No, the serious issue was Colin. How long could she keep Jack from running into the boy? And once he saw him, once he saw an eleven-year-old kid with curly black hair and eyes the color she had always called *Killian blue*...

Nora wondered, sometimes, what Jack's brother thought when he looked at Colin. At first she'd been afraid that he might tell Jack, but that fear had subsided little by little, as the years passed without incident. She always had her story ready, though. The whirlwind romance in Cornwall, the black-haired charmer who had broken her heart.

But no one had ever asked.

Still, if Jack saw Colin, how long would it be before he put the whole picture together? About five minutes?

And then what would he do?

Dear Reader,

I love Christmas so much it's become a joke in my family. When I was six, my uncle came to our house and asked my dad incredulously, "Is Kathleen really out on the porch playing *Christmas* music?" It was July.

Maybe I began loving the season because my parents filled our living room with marvelous presents—life-size dolls, dollhouses with real electric lights and stuffed turtles and crocodiles the size of armchairs. But I still love it, even though I have to do the shopping myself, and the cooking, and the cleaning…and the dreaded opening of the bills in January.

Christmas has everything. It has lilting, emotional music—can anyone listen to Bing Crosby sing "O Holy Night" without tearing up? It has color—what's more visually joyous than a whole neighborhood twinkling with lights? It has great food—when else can you stuff yourself, from the morning's pumpkin muffins to the late-night reheated pecan pie, without feeling guilty? It has family, friends and time off from work. It has cherished rituals that wind like golden threads through our lives, connecting great-grandparents to the generations they'll never see.

And it has that most beautiful of all things: Hope. At Christmas we believe in fresh starts, in second chances. In the promise of angels and the return of innocence. Christmas seemed like the perfect season for Nora Carson and Jack Killian to find each other again, after twelve long years apart. They have many problems to overcome—betrayals, broken hearts and terrible secrets. But the magic of Christmas, surely, is enough to overcome all that. I hope you enjoy their story.

And remember…there really is no law that says you can't play carols in July!

Warmly,

Kathleen

CHRISTMAS IN HAWTHORN BAY

Kathleen O'Brien

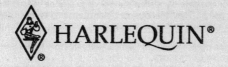

TORONTO • NEW YORK • LONDON
AMSTERDAM • PARIS • SYDNEY • HAMBURG
STOCKHOLM • ATHENS • TOKYO • MILAN • MADRID
PRAGUE • WARSAW • BUDAPEST • AUCKLAND

ISBN-13: 978-0-373-71382-0
ISBN-10:   0-373-71382-7

CHRISTMAS IN HAWTHORN BAY

www.eHarlequin.com

Printed in U.S.A.

ABOUT THE AUTHOR

Four-time finalist for the Romance Writers of America's RITA® Award, Kathleen is the author of more than twenty novels for Harlequin Books. After a short career as a television critic and feature writer, Kathleen traded in journalism for fiction— and the chance to be a stay-at-home mother. A native Floridian, she and her husband live just outside Orlando, only a few miles from their grown children.

Books by Kathleen O'Brien

HARLEQUIN SUPERROMANCE

HARLEQUIN SINGLE TITLE

SIGNATURE SELECT

CHAPTER ONE

NORA CARSON HAD ALWAYS found it hard to say no to Maggie, even when she knew that her bullheaded best friend was being stupid. Though Nora, at nineteen, was only three months older than Maggie, the younger girl had a way of making Nora's common sense sound pathetically boring.

And if making Nora feel like a fuddy-duddy didn't work, Maggie had big sad eyes and a killer pout, a little-girl-lost look that turned Nora—and just about everyone else—straight to mush.

This late-autumn Saturday, Maggie's nineteenth birthday, was no exception. Maggie, who was eight months pregnant, woke up with a hankering to go sailing. Nora knew it was a rotten idea, and so did Dr. Ethan Jacobs, the young obstetrician who had begun as Maggie's doctor when they'd arrived in town three months ago—and ended up more like a love slave with a stethoscope.

But neither of them could resist Maggie in a Mood.

So here they were, halfway to nowhere, with the Maine coast receding as Ethan's sails filled with crisp, clean wind. The cooler at their feet bulged with fried chicken, egg-salad sandwiches and bottled water. Ethan had caved in to Maggie's pressure first, and admitted that he knew a tiny island Maggie would love. Just a couple of miles wide, it had everything, he said—a green forest, a cliff, a small white waterfall.

Best of all, it was completely uninhabited. The perfect place to make the world go away for an afternoon.

They'd been on Ethan's tiny day sailer for almost an hour—the island was about ten miles offshore—when suddenly Maggie hopped up onto her cushioned seat and let out an exhilarated squeal.

"This is the best birthday *ever!* Oh, my God, I *love* this day!"

Nora, who was sitting at the back of the boat, couldn't help smiling. Maggie's spiky brown hair stood straight up in the wind, and her pregnant stomach looked as rounded and full of energetic purpose as the sails above her.

Maggie's moods were always infectious. If she was depressed, everyone around her suffered. But if she was happy…

"And I love *you!*" Maggie climbed down and wrapped Nora in a bear hug. She turned to Ethan, who was angling the tiller, and, taking his face in her hands, covered his parted lips with a loud, smacking kiss. "And you, my dashing seafarer!"

Then she whirled away, and, with a contented sigh, leaned over to drag her fingers in the green current that rushed along the side of the boat.

Nora caught Ethan's gaze. Behind his wire-rimmed glasses, he looked stunned, as if he'd never been this close to anything as dazzling as Maggie. The sails began to luff, as Ethan forgot to steer, but he corrected the mistake and shrugged sheepishly, his cheeks pink.

Just last night, he had confessed to Nora that he was in love with Maggie. When Ethan had finished rubbing Maggie's feet, which had been sore after a long day waiting tables at the lobster shack, she had stumbled off to bed, leaving Nora and Ethan alone together.

He had flushed the entire time he spoke. He knew it was inappropriate, he said, given that Maggie was his patient, but he couldn't help it. She'd made her way into his blood, and he was going to ask her to marry him.

What did Nora think? Would Maggie say yes?

Nora wasn't sure. For all her childlike displays of emotion, Maggie kept her deepest truths in darkest secret. That's how you knew something really mattered to her—the bubbling stream of chatter suddenly dried up to dust.

Though they'd been best friends since they'd eaten paste together in kindergarten, Nora had accepted that there were things she'd never learn, no matter how many times she asked.

Like where Maggie got that old-fashioned gold ring she wore on a chain around her neck.

Or who was the father of her baby.

"Land ahoy!" Maggie leaned way out this time, pointing east. "I see it!"

"Maggie," Ethan said sharply, "don't lean out so far! You could fall overboard!"

"Stop being such a worrywart." Maggie cast a sour look at Ethan, then went back to dragging her hand in the water. "Even if I did fall over, I know how to swim."

Nora gave Ethan a look, too. She tried to signal that bossing Maggie around was not a good idea. Maggie hated domineering, patriarchal men—probably because her father was one of the worst. Nora knew that Mr. Nicholson had hit Maggie, at least twice, and she often wondered what else might have happened that Maggie didn't confide.

But Ethan wasn't paying any attention to Nora. He was still watching Maggie, and his mouth was set in an anxious line. Nora looked over at her friend, too. Maggie had both hands on her belly, and her face was gripped in a sudden, strange tension.

"What is it?" Nora leaned forward. "Is something wrong?"

"I'm fine. Carry on."

Ethan's dark brows pulled together. "Are you having contractions?"

"I'm *fine,* sailor." Maggie waved her hand nonchalantly, clearly trying to lighten the mood. Nora couldn't blame her. Ethan did hover a bit. "Colin was just giving me one of his Morse code messages. You know, punch-punch-jab-poke. I think he said something about *nappy turfday.*"

Nora smiled. Maggie always called the baby Colin, though the ultrasound had been inconclusive as to sex. She'd decided it was a boy, and, as usual, the facts didn't really concern her.

But Ethan wasn't buying it. He reached out with a doctor's instinctive authority and put his hand on Maggie's stomach. "I don't like it. You sure he's not saying something about going into labor?"

Maggie stood up and moved beyond Ethan's reach. "My Morse code is pretty rusty, but I think I could tell the difference between 'Happy birthday, Mom,' and 'Look out, here I come!'"

"Could you?"

She glared at him. "Colin is fine. I said *carry on.*" It always frustrated her when the universe didn't fall right in line with her plans. "Look, not only is this my birthday, but this may be the last completely free day I have for—oh, say eighteen years? So don't you two go all smothery and cheat me out of it, okay?"

Ethan adjusted his glasses. "But in the third trimester—"

Maggie stood on the seat, stepped one foot up onto the gunwale and pointed her hands over her head in the classic diving position. "I'm going to that island," she said, "if I have to swim the rest of the way."

Ethan laughed nervously. "Get down, you dork. Do you want to slip?"

He wasn't really concerned that she'd jump. But Nora knew Maggie better than he did. She glanced quickly toward the island, calculating the distance. Only about a hundred yards. Maggie could swim it. And, if he didn't back off, she just might.

"Ethan, don't piss me off." Maggie wasn't laughing. "You're not my father."

"No, I'm your *doctor.* I simply can't allow you to take foolish risks—"

Nora groaned. Too bossy. He even sounded a little like Maggie's father. Maggie despised her father.

She dove into the ocean with an emphatic splash. Ethan lurched. "For God's sake, *Maggie!*"

She ignored him, her arms cutting through the water with a brisk freestyle. Her feet churned up little green-white whirlpools, and soon she was moving faster than the boat.

"She's a great swimmer," Nora said when Ethan turned around to give her a horrified, open-mouthed stare. "At home, we swim all the time."

"But she's eight months pregnant! She has no idea how dangerous that is."

He looked down at the water, and Nora knew he was thinking of diving in after Maggie.

"Bad idea," she said. "You know how stubborn she is. She'll fight you till you both drown."

Though his adoration made him act silly sometimes, Ethan wasn't stupid. He knew when he was outmaneuvered. Obviously the only thing they could do right now was stay close to Maggie, and get to the island as fast as possible.

He sat, wiped his water-speckled glasses on his shirt, and then grabbed hold of the tiller. It took several seconds, but he adjusted the sails until they caught the wind.

They were only a few yards behind Maggie, just a few feet to her left—Ethan was steering as close to the wind as he could, so that they wouldn't separate much. Her small white face kept turning toward them every other stroke. Once, Nora could have sworn Maggie stuck out her tongue at them.

"Little brat," Ethan murmured. But Nora saw that he was smiling—and, in spite of her annoyance with Maggie, she felt happy for her. How great to have someone love you so much they even found your flaws adorable.

Back in high school, Maggie's edgy personality had scared off most of the guys. She'd had only one boyfriend, as far as Nora knew—a short, dumb fling with Mr. Jenkins, their senior biology teacher who shortly afterward had married the English lit teacher and had moved out of town. Nora assumed Mr. J. must be the father of the baby, though of course Maggie wouldn't discuss it.

But perhaps Mr. Jenkins had been a sign. Maggie needed someone a little older, a lot wiser.

Yes. Nice, honest, loyal and *unmarried* Ethan would be good for Maggie.

If only she'd have him.

The wind had shifted, so Ethan had to tack. Maggie beat them to the beach by at least five minutes, and they were coming in several yards west of her.

All they could do was watch as she climbed out of the surf, little bits of foam clinging to her bare legs. She shook water from her ears and ran her fingers through her hair to spike it back up where it belonged. Finally, she assumed a pose of exaggerated boredom, as if they were taking forever.

And then, abruptly, she doubled over, gripping her stomach with both hands.

Ethan made a skeptical sound. "Faker," he said. "I'm not falling for that one."

Was it just a joke? If so, it wasn't one bit funny—it was actually damned scary. Would Maggie really be such a jerk? Nora frowned and moved to the other side of the boat, hoping to make out the details of Maggie's face.

But her chin was tucked down against her breastbone. Her shoulders were hunched, and her hands were still hanging onto her stomach, fingers widespread and curved, like stiff claws.

"No," Nora said through suddenly cold lips. "No, she's not faking. You know how she is. She never pretends to be weak. She always pretends to be strong."

Ethan frowned. They had almost made land. A shrill cry reached them, knifing through the crisp autumn silence. It sounded like a gull, but it was Maggie.

"Oh, my God," he said. His knuckles were stark white around the tiller.

As they watched, Maggie swayed from side to side, as if she were wrestling with something inside her. And then she sank to her knees in the sand.

The sailboat was only fifteen feet from shore. Without thinking, Nora jumped out and waded through the cold, chest-high water as fast as her trembling legs would take her. Behind her, she heard Ethan jump out, too.

Her feet were clumsy on the grainy sand, but she ran as fast as she could. She reached Maggie just as she toppled over onto her side, her hands still wrapped around her stomach.

"Honey, honey, what's wrong?" Nora dropped to her knees beside the moaning girl. "Is it the baby? Is the baby coming?"

"I don't know." Maggie's face was coated with sand. Her voice sounded high, half-strangled with either pain or fear. "Maybe, but…but it's too soon. And it hurts. I think something's wrong."

"How exactly does it feel?"

Maggie turned her face toward the sand. "It hurts."

"Did your water break?" It might be hard to tell, Nora thought, given that Maggie was soaking wet all over.

For the first time, Nora looked down at Maggie's legs. They were streaming with pale, watery blood.

The comforting words Nora had been about to say died away. This wasn't right. This wasn't what she'd been told to expect. She'd been to the birthing classes, and it had all sounded so organized. Step one, step two, step three…

No one had said anything about pale, quivering legs laced in blood that grew a brighter red with every passing second.

She didn't know what to do. But even if she had known, she wouldn't have been able to do it. She was going to faint.

Why, why had she listened to Maggie? Why had they come out here, to the end of the world, all alone? And before that…why hadn't she insisted that they go home to Hawthorn Bay and tell Maggie's parents about the baby? Maggie should have delivered her baby in the little hospital by the bridge, with a dozen brave, experienced adults to see it through.

But Nora had never been able to make Maggie do anything. Maggie was the strong one, the defiant one—she didn't care what anyone thought of her. She didn't need anyone, she always said. Not even Nora.

And maybe she didn't. Maybe she would have been just fine alone. But, though Nora was almost painfully homesick to be back in Hawthorn Bay, back in her own little yellow bedroom at Heron Hill, she hadn't been able to leave Maggie behind.

Under all that defiance, there was something…something tragic and vulnerable about Maggie. Nora had decided to stay with her, at least until the baby was born.

After that they'd decide what to do next.

Ethan was still thigh-deep in the water, trudging toward them, pulling the small sailboat along by a tug line. Intellectually, Nora knew he was right to take the time—they couldn't afford to let the boat drift away. No one knew where they were. Even Ethan's father, who was also a doctor, just thought they were having a picnic in the park.

But emotionally she wanted him to just drop the line and race over here. He was one of the brave, experienced adults they needed. She was only a teenager, and she wasn't ready for this.

Maggie had begun to weep. "It hurts," she said again, and she reached out for Nora's hand.

Ethan finally dragged the boat onto the sand. A couple of gulls landed near it, obviously hoping for dinner. Ethan reached into the cockpit and extracted their beach towels and his cell phone.

Oh, God, hurry.

He punched numbers into the phone as he ran toward them. He listened, then clicked off and started over.

It was like watching a mime. Even from this distance, Nora could read the significance of that wordless message. They had no phone signal. They were officially in the middle of nowhere.

And they were officially alone.

When he reached them, Nora focused on his eyes—she knew the truth would be there. She'd known him only a few months, but she had already learned that he was a terrible liar.

For just a second, when he saw the blood, his eyes went black. For that same second, so did Nora's heart.

She felt an irrational spurt of fury toward him, as if by confirming her fears he had somehow betrayed Maggie. She turned resolutely away from his anguished gaze.

"You're going to be okay, honey," she said, but she heard the note of rising panic in her voice and wished she hadn't spoken.

Maggie stared at her with wild eyes. "There shouldn't be blood," she said. "There shouldn't be blood."

Ethan touched Maggie's shoulder gently. "We have to see what's causing it. And we need to see what's going on with the baby. I need to know if you're dilated."

Maggie moaned in response.

"Nora," he said without looking at her. "Please get the water bottles out of the cooler." He held out the phone. "And take this. I don't think it's going to work, but keep trying."

She clutched the phone and started to run, her sodden tennis shoes squishing with every step, making mud of the sand. Though there were no bars on the cell phone's display, indicating they had no service, her fingers kept hitting 911 over and over.

By the time she had gathered the little plastic bottles in her arms and run back to the others, she'd tried 911 a dozen times.

Nothing.

While she'd been gone, Ethan had somehow spread out the towels, arranged Maggie on them, and removed her shorts and shoes.

Nora didn't look at anything below Maggie's face. She couldn't allow herself to see how much blood there was. She couldn't even think about how the baby might be coming. Here, in this empty place. A full month too early...

She gave Ethan the water, and then she took her place at Maggie's shoulder.

Maggie rolled her face toward Nora, and the whites of her eyes were so huge that for a minute she looked like a frightened colt.

"Ethan will take care of everything," Nora said numbly as she took Maggie's hand. She felt like the recording of a person, programmed to speak words she didn't even understand, much less believe.

Maggie's face was so white. Was that what happened when you lost too much blood? Nora wanted to ask Ethan, but she didn't want Maggie to hear the answer.

She didn't want to hear the answer, either.

Ethan had positioned himself between Maggie's knees. He'd opened some of the water, and poured it onto a small towel. He must have been hurting her, because Maggie's grip on Nora's hand kept tightening, until she thought the bones might break.

"Ethan will fix it." She realized she was speaking as much to Ethan as to Maggie, telling him that he had no choice, he had to make this right. "Ethan won't let anything happen to you."

"I don't care about me," Maggie said, shutting her eyes and squeezing her fingers again. "Just be sure the baby is all right, that's all that matters."

Nora nodded. "Yes. Of course the baby—both of you will be fine."

"You've got to relax, Maggie." Ethan shook his head. "I need you to relax so I can find out what's going on." He glanced at Nora, the consummate doctor now, all business and no emotion. "Talk to her," he said.

About what? About the blood? About the cell phone that was no more useful than a lump of scrap metal? About the miles of ocean that stretched out all the way to the horizon?

Over by the boat, more gulls were arriving, screaming overhead and diving for crumbs, like vultures.

She swallowed, her mind casting about. "Did you ever tell Ethan why you call the baby Colin, Maggie? Did you ever tell him about Cornwall?"

Amazingly, she seemed to have hit on the right subject. Maggie seemed to be trying to smile. "We were happy in Cornwall," she whispered.

"Yes." Nora nodded. It had been a lovely summer—and it was, she thought, the only time she'd ever seen Maggie completely relax. It was the only time the underlying vulnerability had seemed to vanish.

"You tell him, Nora." Maggie nudged her hand. "Tell Ethan about Colin."

Ethan wasn't listening, Nora knew, but it wouldn't hurt to talk. It was a good memory, and it would at least distract Maggie for a minute or two.

"When we graduated last spring, my parents gave us a trip to England," she began awkwardly. She smiled down at Maggie. "Four whole months abroad, just the two of us. We couldn't believe our luck."

Maggie shut her eyes. "And all thanks to Jack," she said with a hint of her normal dry sarcasm.

Nora let that part go. Ethan didn't need to hear about Jack Killian. But it was true—the trip had been partly to celebrate their high-school graduation, and partly, Nora's parents hoped, to help Nora get over the broken heart handed her by Black Jack Killian.

"We liked London," she went on. "But we really fell in love with Cornwall, didn't we, Maggie?"

Maggie's eyes were still shut, but she nodded, just a fraction of an inch, and she once again tried to smile. It had shocked Nora to see Maggie, whose punk sassiness seemed much better suited to the London club scene, bloom like an English rose among the brutal cliffs, stoic stone houses and secret, windswept gardens of Cornwall.

But from their first night in the West Country, which they'd spent in a tiny fishing village that echoed with the cries of cormorants and the strange, musical accents of the locals, Maggie had clearly been at *home*.

"We met Colin Trenwith in Cornwall," Nora said. "I think it was love at first sight for Maggie."

Finally, Ethan looked up. Nora knew he'd always thought Colin might be the name of the baby's father.

She smiled. "Or at least we met his ghost," she added. "Maggie found his tombstone. He was a pirate who died in the 1700s. I think she fell in love with that name, right from the start."

Ethan blinked behind his glasses, then returned to his work.

Nora tried not to see what he was doing. Instead she pictured Maggie, kneeling in front of the tilted tombstone in that half-forgotten cemetery over-looking the Atlantic.

"Nora, listen," she'd called out excitedly. "Colin Trenwith, 1756–1775. Once a Pirate, Twice a Father, Now at Rest with his Lord." She'd run her fingers over the carving. "Isn't that the most poetic epitaph you've ever heard?"

Maggie hadn't been able to tear herself away. She'd begged Nora to linger another week in Cornwall, and then another. They'd changed their tickets, and, cloaked and hooded against the wind, they'd hiked every day to the graveyard.

While Nora read, Maggie used Colin's stone as a backrest and invented romantic stories about the boy who had packed so much life into his nineteen short years.

It was there, in that cemetery, that Nora had realized her parents were right—a new perspective had been just what she needed. Jack Killian had hurt her, yes, but her heartache was neither as immense as the Atlantic beside these ancient tomb-stones, nor as permanent as the deaths recorded on them.

And it was there, in that cemetery, breaking off impulsively in the middle of a tragic tale, that Maggie had first confessed her secret.

She was pregnant.

She was going to name her son Colin.

And she was never going home to Hawthorn Bay again.

So far, she hadn't. Though they'd left England, having run out of money, they hadn't gone home. They'd taken a bus from New York's airport to small-town Maine and found menial jobs here, so that Maggie could have her baby in secret. Nora had called her parents, to let them know they were all right, though for Maggie's sake she couldn't tell them exactly where they were.

Maggie hadn't called her family at all.

"We have to get back to the mainland," Ethan interrupted tersely. "Right away. We have to get her back on the boat."

Maggie cried out and her body jackknifed, as if someone had stabbed her from the inside.

"No," she said, her voice tortured. "No. Do it here. The baby's coming, Ethan. It's too late to go back."

Nora balanced herself with one hand on the wet sand. "Is it true? Is the baby coming?"

He nodded. "She's already seven centimeters." He gazed down at Maggie. "You must have been having contractions all morning, you little fool."

Maggie shifted her head on the beach towel, grimacing. "Just twinges. Braxton-Hicks, I thought."

Nora knew what that meant. When she'd agreed to stay in Maine with Maggie until the baby was born, she'd agreed to be her labor coach. Braxton-Hicks. False labour. Not uncommon in the weeks prior to delivery.

Maggie looked at Nora, as if she needed absolution for the sin of such dangerous foolishness. "Honestly, I didn't think— Everyone says it takes so long the first time—"

"Well, it's not going to take long for you." Ethan sounded tense. "We have to get you back on the boat. Even if the baby is born there, we have to do it."

Nora twitched her brows together, silently asking the question. Why? Why did they have to take such a risk? Surely it was safer here, where they at least had solid ground under their feet. *Why go?*

For answer, Ethan simply held up his hand. It was covered in blood, from fingertip to wrist, like a red rubber glove.

Nora felt the beach tilt. She thought for a minute she might pass out. It wasn't just the baby coming early, then. Maggie was in real trouble. She was losing too much blood.

Maggie must have seen Ethan's hand, too, though they both thought her eyes had been closed. Her whole body clenched, and then once again she reached for Nora's fingers.

"Nora. Listen to me. If anything happens, I want you to take the baby."

Nora pulled back instinctively, as if the words had burned her. Her heart was beating triple time, and her flesh felt cold.

"Don't talk like that, Megs," she said. She forced a teasing note into her voice. "It's absurd. I know you love melodrama, but this isn't the time. You need to focus on your breathing."

"Not yet." Maggie's gaze bore into hers. "If it's absurd, we'll all have a good laugh about it later. But just in case. I want you to promise me that you'll take the baby."

Ethan was wrapping the towels around her. He must have done something that hurt. Maggie cried out, and her legs stiffened.

"I'm sorry," he whispered. Nora saw a bead of sweat make its way down his hairline and mingle with a smear of blood on his cheek.

"Promise me, Nora."

"Okay," Nora said as she began to shiver. "Okay, Maggie, I promise. Now please. Focus."

"And you must never let my parents know. About Colin. They can't have him. My father—"

Maggie bent over again, making a sound like a small animal.

Ethan cleared his throat. "Nora, you have to help me carry her."

When had Ethan stood up? Nora felt confused. This was a nightmare, where things happened in confusing, nonsequential jerks. But she had her part to play in the nightmare, too, so she struggled to her feet, though she no could longer feel them or trust that they were rigid enough to carry her own weight, let alone a bleeding woman and an unborn baby.

Maggie was so light, though, frighteningly light, as if part of her had bled away into the beach. They tried not to jostle her, but once or twice she seemed to pass out, then come back to consciousness with a groan.

Ethan cradled her in his arms while Nora made a pallet out of blood-soaked beach towels on the floor of the cockpit. As they placed her on it, Maggie seemed to rally a little. With one hand that, though it shook, seemed surprisingly strong, she pulled off the chain that held the mysterious gold ring.

She held it out to Nora.

"For you," she said. Her voice seemed slurred. "For Colin."

Nora took it, and her first tear fell.

Colin Trenwith.

Once a pirate, twice a father, now at rest with his Lord.

While Ethan towed the boat out to deeper water, Nora chanted the epitaph silently, over and over, like a prayer.

And then, with the words still circling through her mind, like a slender chain wrapping its fractured pieces together, Nora watched Ethan climb into the little boat, and the three of them set sail for home.

CHAPTER TWO

Eleven years later

MOTHERHOOD, NORA CARSON decided as she retreated to the kitchen, leaving her eleven-year-old son pouting in the living room, was not for the faint of heart.

Nora had three jobs—mayor of Hawthorn Bay, co-owner of Heron Hill Preserves and mom to Colin Trenwith Carson.

Of the three, being Colin's mom was by far the toughest.

At least it was *this* week. Last week, when the Hawthorn Bay City Council had been sued by a recently fired male secretary claiming sexual discrimination, *mayor* had been at the top of Nora's tough list.

Luckily, Nora had kept some of the secretary's letters, all of which began *Deer Sir.* She produced them at her deposition, explaining that she didn't give a hoot whether their secretaries were male, female or Martian, as long as they could spell.

The lawyers withdrew the suit the next day.

Now if only she could make this problem with Colin go away as easily. But she had a sinking feeling that it was going to prove much thornier.

She put the blackberries and pectin on to boil—she had orders piled up through next Easter, so she couldn't afford a full day off. She read the letter from Colin's teacher while she stirred.

Cheating.

Fighting.

Completely unrepentant.

These weren't words she ordinarily heard in connection with Colin. He wasn't perfect, not by a long shot. He was a mischievous rascal and too smart for his own good. But he wasn't *bad*.

This time, though—

"Nora, thank heaven you're home!" Stacy Holtsinger knocked on the back door and opened it at the same time. She was practically family, after eight years as business partner and best friend, and she didn't bother with ceremony much anymore.

Nora folded the letter and slid it into the pocket of the World's Greatest Mom apron Colin had given her for her birthday. "Where else would I be, with all these orders to fill? Out dancing?"

Stacy, a tall brunette with a chunky pair of tortoiseshell glasses that she alternately used as a headband, a pointer or a chew toy, but never as glasses, went straight to the refrigerator and got herself a bottled water. She wanted to lose ten pounds by Christmas and was convinced she could flood them out on a tidal wave of H_2O.

Nora thought privately that Stacy would look emaciated if she lost any more weight, but the water sure did give her olive skin a gorgeous glow. She wondered if Stacy had her eye on a new man. She hoped so.

"Well," Stacy said, raking her glasses back through her hair as she slipped onto a stool, "you could be down at city hall, I guess, trying to knock sense into those Neanderthals. Which would be disastrous right now, because I need you to make an executive decision about the new labels."

Nora groaned as she added the sugar to the blackberries. Her mind was already packed to popping with decisions to make. What to do about the latest city-council idiocy—trying to claim eminent domain over Sweet Tides, the old Killian estate by the water? What to do about that crack in her living-room wall, which might be the foundation settling, something she could not afford to fix right now?

And, hanging over everything, like a big fat thundercloud—what to do about Colin?

"Labels are your side of the business." The berries were just about ready. Nora pulled out the tablespoon she'd kept waiting in a glass of cold water, and dropped a dollop of the jam on it. *Rats.* Not quite thick enough.

"Come on, Nora. Please?"

Nora looked over her shoulder. "Stacy, do I consult you about whether to buy Cherokee or Brazos? What to do if the jam's too runny? No. I make the product, you figure out how to sell it, remember?"

"Yeah, but—" Stacy held up a proof sheet. "This is a really big change. And I drew the artwork myself. I'm sorry. I'm weak. I need reassurance."

Nora put the spoon down. It was probably true. Stacy was one of the most attractive and capable women Nora knew, but her self-esteem had flat-lined about five years ago when her husband had left her, hypnotized by the dirigible-shaped breasts of their twenty-year-old housekeeper.

Zach was a fool—although rumor had it he was a happy fool, having discovered that The Dirigible was into threesomes with her best friend, whom Stacy had dubbed The Hindenburg.

"Okay." Nora wiped her hands. "Show me."

Nora would have said she loved it no matter what, but luckily the new label was gorgeous. Done in an appropriate palette of plums, purples, roses and blues—all the best berry colors—it showed a young beauty on a tree swing, with a house in the background that was the home of everyone's fan-tasies—wide, sunny porch, rose-twined columns and lace curtains fluttering at cheerful windows.

Everyone wished they'd grown up in that house.

But Nora really had.

She looked up at Stacy. "You used the real Heron Hill?"

The other woman nodded. "You don't mind, do you? I changed it a little, so that no one could sue or anything. But it is the ultimate dream house, don't you think? It was our business name before you sold the house, and we've worked that out legally with the new owners, so—" She broke off, fidgeting with her glasses. "I mean…you really don't mind, do you?"

"Of course not." Nora smiled. She'd been born at Heron Hill. And Colin had spent his first few years there. It had indeed been the dream house. But when her father had died, and Nora discovered that the Carson fortune was somewhat overrated, she and her mother had decided to sell it.

Heron Hill was now a very popular local bed-and-breakfast. Nora's mother had moved to Florida last year, so she didn't have to pine over the loss. It stung Nora, though, sometimes, when she passed it and spotted a stranger standing at the window of her old bedroom. But whenever that happened, she just reminded herself of the big fat trust fund they'd set up for Colin with the proceeds from the house, and she'd walk on by, with her chin up and no regret.

"The label is gorgeous," she said. "It will sell so well I won't be able to keep up with the demand."

"Great. I'll tell the printers today." Stacy tucked the proof back into its protective folder and gazed happily up at Nora. "Now, can I return the favor? I haven't a clue whether Cherokee or Brazos blackberries taste better, but I do have a breakdown of their sales figures for the past three years, which might—"

Nora laughed. "No, no, I've got that part covered. But I—I could use some advice about

Colin. He's gotten himself into some trouble, and I'm not sure how to handle it."

Stacy raised one eyebrow. "Colin's in trouble? Trouble he can't charm his way out of? I didn't know there was such a thing."

Nora knew that wasn't just empty flattery. With his curly black hair, big blue eyes and dimpled smile, Colin was already so handsome and winning that most adults couldn't stay mad, no matter what he did. He'd get caught right in the act of something devilish, like the time he'd learned the signs for several off-color words and had the class rolling out of their seats with laughter while his poor teacher tried to figure out what the joke was. Or the time he and a few friends had fiddled with the school's front marquee and changed the phrase We Love Our Students to We Love Our Stud Nest.

Both times, Colin had apologized so humbly—even, in a nice touch, using the sign for *ashamed*—that the principal had ended up praising his honesty instead of kicking him out of class.

"I know, but this time it's different," Nora said. The jam was ready, and she began to pour it into the sterilized jars she had lined up on the central island. This little house, which she'd bought after selling Heron Hill, wasn't much to look at, but it had a fantastic kitchen.

"Different how?"

Nora sighed. "They say he and Mickey Dickson cheated on their math test."

Stacy raised her brows. "What? He hates Mickey

Dickson. Heck, I hate Mickey Dickson. Sorry, I know he's some kind of cousin of yours, but the kid is a brat. And an idiot. I take it Mickey cheated off Colin's paper, not vice versa?"

"Yes, but Colin let him. He said he knew Mickey had been doing it for months, so this time he made it easy…and he deliberately answered all the questions wrong, so that Mickey would get caught. He said he didn't mind going down, as long as he brought Mickey down with him."

"Yikes." Stacy shook her head. "That's gutsy. Dumb, but gutsy."

"Yeah, and that's not all. After school he and Mickey had a fistfight on the softball field. Tom called about an hour ago. He and Mickey just got back from the emergency room. They thought his nose might be broken, but apparently not, thank God."

Stacy twirled her glasses thoughtfully and let out a low whistle. "Wow. It does sound as if Colin has slipped off the leash. What are you going to do?"

"I have no idea. He starts his Christmas break soon, which is both good and bad. Good, because he won't have to see Mickey, but bad because he'll have way too much spare time. Colin and 'free time' are a recipe for disaster."

"Maybe you can get him to help you with the jams."

Nora laughed as she screwed the lid onto the first of the filled jars. "No way. He's a bull in a china shop. Last time he helped, he broke a gross of jars and ate more berries than he canned. We'd be out of business by New Year's."

Stacy laughed, too, but she kept twirling her glasses, which meant she took the problem seriously.

"Besides," Nora went on. "Hanging out here with me is too easy. We'd have fun. I want to give him some chore that really hurts. Something he'll hate so much he won't even think about getting in trouble again."

Stacy scrunched up her brow, thinking hard. "Man, I don't know. What did your parents do when you got in trouble?"

Nora tilted her head and cocked one side of her mouth up wryly.

"Oh, that's right," Stacy said, laughing. "I forgot you were the reigning Miss Perfect for a couple of decades there."

"Miss Boring is more like it." Nora began wiping down the countertop, though she hadn't spilled much. "My friend Maggie used to say that if she weren't around to keep things stirred up I would probably turn to stone."

"I wish I could have met her," Stacy said. "You always make her sound like a human stick of dynamite. I'll bet she'd know how to handle Colin."

Nora's eyes stung suddenly. She turned around so that Stacy couldn't read her face too easily. "Yes," she agreed. "She probably would."

"Well, okay, let's think. I wasn't exactly

dynamite, but I wasn't Miss Perfect, either. I remember one summer, when I was about sixteen, and I'd just met Zach. I stayed out until dawn. I thought my dad was going to kill Zach, but my mom held him back. They made me spend the rest of my summer volunteering every night at the local nursing home."

"Oh, yeah? How did that go?"

"It was hell. I wanted to be wrapped in Zach's manly arms, and instead I was reading the sports section to an old guy who hacked up phlegm into his plastic cup every few sentences and kept yelling, *'Nothin' but net!'* every time I mentioned the Gamecocks."

Nora laughed.

"It's not funny," Stacy said, though there was a twinkle in her eye. "It could have scarred me for life. To this day, whenever I see a basketball, I twitch."

"Okay, then, I won't send Colin to the nursing home just yet. I'll reserve that for the day he comes home at dawn smelling of Chanel."

She looked toward the living room, which was suspiciously quiet. "Right now he's in there stuffing candy canes into the goody bags for the Christmas party. Even that little punishment annoyed him. He seemed to think nearly breaking Mickey's nose was a gift to mankind, something to be applauded."

"In there?" Stacy pointed with her tortoiseshell glasses. "Sorry, but I don't think so. I'm pretty sure I saw him climbing the tree when I came in."

Nora frowned, then, without stopping to say a

word, reached for the latch. She yanked the door open and, pulling her sweater closed against the blast of December wind, took the steps down to ground level quickly.

Oh, good grief. Stacy was right. Colin wasn't indoors, working through his punishment. He was about six feet up the leafless maple tree, hanging by his knees from a large, spreading branch. His sweater nearly smothered his face, leaving his skinny rib cage exposed and probably freezing.

Beneath him, his friend Brad Butterfield squatted in the middle of about two dozen scattered candy canes, some broken to bits inside their plastic wrappers. Both Brad and Colin were eating candy canes themselves, letting them dangle from their lips like red-striped cigarettes.

"Come on, Colin, you're only hitting like thirty percent. Let me try. It'll take us all day to do these damn bags at this rate."

"Shut up, butt-head," Colin said, his voice muffled under folds of wool. "You're the boat, and I'm the bomber. That's the deal. Now…target ready?"

With a heavy sigh of irritation, Brad began moving the paper bag slowly across the winter-brown grass. When he was directly under Colin's head, a candy cane came sailing down. It fell squarely into the bag, and both Colin and Brad made triumphant booming sounds.

Stacy, who now stood at Nora's shoulder,

chuckled softly. "Well, what a coincidence," she said. "Nothing but net."

MOST PEOPLE IN HAWTHORN BAY said the Killian men had an unhealthy obsession with gold. A Civil War Killian ancestor supposedly buried his fortune in small caches all over the Sweet Tides acreage, and no Killian since had been able to drag himself away from the house, no matter how hard the community tried to run them off.

But Jack Killian, who hadn't set foot in Hawthorn Bay for twelve years and therefore had a more objective perspective, didn't think their problem was the gold.

It was the water.

Living in the South Carolina lowlands meant your feet weren't ever quite dry. Thousands of acres of spartina marshland, endless blue miles of Atlantic coastline, haunted black swamps and twisting ribbons of tea-colored rivers—that was what Jack saw when he dreamed of home, not the antebellum columns and jasmine-scented porches of Sweet Tides.

And certainly not the gold.

Almost every major incident in his life was tied to the water. He'd been four the day they'd dragged his grandmother out of the river behind Sweet Tides, where she'd unsuccessfully tried to drown herself. He'd been nine the day he'd broken his fibula learning to water-ski behind their new boat— Killian luck never lasted long, and that boat had been sold, dime on the dollar, before the cast had come off Jack's leg. He'd been sixteen the day his mother, lying on the floor in a pool of her own blood, had sent him to find his father, who'd been drinking malt liquor at a shanty on the edge of Big Mosquito Swamp. It was the first time Jack had driven a car alone.

And, of course, he had won Nora Carson on the water—the day they'd wandered away from a high school science trip to a loblolly pine hammock, and he'd kissed her beside a cluster of yellow water lilies.

He'd lost her on the water, too, the day he'd taken her filthy cousin Tom out to a deserted spoil island, beat the crap out of him and left him there to swim home on his own. He hadn't realized that he'd broken Tom's arm, rendering the jerk unable to swim an inch, but the cops had decided ignorance was no excuse.

Jack had escaped an attempted murder charge by the skin of his teeth, and by a timely enlistment in the United States Army.

He hadn't been home since. Until today.

He drove his Jaguar around back, between the house and the river. In Jack's lifetime, no one but the sheriff had ever entered Sweet Tides from the fancy front, where gray, peeling Doric columns guarded the portico like ghosts from a long-lost world.

Yeah, the front of Sweet Tides was pure Greek tragedy, but the back was merely pleasantly ragged, with mossy oaks, leggy camellias, crooked steps and weathered paint that all needed a lot more tending than they ever got.

Jack's brother, Sean, stood at the back porch. When Jack killed his engine, Sean loped down the uneven steps, arms open, a huge grin on the face that looked so eerily like Jack's own.

"You made it! I thought surely the minute you hit the marsh flats you'd break out in hives and make a U-turn back to Kansas City!"

Jack folded Sean in with one arm and ruffled his unkempt black curls with the other. They both still wore their hair a little longer than other men—it was Jack's one rebellion against the establishment. But while Sean clearly still cut his own with the kitchen scissors, Jack paid a small fortune to someone named Ambrosia, who knew how to keep the uptown-edgy-lawyer look from revealing its roots as backwoods bad boy.

"I thought about it," he admitted. "But curiosity got the better of me."

Sean raised one eyebrow into a high, skeptical arch, a favorite Killian trick. "You managed to keep your curiosity under control for twelve long years."

"Yeah, but this time you sweetened the pot. I couldn't pass up the chance to thwart the evil plans of that lowlife Tom Dickson and his cronies." Jack popped the trunk, exposing a suitcase and a garment bag. "Give me a hand with these, okay? I brought some extra suits, in case the bastard puts up a fight."

Sean smiled. "Oh, he'll fight, especially once he realizes you're his opponent. Somehow I don't think he's ever forgiven you for trying to kill him."

Jack hoisted one of the black leather cases and extended the other to his brother. He held onto the handle an extra second.

"Just for the record. If I'd ever tried to kill Tom Dickson, he'd be dead."

"Point taken." Sean chuckled as he led the way into the house. "Though I'm not sure that logic will cut much ice with Tom."

Given the dilapidated state of the exterior, Jack was surprised to see how neat and clean—if somewhat Spartan—the interior of the mansion had been kept. The rooms had all been painted recently enough to shine a little, and the heart-of-pine floors were freshly varnished.

There wasn't much furniture. Their dad—Crazy Kelly, his friends called him—had sold all the antiques years ago, in his attempt to set the world record for butt-stupid poker playing. He'd lost the grand piano betting on a pair of tens.

But the few pieces Sean had scattered around were sensible and high quality. Even Kelly Killian hadn't found a way to sell the marble off the walls, or the carvings off the cornices, so the interior still made quite an impression.

As they walked past the elaborate painted-brick archway that led to the living room, Jack realized he was tensing up instinctively. Their mother had kept her collection of miniature glass unicorns in there, and it still made Jack cringe to remember how he and Sean had occasionally joined in their father's mocking laughter. "Unicorns! Are you daft in the head, Bridey, or just a goddamn fool?"

When she'd fallen that day, she'd hit the case and broken every one. Jack didn't look into the living room as they passed, but out of the corner of his eye he imagined he still saw the twinkle and glitter of shattered glass.

So, he thought. Not all the ghosts had moved out.

But overall, the place had definitely changed for the better. It didn't smell damp and defeated anymore, as if it stood in a stagnant bog of booze and tears.

"I put you in your old room," Sean said. "But let's have a drink first, okay? There's some stuff I probably ought to fill you in on."

They dropped the cases at the foot of the wide, curving staircase and headed toward the smoking room, where the liquor cabinet had always been kept. Jack didn't wonder, even for a second, what kind of drink Sean intended to offer him. Neither of them had ever drunk liquor in their lives—except for that one night, the night before Jack had joined the Army. Jack had gotten plastered that night, and it had scared the tar out of him. There was no nightmare more terrifying than the fear that they'd turn into their father.

"Soda? Or iced tea?" Sean had obviously tossed out the cherry-inlaid liquor cabinet, with its front scarred from Kelly's fury when Bridey had dared to try to lock him out. Instead, Sean had installed a handsome modern marble wet bar. "I've got water in six flavors. The chicks love it."

"I'll take a Coke," Jack said. He parked himself on one of the bar stools and looked around the mostly bare room. "I have to tell you, buddy. For a junk dealer, you have remarkably little *junk.*"

Sean handed over the cold can and shrugged. "Yeah, well, I buy to sell. I don't keep. I don't care much about stuff, you know? All these people, they accumulate these expensive trinkets, hoping the stuff will define them, or save them, or…whatever. Bull. If material things had any power, then Mom…"

He didn't finish the sentence. He didn't need to. A hundred crystal unicorns, and not enough magic in the lot to stop a single tear from falling.

Jack's apartment in Kansas City was equally spare.

"Anyhow," Jack said to cover the silence. "Fill me in. You said that the city council has let you know they want to buy Sweet Tides. And that they've hinted that, if you don't sell willingly, they'll find a way to claim eminent domain. Somebody wants to put up a shopping plaza or condo complex or something like that, right?"

"Yeah. They brought it up earlier this year, but I thought they were just trying to rattle my chains, you know? I thought they'd back off, because it's such a stupid idea. Unless they can claim that Sweet

Tides is a blight, it's going to be hella hard to assert eminent domain. But they haven't let go of the idea. They've already tried, informally, of course, to talk numbers with me."

"And what kind of number did they suggest?" Jack knew that, unfortunately, the people displaced by eminent domain often ended up taking less than their property was worth, just because they didn't have the savvy to know how to fight back. "Was it even in the ballpark?"

"That's what made me nervous. They offered top dollar. Does that make sense to you?"

Jack shook his head slowly. "Not as a first offer. They have to know they need bargaining room."

"That's what I thought."

"So what's going on? You know these people better than I do. Do they really want to put a shopping plaza out here that bad? Didn't look to me as if the commercial area had spread out this far yet anyhow."

"It hasn't. And no, they don't want that blasted shopping center. They couldn't. The one they built last year doesn't have full occupancy yet."

Jack sighed. "So. Can I assume this is just a new case of Killian fever? Someone has decided that the trashy Killians can't be allowed to live this close to decent folk?"

"Maybe." Sean looked thoughtful. He came out from behind the bar and stood at the picture window, which looked out toward the river. "Or maybe it's a different kind of fever. Maybe it's the gold."

"Oh, for God's sake, Sean. No one really believes that anymore. Everyone knows that, if there had been gold on this property, dad would have found it and bet it all on a pair of tens."

Sean was quiet a long time, just staring out the window, as if he was hypnotized by the moss swaying from the oaks. Finally he turned around.

"But what if there is? We used to think we'd find it, remember, Jack?"

Of course he remembered. The two of them had sneaked out almost every night for a year, right after their mother had gotten sick, and had dug holes until they'd been so tired and dirty all they could do was lie on their backs and stare at the stars. And whisper about what they'd do with the gold when they found it.

Sean, who was two years older and much nicer, had always listed a detox center for their dad first. Jack had called him a moron. Betting that Kelly Killian could get off the bottle? You might as well throw the whole treasure away on a pair of tens.

"I remember," Jack said. "That's about a thousand hours of our lives we'll never get back, huh?"

Sean shrugged. "Another piece washed up last month. We got six inches of rain in two hours. When it stopped, there was a Confederate coin out on the South Forty."

Jake wasn't impressed. Coins had washed up at odd intervals for the past hundred and fifty years. Just enough to keep the rumor alive. Never enough to make anybody rich.

"So, look, Sean, what exactly do you want me to do? I can try to get an injunction against the city council, preventing them from pursuing the eminent domain claim. But it'll only slow it down. If they're determined, they just might win in the end. The Supreme Court has ruled that this sort of thing, to bring in necessary revenues, is legal."

"Slowing them down is enough." Sean looked tired, Jack suddenly realized. "Truth is, Jack, I don't really care about the house. I'm ready to let go of it. Too many memories, I guess. I've done everything short of an exorcism, but the damn place is still haunted, you know?"

Jack nodded. He'd never understood why Sean stayed in the first place. Their only living relative was their grandfather, Patrick, who had once been a strong force in their lives, but who now resided in the local nursing home.

A major stroke had brought him down—no one was sure how clear his mind was now, Sean had explained when he'd called Jack after the stroke. Patrick had almost complete loss of motor control on his left side. He couldn't even leave his bed, unless the nurses hoisted him into a wheelchair and strapped him in.

Surely he could be moved to another nursing home, in some other city, if Sean really wanted to get away.

Jack certainly had wanted to. Once Nora Carson had made it clear she never wanted to see Jack again, Hawthorn Bay had held nothing for him. He was sick of fighting the Killian reputation—even if he had contributed plenty to it himself.

And he wouldn't have lived in this house for all the gold in the world.

"Okay. But if you don't want to save Sweet Tides, why did you need to import a big-shot Kansas City lawyer like me?"

Finally Sean smiled. "To slow them down, like you said. I want time, Jack. I want time to find the gold. And I want you to help me."

Jack hesitated. Then he laughed. "You sure you haven't taken up the bottle? You're talking crazy now."

"No, I'm not. A friend of mine, a woman named Stacy Holtsinger, she's found something. You don't know her, she came here after you'd already left. But she's doing a master's in history, and she's going through a lot of the old Killian letters for her thesis. She found one that seems to talk about the gold."

"Everyone talks about the gold," Jack said irritably. "Words are cheap."

"She's got the letter now, but I'll show it to you tonight. I think you'll see what I mean. It feels important. It feels real."

"Sean, look, you told me you needed a lawyer, not a treasure hunter. I'm afraid I left my metal detector at home. Besides, I've got a job. I've got cases in Kansas City that—"

"A month. That's all I'm asking. Every big shot can get at least a month off, can't they? It'll mean we have Christmas together. And you can see Grandfather."

That would be nice. He and his grandfather had been close when Jack was little. Patrick had provided the only affectionate "fathering" Jack had ever gotten. Some of his happiest memories were of walking through the marshes with his grandfather, bending over to inspect the bugs and butterflies Patrick pointed out.

When Patrick and Jack's dad had fought for the last time, Patrick and Jack's grandmother Ginny had moved away. Through the years, he'd visited them often—glad that he didn't have to return to Hawthorn Bay to do it.

But he hadn't seen Patrick since his grandmother's funeral last year. He hadn't seen him since the stroke. He had to admit, it was tempting.

"And hey," Sean said, "we can clear out the rest of the stuff in the attic while you're here. So even if we find nothing, the time won't be a waste."

Sean put his tea down on the bar and shoved his hands into the pockets of his jeans. He stared at Jack, and his face had that mulish look that all Killians got when they weren't planning to back down, come hell or Union soldiers.

"Come on, Jack. I haven't asked for a damn thing in twelve years. Can't you give me one month?"

Jack couldn't say no. He'd started out tough, and the Army and the law had only made him tougher. But not tough enough to say no to Sean when he sounded like this.

Besides, Jack was already here. That had been the biggest hurdle. Now he might as well look around. And if Sweet Tides was going to get bulldozed to make room for Slice O'Pizza and Yuppies R Us, he might as well stick around long enough to say a proper goodbye.

He'd say goodbye to old Patrick, too.

He stood. "Okay. I'll stay till after Christmas. Meanwhile, I'll go talk to the city attorney and see what this band of weasels is planning. I'll pretend we're going to fight tooth and nail. I'll see if I can buy you some time."

"Thanks, Jack. Really, thanks a lot." Sean looked pleased, but still, oddly, a little uncomfortable. "I— Well, if you're going right now I guess there's one other thing I probably should tell you."

"Yeah?" Jack raised the Killian brow. "What's that?"

"Know how I told you Tom Dickson is on the city council?"

"Of course. That's how you got me to come, remember?" Jack grinned. "Actually, I could probably have guessed that anywhere there's a band of weasels, Tom Dickson will be nearby. What else is there? Have I got some other old friends on the council?"

"Sort of. Not exactly a friend, and not exactly a councilman. You see, it's the mayor."

"Okay. Tell me. Who is mayor these days?"

Sean paused.

"I'm sorry, Jack. It's Nora Carson."

CHAPTER THREE

1862

JOE KILLIAN WASHED UP in the river, though the December air was frigid. He was too covered in dirt and sweat to use the basin in the bedroom. Julia slept lightly on her perfumed sheets, and the stink of wet earth would wake her.

His shoulders ached. He'd worked hard all his life, but only with his mind, not with his arms and legs. Though he had inherited Sweet Tides and the one thousand acres of rice fields all around it, he'd never planted anything with his own hands.

Until tonight.

Tonight he had planted the crop that would, he prayed, secure his future. Billings and Pringle were arriving in the morning. They would take his gold for the Cause, and in return they'd give him piles and piles of Confederate paper.

Joe was a Southerner by birth, and his father before him. But Joe had married a Philadelphia woman, and he'd visited there many times. He knew facts, hard realities about the differences between the two places. He knew things that these naive Hawthorn Bay zealots—men who thought the South Carolina state line was the edge of the civilized world—couldn't even imagine.

He knew that, unless God intervened with a miracle, Confederate paper would be worthless within the year.

And he knew that Julia, with her divided loyalties and her love of all things graceful and easy, would despise him for a fool. She had already hinted that, if foodstuff were to be rationed any further, she might have to make her way home to Daddy.

Joe wasn't afraid to live without coffee and sugar and meat. He wasn't even afraid to die, although that didn't seem likely, since, bowing to Julia's charming entreaties, Dr. Hartnett had certified him unfit for fighting.

But Joe couldn't live without Julia.

And so he had buried the gold. Dozens of heavy bars, hundreds of elegant coins, all gleaming dully under the cloudy moonlight, their fire winking out as he shoveled the black dirt over them, spade by spade. When Billings and Pringle came tomorrow, Joe would toss them a few bars, like scraps to the hogs. They'd be surprised, maybe even suspicious, but what could they do?

Julia would know, of course. She was as clever as she was lovely. She would give Joe one long look, and then she'd bewitch Billings and Pringle until they forgot to be suspicious.

When he was through, Joe made his way to the bedroom quickly. He'd begun to shake from the cold and the exhaustion of his limbs. As he climbed into bed, a shaft of moonlight fell on Julia's ivory face, and he told himself it would be all right.

But, in spite of the perfumed sheets, in spite of Julia's warmth beside him, the sleep that finally came to him was thick with dreams.

He dreamed of dead men bursting from black-sod graves. They rose and, like an army, marched slowly toward Sweet Tides to avenge their terrible deaths.

They had no skin, no flesh to soften their skulls, no eyeballs to gentle their pitiless stares. But their bones shone in the moonlight.

Bones made entirely of gold.

WHEN JACK SAW THE BUSTLE in the town square, with the Santa in the band shell and the Christmas tree in the center, he wasn't a bit surprised.

Like most little towns, Hawthorn Bay loved a good festival. Without the museums and theaters and operas and bars of a big city, the good people of the community had to break their boredom other ways. So they held parades and picnics and rodeos, carnivals and cook-offs and white elephant jumbles. Any excuse to string the town square with fairy lights would do.

Jack had actually liked the festivals, back in high school. As the reigning community leaders, "Boss" Carson and his society wife, Angela, had always been in the thick of things, busy with committees and volunteers, organizing the dances and pouring the lemonade. Which had given Jack the perfect chance to sneak away with Nora.

Back then, he'd always been burning up with the need to touch her. With a girl like Nora, you had to go slow, but over the six months of their romance he had been claiming her, inch by tormenting inch. He'd already owned her soft, sunshine-golden hair, her lips, her cheeks, her ears, her eyelids. He had left his mark on her neck, her collarbone, the inside of her elbow, her swelling, rose-tipped breasts.

He'd win her all someday, he'd been sure of that. The fire lay so deep inside her that it didn't often show on the outside, but he knew it was there. He could taste it in the heat of her lips. He could hear it in the trapped-butterfly beat of her heart.

And then, one day, in a black Killian temper, he'd put the fire out for good.

But that was ancient history. He gave himself an internal shake and put the memories back in cold storage.

It had been late afternoon when he'd left Sean at Sweet Tides, and by the time he got to City Hall, though it was only about four thirty, the offices were closed. At The Christmas Jubilee, the sign on the door read.

He left his car by the municipal complex and walked back to the town square. It was growing colder, and the trees were already casting long shadows on the sidewalk. The sun would probably go down in about an hour or so—he could tell by the light on the river behind City Hall, which was morphing from dark blue to dirty pink.

The sky was a little busier, too, as the birds made their last-minute flights back to their nests.

Funny how quickly he could fall back into the rhythms of coastal life. He might have been gone for only twelve days, instead of twelve years.

He stood at the edge of the square for several minutes, just absorbing the scene. They'd gone all out for this particular festival. Main Street was lined with life-size, blow-up snowmen, which would have been right at home in the Macy's parade. Every tree, large and small, twinkled with colored lights. At the south edge of the square, an ornate merry-go-round in which every horse was a reindeer twirled to the tinkling sounds of "Jingle Bells."

But most of the activity was concentrated at the north end, up by the band shell. That was where Santa was holding court, enthroned in red velvet under the bright lights that usually illuminated the Hawthorn Barbershop Quartet. A long line of children wound down the band shell stairs and out into the square, waiting to sit on Santa's lap.

Boss Carson used to do the Santa bit, but Jack knew that Nora's dad had died quite a few years ago. He wondered who had taken over. He moved up a few yards, to the edge of the bank of folding chairs, to get a better look.

Well, how about that? It was Farley Hastert. Talk

about casting against type. Farley had been the
tallest, skinniest boy in Blackberry High. A couple
of years older than Jack, he'd been a basketball
jock and a straight-A student, on top of having a
very nice, very rich father. Naturally, Farley was
never without a gorgeous girl on his skinny arm.

Jack had been so jealous of Farley Hastert, he
hadn't been able to see straight. Once, Nora had let
Farley give her a ride home from school, and Jack
had gone caveman, getting up close into Farley's
long, hound-dog face and ordering him to stay
away from his girl, or something equally Neanderthal.

Nora had broken up with Jack on the spot, and
the week before she forgave him had been pure
hell.

True to form, Farley still had a gorgeous girl
with him. Santa had a sexy elf helper this year,
dressed in a tight-fitting, very short red satin mini-
dress trimmed in white fur. Red tights set off fantastic legs, and a perky red cap perched on top of
bouncing blond curls.

Jack stood up straighter.

That was no elf. That was Nora.

"Well, knock me down with a feather! If it isn't
Black Jack Killian himself, all dressed up like a
banker!"

Jack turned. It took him a minute to place the
face, which looked like the much-older version of
someone he once knew. The red hair was a clue,
and finally he made the connection.

"Amy!" He gave her a hug, hoping his face didn't register surprise. Amy Grantham was actually two years younger than he was—maybe twenty-nine or so? But she looked forty-five and exhausted. "I didn't know you were back in Hawthorn Bay."

"It sucked me back," she said with a dry smile. "I married Eddie Folger, he's got a charter boat business. We…we don't have any kids yet, but we're still trying. We do all right."

"I'm glad," he said, but it hurt to see her so drawn and discouraged. He had hoped her life had improved.

They'd met at an Al-Anon meeting his first year of high school. Amy's father had been an alcoholic, too. And they'd both been poor. That had been enough to make them friends. Secretly, they'd bonded against all the happy families in Hawthorn Bay—*secretly* because Amy hadn't wanted anyone to guess how much being an alcoholic's child could define you.

Jack had already accepted his fate as an outcast—what was the point, after five generations of Killian hatred, in fighting it?—but Amy was still pretending she was just like everyone else.

They still exchanged Christmas cards sometimes…or at least his firm used to send his. He tried to remember whether they'd started to bounce back, after she'd moved. He was ashamed to realize he had no idea.

"What about you?" She smiled at him. "What

are you doing here? Don't tell me this place has got hold of you again, too?"

He shuddered inwardly at the thought. "Nope. I'm just here to see Sean. He's in a tangle with the city council, and he needed some legal advice."

Amy rolled her eyes. "*Them!* Yeah, I heard about them wanting Sweet Tides. They're just a bunch of vultures, the lot of them. But they've got the power, just like they always did. Tom Dickson is one of them, did you know that?"

Jack smiled. "Sure. That's the icing on the cake. Made the whole trip down here worthwhile."

Amy glanced at the band-shell stage. "And *she's* one of them. In fact, she's the head buzzard. I guess you knew that, too."

"Yeah."

"Have you seen her yet? I mean, to talk to her? Does she know you're in town?"

"Not yet." He watched Nora lead a little girl up and lift her into Santa's lap. The little girl began to cry, so Nora knelt beside her, soothing her tears. "I don't think she'll exactly be thrilled to see me."

"You two never made up, then?" Amy's pursed mouth moved nervously. "You never—explained things to her?"

He put his hand on the woman's arm. It was painfully thin. Amy had been anorexic back in high school. He wondered if she still was. Her neck was stringy, like an old woman's.

"I promised you I'd never tell anyone about all

that," he said. Had she carried this fear around with her for the past twelve years? "I meant it."

"But…" Amy's eyes looked watery and pale. "She never forgave you for what you did to Tom, did she? Surely you were tempted to explain—"

"Explaining wouldn't change anything," he said. "Nora didn't want the kind of man who would try to murder anyone."

"But—"

"And I didn't want a woman who thought I was that kind of man."

Amy gazed at him a long moment, then nodded slowly. "I guess I can see that," she said. She drew herself up a little straighter. "I should be getting on home. Eddie will be docking soon, and he'll want dinner."

They hugged goodbye, and Jack watched her go. Even from the back she looked like a tired, middle-aged woman. He couldn't help comparing her to Nora. In that ridiculous but strangely seductive elf suit, Nora could have been mistaken for a teenager.

He looked at the stage again. There seemed to be some kind of commotion. Nora was talking to a group of kids, and Santa was walking slowly down the stairs. As soon as she herded the kids back to the line, she posted a sign that said Santa Will Be Back In Five Minutes. Then she turned quickly and followed the man in the red suit.

Looked as if they were taking a break.

If Jack wanted to talk to her, now was the time.

But did he? What did they have to say, after more than a decade? Wouldn't it just open up a wound that had healed nicely over the years, hardly giving him so much as a twinge anymore?

The questions were purely rhetorical. Jack was already moving toward the stage.

NORA HADN'T EVER BEEN IN a men's restroom before. And if she never went into another one, that would be fine with her.

But this time she'd had no choice. The minute she'd realized Farley was drunk, she'd had to do something. The kids had been crushed, of course, and a couple of parents were annoyed, but she'd explained in her best elf voice that Santa had an emergency call from the North Pole, and he'd be right back.

She'd managed to get him in here before he started vomiting. But unfortunately, she hadn't pulled his beard off in time. When he was finished groaning into the bowl, she unhooked the elastic carefully, and deposited the beard in the trash can.

As an afterthought, she covered it over with paper towels. No point shocking innocent kids.

"Thank you, darlin'," Farley said in a little boy voice as she wiped his face with a cool paper towel. "I think you saved my life. My lunch must have disagreed with me."

Nora felt too grumpy to participate in the charade. "More likely the bottle of wine you drank *with* lunch, don't you think?" She scrubbed at his white fur collar, which wasn't quite white anymore. "Look at you. What are we going to do about that line of kids waiting to see Santa?"

"Tell them Santa's been distracted." He reached up and caught Nora's hand. "Tell them Santa's fallen in love with his beautiful little elf."

"Gross." She batted his fingers away unemotionally. "I'm not kidding, Farley. There are at least fifty kids out there. You'd better call one of your friends and get them to take over."

"Whatever you say." He smiled. He might have thought the smile was sexy, but he was wrong. Farley had been sexy in high school, and even in college, but from the time he'd started drinking heavily a couple of years ago, all that had disappeared like smoke in the wind.

"I'll call Mac," he said. "But only if you give me a kiss."

Nora turned away and tossed the paper towel into the trash. "Your mouth smells like a toilet, Farley. Nobody's going to be kissing you tonight. I'll go stall the kids. You stay here and make that call."

She would have thought he was too wobbly even to stand up. But she had just exited the men's room when she felt him wrap his gloved hand around her waist.

"I'm serious, Nora," he whispered in her ear. She nearly vomited, too, as she recognized the odor of half-digested seafood. "I think I love you."

"Farley Hastert," she said through gritted teeth.

She kept her voice low, in case any children were nearby. "Let go of me."

"But Nora—" He brought his other hand up to her waist and began trying to spin her around to face him. "Nora, you're so beautiful."

"Goddamn it, Farley." She put the heel of her hand on his chin and shoved his face up, so that at least he wasn't exhaling rotten food into her nose. "Get a grip."

He was so tall, and though he was as thin as a stick he was pretty strong, from all those years playing basketball. Her arm was failing. His face was getting closer and closer.

Oh, hell. She brought her left knee up hard.

Farley made a sound somewhere between a curse and a kitten's mew, and then he slid to the ground, clutching his red velvet-covered crotch.

She looked down at him, just to be sure he hadn't cracked his head on the sidewalk. Nope, he was fine. She felt kind of sorry for him, but not sorry enough to stay and face the wrath when he recovered. She brushed the front of her elf dress, in case he'd left anything disgusting there, then turned to go back to the band shell.

She'd have to think of something to tell the kids. *Santa's a drunken letch* probably wasn't the right approach.

But she never made it to the stage.

She got only about ten feet, and then, there on the path, clearly watching the whole thing with a broad grin on his face, stood a man she hadn't seen for a dozen years. A man she'd hoped never to see again.

Jack Killian.

Her heart raced painfully—from normal to breathless in less than a second. She had a sudden, mindless urge to knee him in the groin, too, and make her escape.

She couldn't do this right now. She couldn't do this *ever.*

But he wouldn't be as easy to subdue as Farley. Farley was basically a spoiled man-boy who thought the world was his box of candy. Jack Killian had been a street fighter from the day he was born. He didn't expect life to be simple or sweet.

And he didn't know how to lose.

She had loved that about him once. Before she'd realized the twisted things it had done to his soul.

"Hello, Nora," he said with a maddening composure. "Been explaining to Santa that all you want for Christmas is to be left the hell alone?"

She smiled in spite of herself. "Something like that," she said. She adjusted her elf hat, which had slipped sideways, and tried to look semi-dignified. "It's nice to see you, Jack. I didn't know you were in town."

How stupid she'd been not to consider this possibility. She knew that he and Sean were still close. Through the years Sean had traveled to Kansas City frequently to visit Jack, but the only time Jack had come back here was for his mother's funeral, which had been held while Nora had been in Europe.

She had naively assumed she was safe.

Why hadn't it occurred to her that the council's bid to confiscate Sweet Tides would be the one battle he'd be willing to fight in person?

"Is it, Nora?"

"Is it what?"

"Nice to see me."

She willed herself not to flush. But, as she looked at him standing there with his curly black hair and his piercing blue eyes, a dizzy confusion swept over her. For just a moment, she was transported back a dozen years, to a cold Christmas dawn rising over the water in wisps of blue and gold. Jack's lips had tasted like the chocolate he'd stolen from her stocking, and his arms had been hotter than the bonfire they'd built on the beach.

In another instant the memory dissolved. All that was left was the awkward present.

"Of course it's nice," she said. She would not give him the satisfaction of knowing how easily her composure could unravel right now. She had to keep it distant, keep it professional. "I know we're going to be on opposite sides of the eminent domain issue, but still…I'm glad to see you looking so well. Apparently the Army agreed with you."

"Not really, but getting out of it did. And I enjoy practicing law. It's a relief to be on the right side of it for a change."

She laughed politely. "I can imagine."

God, who were these two people? Years ago, they'd sat in this very park, in a twilight much like this one. They'd shared a cold park bench, and she'd laid her head in his lap. He had hummed a love song—he had a beautiful baritone—and had lifted her long curls to his lips, the gesture so sexy it had burned her scalp.

"I should go," she said. "The children—"

"Yes." He stepped out of the way. "I'll look after Santa for you."

"Thanks." She paused, a sudden anxiety passing through her. Jack's temper. If he'd seen Farley pawing her, grabbing her against her will…

"He's been punished enough," she said carefully, hoping Jack would get her meaning. "He drinks a little too much, but he's not a bad guy."

Jack understood her alright.

His familiar blue eyes narrowed briefly, and then he raised one eyebrow high. Oh, God, she thought. She knew that expression. She knew it so well it took her breath away.

"I think I can control myself, Nora. After all, I have no reason to hurt him, do I? He hasn't messed with anything that belongs to me."

"No." She felt like an idiot. The man who stood here, with his expensive suit and his expensive haircut and his sardonic voice…he wasn't going to get in a brawl over some woman he'd forgotten a decade ago.

He didn't lust after Nora Carson's body anymore, or her heart, for that matter.

But that didn't mean she was safe.

She might still have something he wanted.

Something he'd battle for. Something that would bring out the bare-knuckled street fighter she used to know. Just thinking of it made her racing heart come to a dead standstill.

She just might have his son.

CHAPTER FOUR

"I'M OUT," THE MAN in the camel-hair suit said, slapping his cards facedown on the game table set up in the gun room of Sweet Tides. "My wife will kill me if I lose any more. You're too damn lucky this week, Killian."

"He's too lucky every week," the older man across from him, who had a strangely bouffant set of gray curls, grumbled around his unlit cigar.

"What can I say?" Sean laughed. "The angels love me. You in or out, Curly?"

"In, damn it. I'm not afraid of you." Curly held onto his cards, but he kept rearranging them nervously while his cigar bobbed up and down.

Jack, who had spent the past hour sitting by the window reading through some eminent domain research, could see even from this distance that Curly's knuckles were white with tension.

Jack smiled, bending his head back to the boring papers. Damn if Sean wasn't going to take this hand, too.

It had been the same all night. One by one, the yellow and blue mother-of-pearl chips had marched their way across the green felt, as if under military orders, to stand in neat piles at Sean's elbow.

Frankly, Jack had been shocked to hear that Sean even had a regular poker game. Like drinking, gambling had always been something the brothers avoided. Too much like dear old dad.

But, just before his friends had arrived, Sean had given Jack the quick rundown. About five years ago, Sean had decided to give cards a try, and he'd discovered that, unlike Crazy Kelly, he was pretty good.

Jack couldn't bring himself to join in the game— technically, it was illegal, and he knew there were people in this town who would love any excuse to put a Killian behind bars, even if it was just for jaywalking or quarter stakes in a friendly neighborhood game.

But he'd enjoyed watching. He'd learned a lot about his brother. Sure, they'd spent plenty of time together on Sean's trips out to Kansas City, but this was different. Like observing a very clever wild animal in its natural habitat.

He'd also learned a lot about the pretty brunette grad student Stacy Holtsinger, the one Sean had mentioned earlier. Stacy had climbed down from the attic about an hour ago, brushed the dust from her hair and had immediately started refilling glasses and peanut bowls.

Apparently Stacy had been studying Sweet Tides history long enough to become the unofficial hostess of the Saturday-night game.

And what else, Jack wondered?

Curly grudgingly tossed a couple of blue chips into the pile. "Okay, big shot. Show me."

Sean smiled. He had a Killian smile, equal parts cocky bastard and pure good humor. The cocky part had made people around here yearn to tar and feather Killian men for generations. The good-humored part had kept them from doing it. Usually.

Sean splayed out his cards on the table. "Straight. King high."

The other man took a deep breath. "Crap."

Chuckling, Sean started picking up his winnings. As if on cue, Stacy appeared at his shoulder, grinning happily, and refilled his sweet tea.

"More beer, anyone?" She tore her gaze from Sean—reluctantly, Jack thought with a new twinge of curiosity—and she scanned the table. "Or is it time to switch to coffee?"

The other men began looking at their watches, as Stacy had no doubt intended they should. As the big winner, Sean couldn't suggest quitting, so obviously she'd stepped in with the gentle hint. Within minutes, everyone had cashed out. Then they pulled on their overcoats and headed for the door.

After seeing the men out together like an old married couple, Sean and Stacy came back into the gun room, still grinning. He high-fived Jack, then went over to the game table and flicked the first stack of chips. It fell sideways, knocking down the next stack, then the next, like dominos. Apparently Sean had won often enough to have perfected his technique.

"Okay, I'm impressed," Jack said. "What's your secret? Marked cards?"

"Hell, no." Sean tilted his head back and finished off his tea in a long swig. "Why would I need to cheat? Poker's not exactly rocket science. I just have three unbreakable rules."

"Yeah? What are they?"

Jack noticed that Stacy was already smiling. She knew the rules, obviously. She knew a lot, for someone who supposedly was only interested in dead Killians.

"One, I never bet big when I'm broke, tired, pissed off or in love. Two, I never bet big unless I'm holding something better than a pair of tens. Three, I never bet big, period."

He held up four five-dollar bills. "My total winnings tonight."

Jack laughed. "In other words, you're the anti-Kelly."

"Pretty much." Sean put his hand out and stopped Stacy, who had begun to clear away the beer bottles and peanuts. "Leave this stuff. I'll get it in the morning. I want you to show Jack the letter."

She hesitated, but then, with one last look at Sean, she went over to the mantel, an ornate marble affair carved with a hunting scene, and picked up a plastic sleeve into which a yellowed document had been slipped.

She brought it over to where Jack had been reading. She twisted the knob on the desk lamp, increasing the wattage.

"It's from 1864," she said, holding it out for him to take. She looked uncertain, as if she thought he might reject it. He wondered what she'd heard about him—from Sean, and from everyone else in Hawthorn Bay. Probably the attempted-murder story had grown claws and fangs over the past twelve years.

"Who wrote it?" He took the letter, even though he still believed the whole thing was a wild goose chase. Every now and then, someone would heat up the search for the gold. Sometimes it was greedy treasure-hunters. More often it was someone young and naive, like this woman. Either way, it always ended in disappointment.

Because there *was* no gold. There was only a harvest of dreams, lying tender on the ground, ready to be stomped flat by reality.

Even worse, he had a feeling that finding the gold wasn't Stacy Holtsinger's only dream. If he were a betting man, he'd bet that she had a thing for Sean.

Jack felt vaguely sorry for the woman, who seemed very nice but innocent, younger than the thirty or so Sean had said she was. And needy. Definitely needy.

He wondered if he should give her a heads-up.

Her boyish figure, her tortoiseshell glasses and her baggy jeans and sweater were the wrong recipe for snagging Sean's attention. Sean had no interest in settling down with a refined, well-educated woman. He liked his females lusty, busty and loud.

Or at least he used to. Of course, he also used to say he had no interest in following their dad down the poker trail, too, so maybe Jack didn't know as much as he thought he did.

He turned his attention to the letter, deciding it would be premature to nudge poor Stacy Holtsinger toward contact lenses and implants just yet.

"It was written by Joe Killian," Stacy said. She cleared her throat. "It was written to his wife, Julia. She seems to have left him, a year or two before, ostensibly to wait out the war with her family back in Philadelphia. But this letter makes it sound as if she left because of a quarrel."

"Okay." He glanced at the faded handwriting, which crisscrossed the page in both directions. "And? I'm sure this letter has been looked at a million times through the years. If it had confirmed the existence of the gold—"

"That's just it," she said. Her voice sounded a little more confident. She was clearly sure of her ground on this topic. "I'm sure it has been 'looked at,' but I'm not sure it's really been read. Not all the way through."

"She's right," Sean said, as he tossed himself onto the leather sofa. "I tried to read it myself, the day Stacy found it. I just couldn't. It's this endless regurgitation of love-mush. Julia is more beautiful than the gold of twilight, the pearl of dawn. He'll become a living ghost if she doesn't return to him."

Sean shook his head. "Disgusting. The man needed a spine implant, that's for sure."

"So…?"

"Well, you have to get past that stuff," Stacy said, shooting a stern look at Sean. "And then his words seem more pertinent. He tells her that if she comes back—"

Stacy held out a hand for the plastic sheet, which Jack relinquished willingly. She turned it over and squinted at the back. "Let me find it, so I can really… Here it is! He writes, 'For you, I have dirtied my hands and stood in my own grave. If you will come back to me, I will unearth the golden love, the priceless happiness we once had. Come home, my treasure, and you shall want for nothing.'"

Stacy's voice lowered on the last words, as if old Joe's begging had moved her. She blinked, cleared her throat, and then looked up at Jack.

"He must be referring to the gold," she said. "He buried it rather than turn it over to the Confederacy, just as the rumor always said he did. He's promising her that, if she comes home, he'll dig it up and give it all to her."

"That's one way to read it. But who knows? He sounds like a windbag. In love with his metaphors, don't you think?"

Clearly she didn't think. She lowered her brows and held the letter against her chest, as if to protect it from his cynicism.

"Come on, Jack, don't be such a buzz kill." Sean

was tossing a blue poker chip up and down, catching it with first one hand, then the other. "Treasure, dirt, unearth, golden. Those are some pretty pointed images, if you ask me. Maybe he buried it up on the cemetery hill."

Was Sean really buying this? Jack couldn't tell. Sean might just be trying to make Stacy feel good about her discovery.

"Even if you're right, what happened then? Julia came home, didn't she? My family history is a little hazy, but I'm pretty sure their son was born after the war. So why didn't old Joe dig up the gold and shower her in gifts, as he promised?"

"I don't know." Stacy bit her lower lip. "Maybe when Julia returned, she told her husband she loved him with or without the treasure."

"Sure," Jack said with a laugh. "And maybe tomorrow it'll snow sugar and rain roses."

Stacy flushed. "I should have known you were too cynical to take any of this seriously. Nora told me about you. She told me you were—"

She stopped herself abruptly, clearly aware that she'd been about to cross an invisible but electrically charged line.

"I was what?"

She glanced anxiously at Sean, but Sean didn't look disturbed.

"Stacy and Nora are best friends," he explained to Jack. "Partners, too. They're in the jam business."

So that was why Stacy had been subtly hostile ever since she'd laid eyes on him. As Nora Carson's best buddy, she'd probably taken a blood oath to despise Jack Killian sight unseen.

He could easily imagine what Nora had said about him. Still, some perversity made him push. "So…she said I was *what?*"

"She… I… Just—" The woman swallowed. "She said you were cynical. And…unkind."

"Unkind?" Sean laughed out loud. "Damn. That's probably the least offensive thing that's been said about a Killian in two hundred years."

"I suspect that's the edited version." Jack shrugged. "But she was right, Stacy. If *cynical* means I don't believe the Killians have been squatting on a fortune in gold like mindless brood hens ever since the Civil War, then I'm cynical. If *unkind* means that I won't pretend I do believe, just to make you two dreamers feel good, then okay. I'm unkind."

Stacy narrowed her eyes. Something he'd said had struck a nerve. He wondered if it might have been the "dreamer" comment. Perhaps she'd been called that before.

"Yes. Well. The unedited version? She also said you were *dangerous.*"

Jack took a breath. Stacy couldn't know what a direct hit that was.

He tried not to hear Nora's soft voice saying the word, wrapped in shock and tears. *They all warned me about you, Jack. They told me you would break my heart. They told me you were dangerous.*

He pushed the voice away. Dangerous? You bet he was.

Somehow, he found the customary Killian smile. "Right again," he said.

"NORA, SLOW DOWN. I HAVE TO talk to you about the goddamn Killians."

Nora looked around. Bill Freeman, Hawthorn Bay's white-haired, sixty-something city attorney, chugged up behind her on the sidewalk in front of the hospital.

Nora frowned, tilting her head at Colin, who had joined her for the ribbon-cutting at the hospital's new cardiac wing. Bill grimaced, mouthing an *oops* as apology for the profanity. He shifted his battered briefcase from one hand to the other as he caught up.

"Gawd, I'm out of shape," he complained. Though it was only about forty-five degrees outside, he was sweating. He pinched his upper lip to get rid of the perspiration. "Teresa says I've got to either give up the pecan pie or take out more life insurance. Says if she has to be a widow, she wants to be a rich one."

Nora was well aware that Teresa Freeman adored her husband and had no intentions of being any kind of widow. She'd probably subbed in a low-calorie version of that pecan-pie recipe years ago. She'd been secretly ordering sugar-free jam from Nora ever since Bill's sixtieth birthday.

Nora slowed down just a little. "What about the Killians?"

"I had a visit from Jack this morning. That boy

certainly has changed. Have you seen him since he got back to town?"

Nora checked Colin out of the corner of her eye. Good—he was still absorbed in his video game. You couldn't ever be sure what kind of dumb comment Bill might make. He knew all about Nora's high-school romance with Jack. Almost everyone in Hawthorn Bay did.

That was one of the reasons she hadn't returned, at first. She didn't want to answer a million questions from people who would take it for granted that Colin was Jack's illegitimate son.

Even more importantly, she hadn't dared to return as long as Maggie's parents had been alive. But, when Colin had been only about eighteen months old, they had died in a car crash, hit by a drunk driver going over the Hawthorn Bay Bridge.

And then, gossip or no gossip, Nora had made a beeline for home. Single motherhood was hard. She'd wanted to be with her own mother, the only person, other than Ethan, who knew the truth. Nora had known that her charming, dignified mother could handle the curiosity of friends and neighbors. She could even handle Nora's father, Boss.

It had worked. Though Boss had probably been disappointed in his daughter for bringing home a fatherless baby he'd never shown it—to her, or to anyone else.

The Carson family, once united, had presented a formidable front. No one had dared to probe.

As the years had passed, it had become a

nonissue. Nora was a model mom—and people admired her work, first on the city council, and now as mayor. Jack had never returned, and his brother, Sean, had never shown any particular interest in the boy, so most people had lost interest.

"I said, have you seen him?" Bill looked curious, and Nora realized that she'd let her thoughts get away with her.

"Yes. I ran into him at the tree-lighting ceremony."

"Quite a transformation, isn't it?"

Nora actually thought most of Jack's changes were superficial. Behind that suave suit and lazy poise, he still hummed with the edgy energy of a wild animal. And behind those eyes, the fire was merely banked, not extinguished.

"Yes," she agreed blandly. "So how did the meeting go? I assume he wanted to discuss the city's bid to buy Sweet Tides."

They had reached Nora's car. Bill leaned against it, dropping his briefcase as if it were loaded with lead, and pulled out his handkerchief to wipe his face.

Colin glanced at the older man. He obviously understood that Mom was detained again, so with a dramatic sigh he hoisted himself onto the hood of the car and bent over his video game. He kicked the side of the car with his sneakers, until Nora reached out and stilled them.

"Well, now, I wouldn't exactly call it a discussion," Bill said with a smile. "Jack's become a lawyer, you know. And the boy knows his stuff. He doesn't appear to have inherited his father's slacker gene, even if he did get the—"

He broke off awkwardly.

"The *mean* gene," Nora supplied. "So what did he say?"

"He said that they had no intention of selling at any price, and that as the city had no legitimate grounds for condemnation, he assumed that would be the end of it. But he wanted us to know that, if we decided to pursue eminent domain on any grounds, he had already drawn up an action challenging the condemner's right to take."

Nora widened her eyes. "Wow," she said. "He doesn't waste time."

"Nope. And he's right, of course. Any pretext we could trump up for claiming eminent domain would be as phony as a stripper's—"

"Bill."

"Oops," he said again. "Well, you know what I mean. These days, in spite of the Supreme Court ruling, any economic-development takings are risky as hell—*oops*. And though the mansion could stand a new coat of paint, it would be pretty hard to prove it's a blight."

Nora agreed, of course. Both she and Bill had argued all these points to the city council for hours when the eminent domain issue had first come up. But unfortunately, in Hawthorn Bay, the charter had created a "weak" mayor position, which meant she had only one vote, like every other councilman.

She couldn't veto anything, even something as stupid as this.

And, on this issue, Tom Dickson was like a dog with a bone. For whatever reason, fair or foul, he wanted that new retail development to go in on Sweet Tides property, and he wasn't giving up the idea just because it was incredibly venal and unfair.

"Anyhow," Bill went on, "Jack plans to fight, and apparently he knows how. For us to win in court, we'd have to find a judge who literally eats out of Tom Dickson's hand."

"Unfortunately, that wouldn't be all that hard, would it?"

Though she'd been fond of Tom when they'd been teenagers, Nora had learned a lot about her cousin through the years. He knew how to work the system, and had no ethics to prevent him sinking as low as he needed to go. His boot-licking and back-scratching with the other lawyers and judges might not legally constitute bribery, but it sure didn't smell right.

And the stink rubbed off on the whole city council, which she resented.

Bill sighed. "I don't know how many judges he owns, and I don't want to find out. I just want the whole thing to go away. I heard Tom say he's planning to raise the offer. I hope to God the Killian boys will decide to take it."

Though she knew it was completely selfish, she half hoped they would, too. It would make her life so much easier if Jack would just go back to Kansas City.

It wasn't just that his arrival had set all the old emotions bubbling. She was a strong woman, and she could handle a little leftover yearning and angst. She had an old scar on her knee, from the chaos that day on the boat with Maggie. That scar hurt sometimes, too. She took an aspirin and went on with her life.

No, the serious issue was Colin. How long could she keep Jack from running into the boy? And once he saw him, once he saw an eleven-year-old kid with curly black hair and eyes that sparkled with a color she had always called *Killian-blue*...

Ironically, it had taken Nora a few years to figure out the truth. Thanks to the loving cocoon her parents had raised her in, she'd always been ridiculously naive, almost childish when it came to the real world.

Besides, she'd been at a disadvantage. She would never in a million years have suspected that Maggie, her best friend, might have slept with Jack. With the man Nora had loved.

Even after Colin's features had begun to take shape, Nora had innocently assumed it must have been a coincidence. Then she'd tried to tell herself it must have been Sean. But Sean, a couple of years older than Jack, had been away at college that spring.

Finally she couldn't deny the truth any longer. Maggie and Jack must have...

Betrayed her.

Nora wondered, sometimes, what Sean thought

when he looked at Colin. At first, she'd been afraid that he might tell Jack, but that fear had subsided, little by little, as the months, then years, had passed without incident. She always had her story ready, though. The whirlwind romance in Cornwall, the black-haired charmer who had broken her heart.

But no one had ever asked.

Still, if Jack saw Colin…

He already possessed one of the key pieces of the puzzle. He already knew that he'd betrayed Nora with Maggie.

How long would it be before he put the whole sordid picture together? About five minutes?

And what would he do then?

Oh, yes, she wanted him to take the money and run. But she knew how selfish that was. Sweet Tides had been the Killian family home for almost three hundred years. It was Sean's home still.

So she tried to push the thought away. This wasn't about her. It was about justice. She'd have to talk to Tom again, and try to make him see reason. If the council would just drop the issue, that would accomplish the same thing.

Jack would go back where he belonged.

And she and Colin would be safe.

She glanced toward her son, who was using the windshield as a backrest while he punched buttons on the small display. Over his head, the metallic Christmas garland wrapped around the streetlight cable swayed in the wind, casting flashes of green across his ivory wool sweater.

He sensed her attention. He looked up with wide blue eyes and smiled angelically.

That set off her baloney meter. Why was he accepting this delay so patiently? Ordinarily, he hated ribbon-cuttings and groundbreakings and speechifying and couldn't wait to get back home where he could play with his friends.

And then she remembered. Their next stop was the nursing home, where Colin had been doing volunteer work reading books and newspapers to the residents.

He hadn't seemed to hate it as much lately, but still, he'd probably welcome a reprieve. If they were delayed here a hundred years, he wouldn't utter a syllable of complaint.

She shook her head. *The rascal.* It was disgusting how much she loved him. She had the most spineless impulse to go ruffle those silky curls and tell him he didn't have to do it today, not if he really didn't want to.

But she put her hands in her sweater pockets and looked away. She had to stay strong. He mustn't be allowed to believe that he could get off without paying for his sins.

Nobody could, in the end.

CHAPTER FIVE

WHEN JACK WALKED INTO the Bayside Assisted Living Facility, he was glad to see what a nice place it was. Cheerful, clean and brightly decorated for Christmas, it looked more like a condo than an institution.

Still, he found it difficult to believe that Patrick Killian was here. Could he really have become one of these frail old people?

Standing about six-five, Patrick had always looked more like a lumberjack than the accountant he was. His physical and moral strength, frequently put to the test by his wife, who had what today would probably be diagnosed as a bipolar disorder, had been legendary in Hawthorn Bay.

Even people who disliked the Killians on principle made an exception for Patrick. *He's a saint,* they'd say. What they meant, of course, was how did he stand it, living with a trashy son, a crazy wife and those two grandsons who were clearly doomed to be hooligans just like their dad?

Jack scanned the white-haired gentlemen who sat in wheelchairs by the window of the reception area. It gave him a strangely hollow feeling to realize that his tough grandfather might lose this last fight.

"May I help you, sir?" An attractive middle-aged woman stood behind the volunteer desk. She wore a lapel pin in the shape of a reindeer with a blinking red nose. "Are you looking for someone?"

"Yes. Patrick Killian. Room twelve, I think."

"Oh, yes." She smiled at him. "You must be his other grandson. How nice. Just turn right at the next corridor, and you can't miss it. He'll be so happy to see you."

Not half as happy as Jack would be to see him. Patrick had always been the one sane center of Jack's dangerous childhood universe. He still made Jack feel just slightly more balanced, and since seeing Nora the other day, Jack needed a little of that.

The door to number twelve was standing open, and when Jack was still two rooms away he could hear the noises emanating from it. A boy's voice shouted odd words, alternated with a guttural grunt from an old man.

"Thundering apoplexy!" The child was trying to imitate an adult's voice, his tones artificially deep and rounded. "I tell you, Silver, lay down your sword or meet your end!"

Jack reached the door just as the boy finished this odd speech. The old man's voice began to holler a response with a string of excited syllables that didn't quite make words at all.

Curious, Jack entered the room.

His grandfather lay in the bed. Jack's heart loosened a little, just to see how essentially *himself* the old man still looked. His silver hair was still thickly curling, and still had streaks of the old black. His arrogant profile was pure Killian, and it was turned now toward the window. In his right hand, he held a cane, waving it wildly at shoulder level.

This must be the sword the boy had ordered him to lay down. Obviously, in true Killian fashion, he had refused to surrender.

The boy knelt on a small footstool that sat in front of the window. The light was bright, so Jack saw the child only in silhouette, but he was pretty damn sure the kid was pointing the television remote control at Patrick, as if it were a gun.

At that moment, the kid turned his head and saw Jack. The remote control froze in place.

Patrick was slower to realize that they had a witness. He was still waving the cane and shouting.

The boy lowered the black box slowly. He looked back at Patrick. "Hey, Mr. Killian," he said. "It's okay. Time out. Time out."

Patrick stopped gabbling and frowned at the boy.

"Somebody's here." The boy eased himself off the footstool. "We'll finish the game later, Mr. Killian." He pointed to Jack. "See? Somebody's come to visit you."

Patrick, who apparently could still understand words, though he could no longer speak them, rotated his face slowly toward the door with a fierce scowl clearly designed to terrify whoever had dared to interrupt the game.

Jack almost laughed. He knew that look so well. He'd seen it a million times, whenever he or Sean had stepped out of line.

Suddenly, his throat was as tight as if someone were choking him.

"Hi, Grandfather," he said. That was pretty much all he was capable of right now.

The old man didn't move a muscle. The cane still pointed skyward.

"Grandfather?" Jack moved farther into the room. He took the cane out of the old man's hand, resisting the urge to hold on to the cool, papery fingers. "It's me. It's Jack."

"He's okay," the boy said. "I think he's just surprised, and he always has trouble talking anyhow. We were just playing a game. We've been reading *Treasure Island,* and we decided to have a sword fight. But we only had one sword, so I had to use a blunderbuss, and—"

The boy halted his own stream of words, as if he realized they were silly. He laid the remote control on the metal table that fit over the hospital bed. Then he straightened and faced Jack squarely.

"It was just a game, honest. He likes it."

For the first time, now that the boy had moved out of the sunlight, Jack could really see his features. His full lower lip, his pointed chin. The highly arched brows, and the intense blue eyes beneath.

What the hell?

Jack frowned. "Who are you?"

The question came out more harshly than he'd intended, and immediately the boy's conciliatory expression vanished. He drew his dark eyebrows together over those startling blue eyes, clearly disliking Jack's preemptory tone.

"I'm Colin," he said with an edge of defiance. "I read to Mr. Killian every day." He lifted his pointed chin. "Who are *you?*"

Jack felt the strangest need to sit down. "I'm Jack," he said. "Jack Killian. Mr. Killian is my grandfather."

Colin narrowed his eyes. "I've never seen you here before. Sean is Mr. Killian's grandson, and he's here all the time."

How incredible was this? Jack was getting the third degree from this kid—how old was he, maybe thirteen? He was as long and stiffly skinny as uncooked linguini, so he could have been older…but his face was still young, vaguely unformed. Jack revised his estimate down. Maybe only eleven or twelve.

But as determined and self-confident as an adult. Jack was staring, he knew that. The kid just stared back. He clearly saw himself as Patrick's guardian, at least for the moment, and he didn't intend to flinch first.

"Sean comes more often because he lives right here in Hawthorn Bay. I don't. I live in Kansas City." Jack held out his hand. "I didn't mean to be rude. I was just…surprised to see you. It's nice to meet you, Colin…"

He let the sentence drift off, giving Colin the chance to supply a last name.

But the kid obviously hadn't forgiven Jack for being so curt. Though he put out his hand politely, he volunteered nothing further.

"Nice to meet you, too, Mr. Killian."

He let go of Jack's hand quickly, and moved to the edge of Patrick's bed. The old man had been watching the interchange in complete silence. Jack wondered what he was thinking. Had he noticed, too? Had he looked into the kid's blue eyes and thought…

But maybe Jack was imagining things. Lots of people in this world—even in this town—had bright blue eyes, dark, curly hair and a pointed chin that squared off belligerently when they were angry.

Jack took a breath. Damn, he was getting as delusional as his grandmother, who, when she'd been in a manic phase, used to accuse Patrick of fathering half the children in town. Every pair of blue eyes Ginny Killian saw, whether they belonged to the pretty waitress's daughter or the high-school vice principal's brand new twins, were cause for suspicion and tears.

"Mr. Killian, I have to go now," Colin said, touching the pillow. "My mom is going to be here soon. But I want to be sure…are you up to having visitors? Is it okay if your grandson Jack stays here when I'm gone?"

The old man's eyes, their blue unfaded, moved from Colin to Jack, then back again. He raised his right hand about six inches above the mattress.

Colin turned to Jack. "His neck's stiff, so that's his way of saying yes. When he wants to say no, he shakes his hand sideways."

"Okay," Jack said, though the whole thing felt surreal. He wondered what he would have done if Colin had reported that Patrick's answer was no. Would Colin really have tried to send Jack away?

That would have been quite a feat. But it was sort of amusing to watch the kid play guard dog.

Jack glanced around the large, pleasant room. Not as big as the rooms at Sweet Tides, but more homey, with blue walls and white curtains at the window, and a small Christmas tree on the corner table. A very pricey place, as Jack already knew from the size of the check he wrote each month.

Still. Jack realized how Patrick must hate this. How he must wish he could go back to his own home.

There was a comfortable chair next to the table, but Jack wanted something closer. He reached out to drag a straight chair up to the edge of the bed.

As he did, his gaze fell on the nightstand, where an assortment of pills, water glasses, Christmas cards and pictures had been piled together. One of the pictures was of Patrick himself, as a young man in the Navy.

Jack knew that photo—it had been taken right after Patrick's only son, Kelly, had been born.

Patrick looked so proud and strong at that moment, in the first flush of fatherhood, in the pride of his uniform, unaware of the disappointments that were to come.

Jack stepped back two paces, so that the tableau in front of him encompassed all three—the old man in the bed, the boy beside him and the young father in the photograph.

Good God.

He might as well have been looking at three stages of the same man.

"Oh, shoot, there's my mom." Colin glanced out the window, then spun into action, grabbing a well-worn black corduroy jacket and tossing it over his shoulder. "I'll see you tomorrow, Mr. Killian."

He gave Jack a polite, rather chilly nod as he passed, but Jack hardly saw it. He was crossing the room quickly, heading for the window. Though his mind had instinctively formed a picture of Colin's mother, he had to be sure. He might be wrong.

He wasn't.

As he watched, Colin came barreling around the side of the building, smiling at his mother, who had just started to get out of her car.

Jack spoke the word aloud without meaning to. *"Nora."*

Behind him, he heard Patrick make a noise. It could have been an awkward laugh—or a smothered cry.

Numbly, Jack turned to face the old man. Patrick's eyes were bright and fixed on Jack. With effort, Patrick raised his good right hand and pointed a shaky finger toward the window.

"Killian," he said, as clear as day.

SEAN DID MOST OF HIS JUNK DEALING out of the stable, which had been built in the late 1800s, after the old stable had burned down. All the horses had been lost in that fire, so, though the structure had been rebuilt bigger and better than ever, just to show the townspeople the Killians hadn't been beaten, no one had ever had the heart to fill it with animals again.

Through the years, the empty stable had been used alternately as a servant's quarters, garage, storehouse and lover's tryst. Like the rest of Sweet Tides, it looked run-down now, and tired, the white paint peeling down to pure pine, and the roof stained with mildew and oak pollen.

In the lavender light of early evening, though, with the windows glowing a warm honey-yellow, the stable looked better. Almost inviting. Jack moved through the black shadows of the oak trees, his eye on the bright squares. He could see Sean's silhouette moving back and forth, busy and efficient.

Jack hardly knew what he was going to say when he got there. The questions that had burned through him all the way back from the nursing home seemed almost crazy now.

He knocked at the stable door, though he knew Sean never locked it. Knocking seemed more polite, more restrained. Less like a madman barging in to hurl accusations that might well be insane.

"It's open," Sean called. "Whoever you are, I hope you brought a big bucket of greasy fried chicken, because I'm starving."

Jack shut the door firmly behind him. The stable had a window heater that didn't work particularly well, and the place was already chilly enough without letting in more of the outside air. Tonight's forecast called for a soft freeze.

"Sorry," Jack said. "I've got nothing. I didn't know you hadn't eaten."

Sean tilted up a painting he'd been studying. "This is crap," he said with a sigh, pointing to the wild tangle of colors that appeared to have been flung at the canvas. "I had hoped it might be valuable crap, but no. Just everyday what-were-you-thinking-when-you-bought-this crap. I'll be lucky to get five dollars for the frame."

He let the painting fall back onto the scarred wooden table. "Have you?"

"What? Eaten?" Jack realized suddenly that he hadn't had a meal all day. "No. I've been at the nursing home."

Sean nodded sympathetically. "That could take your appetite away, all right. It's a damn shame, isn't it? A man like Grandfather, and he can't speak a single coherent word, or get himself out of bed."

But Patrick *had* said one word. One word that had damn near cut Jack's knees out from under him.

He couldn't start there, though. He had to start more slowly, with...

With what?

"Sean," he said. His voice sounded funny. Even he could hear that. "Sean, I need to ask you something."

Sean tilted his head quizzically. He slapped the dust from his hands, then swept the dangling curls of black hair behind both ears.

"Okay," he said. He pulled up a chair, flipped it around and sat down backward. "Ask."

"I met Nora Carson's son today. I met Colin."

"Oh." Sean raised one eyebrow. "Technically, that's not a question." Pausing, he picked up a stray Phillips head screwdriver and tapped it on the edge of the table. "But, come to think of it, it might be an answer."

"An answer to what?"

"To the question of why you came busting in here as tense as a kite string in a hurricane."

"I'm sorry." Jack took a breath. "It's just— He's so— I mean, you've gotta admit the kid looks—"

"Like a Killian."

"Yeah. So I'm not crazy? You see it, too?"

"Definitely. I first noticed it a couple of years ago. Before that he was just a blob, you know. The way kids are."

Jack waited. There was no good way to ask what he wanted to know. He hoped Sean wouldn't make him say the words out loud.

Sean tapped the screwdriver in an irregular

rhythm, a light calypso beat. His smile looked lazy and amused.

"Sean," Jack began. "Damn it."

"Okay, okay." Sean dropped the screwdriver. "I ought to make you sweat it out, just for being such an idiot. But I can't really blame you. Those eyes... Anyhow, you want to know if the kid is mine, right? You want to know if, after you left for the Army, I came home from college and comforted your brokenhearted girlfriend. Comforted her all the way into my bed."

"Something like that." Jack could feel the pulse beating in his neck. "So. Did you?"

"Nope."

Jack slowly lowered himself onto the edge of the table. He wiped his hand across his face.

"Okay." He was amazed at how much better he felt, just knowing that. It would have been—impossible. "Then what—"

"Frankly," Sean broke in, "at first I figured the kid had to be yours. Remember a couple of years ago I called you and asked you whether, back in the old days, you'd ever, even once, managed to make the Ice Queen open up?"

Jack had forgotten about that, but he remembered it now. The call had come out of the blue, and Jack had wondered, at the time, what had prompted it. He'd even wondered whether Sean might have developed an interest in Nora himself and was putting out feelers to see if Jack still considered her marked territory.

Jack had assured him that the Ice Queen hadn't ever come close to a meltdown, not even once, in spite of the fact that Jack had applied heat like a blowtorch for two long years.

In fact, he'd warned Sean that there might not even *be* a flesh-and-blood woman under all that ice. The night before he'd left Hawthorn Bay, he'd called her phone number like a madman. He'd been in the park by the river, alternately using the pay phone and dangling on one of the kids' swings with a bottle of vodka in the dirt at his feet, abandoning pride as he got drunker and drunker.

He'd begged her to trust him. To forgive him. To sneak out and come to him. To let him explain. To let him say goodbye.

Nothing. In desperation, he'd sent her best friend Maggie to intercede.

Even Maggie had clearly been shocked by Nora's answer. *No. Never. She never wanted to see him again.* Maggie had had tears in her eyes as she delivered it.

Like the drunken fool he was, Jack had exploded. He'd shouted. He'd called Nora all kinds of barroom names. He'd thrown things. He was pretty sure he'd broken the swing. He had, in fact, confirmed every ugly thing people thought about him. He was difficult, violent, dangerous.

In the end, he'd even scared Maggie away. The last thing he remembered about that night was hearing Maggie's sandals slapping on the sidewalk as she'd run to her car, and then the sound of her tires squealing as she'd peeled off, unable to get away from him fast enough.

He'd puked then, inevitably, into the bushes. As he'd hunched there, heaving, he'd wished he could puke out every last bit of feeling he'd ever had for Nora.

And maybe he had. When he'd woken up, dew had glistened like shards of glass on the grass where he'd lain. And his heart had been as cold and hard as the puny gray moon that had been fading away in the early morning sky.

Sean was watching him now. "You said you'd never made it into her pretty panties. I believed you. You don't want to change the story now, do you?"

Jack shook his head. "No. I dreamed about it a thousand times, you know how it is to be eighteen. But in real life, never. She was locked up tighter than Fort Knox."

Sean nodded. "I figured as much. That's one of the reasons I never even tried. You know I don't like to work that hard. I like women who think sex is a one-way ticket to heaven, not hell."

Jack knew that was true. And Sean had never suffered any shortage of willing women. It was weird how many women were turned on by a bad boy.

Just Jack's luck to fall for the one woman in town who wasn't.

"Okay," Jack said. "So where did the kid get those eyes? And that hair? Were you ever curious enough to snoop around and find out?"

Sean shook his head. "Honestly, I already knew it wasn't me, so when I made sure it wasn't you I just stopped worrying about it. Obviously the lady likes men with dark hair and blue eyes. It's her type. And though it may prick our pride to face it, we're not the only men in the world who have those things."

"Yeah, but—" Jack tried to find the hole in the logic. "The boy looks about eleven, which means she would have had to—"

"Find a new pair of blue eyes pretty quickly after you left? I know." Sean shrugged. "Sorry, Jack, but I'm not sure she nursed that broken heart very long."

Jack reached out and took hold of the junk painting. He scraped it toward him across the table and stared down into its chaotic depths. The longer he looked, the easier it was to make out the pattern. Though it looked like a mess, it was actually a bouquet of flowers.

Maybe Sean was right—maybe the explanation was really that simple. Nora liked tall, thin men with blue eyes and black hair. She'd slept with one. End of story.

So why did it feel so wrong?

Sean cleared his throat. "She went abroad, you know, not long after you enlisted. I know they went to England. Maybe they went to Ireland, too. We get our coloring from our Black Irish forefathers, right? Maybe, when she got over there, she found herself the real thing."

Jack looked up. It made sense, but…

Damn it. He felt hot, suddenly, and pissed off. "Do you really believe that? After two years with me…this…this *stranger* just happened to have the key to Fort Knox in his hip pocket?"

Sean's eyes were gentle, which inexplicably just made Jack feel even madder.

"Maybe…" Sean said softly. "Maybe she was just tired of saying no."

CHAPTER SIX

COLIN'S MOM WAS COOKING dinner while he did a sheet of practice math that she'd assigned him as part of his punishment. He didn't really mind because he liked math. He was good at all kinds of puzzles, and that's what math was, really. Puzzles they graded you on, instead of puzzles you did for fun.

This page was full of "negative integers" problems that she'd downloaded from the Internet. He had finished about half, but he was hungry and his attention was wandering.

He'd started making anagrams with the words *negative integers,* and he was already up to twenty-five. Most of them were easy words, like *egg* and *ten,* but some of them were really good, hard words, like *revenge* and *senate.*

"So how was it at the nursing home?"

He looked up. His mom had her back to him. She was making stir-fry chicken, which smelled so good his stomach was rumbling.

He considered his answer carefully. He knew better than to sound enthusiastic. Once she got the idea that he liked the nursing home, she'd think it wasn't a bad enough punishment anymore, and who knew what she'd come up with next.

"Boring," he lied. Well, not a complete lie. Some of the old people just sat and stared, no matter what he said, and that part *was* boring. But a lot of them did crazy things, like Mr. Pettigrain, who would be real quiet, and then he'd all of a sudden yell, "Turkey bollocks!" The nurses would look at each other and pretend not to be giggling.

And there was Mrs. Ingraham, who would be walking down the hall, making that shuffling sound, looking all innocent. But when she saw Colin she'd get this sneaky smile and she'd open up her hand, and in there would be a bright green, sweaty rabbit's foot. She'd say "Shh," as if they were spies or something, and then she'd close her hand again.

Some of them told him stories about the old days, and Colin knew they exaggerated, but still it was cool. The old people weren't very different from anyone else, really. They just wanted life to be more fun than it was.

He liked Mr. Killian the best. They understood each other. Colin always knew when Mr. Killian had heard enough of *Treasure Island* and was ready for a game. Mr. Killian loved games as much as Colin did, and Colin liked inventing some that Mr. K. could play without words.

"So, when you're there….do you see Mr. Killian very often?"

Colin glanced up curiously. His mom's voice had that fake smooth sound she got when she was trying to pretend a question wasn't important. Like when she said, "So, how did that geography exam go?" or "Do you ever mind that I spend so much time doing mayor stuff?"

He wondered what was important about this question. He wondered if the nurses at the home had been ratting on him. Sometimes they poked their heads in through the door and asked him to keep it down.

"Yeah," he said. He didn't want to lie if he didn't have to. His mom was pretty decent, as moms went. "I read to him almost every time. He likes exciting stories. Some of them just want me to read the newspaper. I hate that."

"Is he a nice man?"

"Yeah, he's cool. I like his family, too. Sean's cool, and his other grandson has started to come see him, too. At first I thought he was a jerk, but he got better."

His mother turned around. That surprised him. Usually, when she was cooking, their conversations were all held with him talking to her back.

She wiped her hands on a dishcloth. "You mean Jack?"

"Yeah. He said he used to know you."

She nodded. "It was a long time ago, though. I was in high school."

"Oh. Was he like your boyfriend?" Colin tried to make his own voice sound smooth and casual, and he wondered if she would recognize the trick. He looked down at his math paper so that she couldn't read his face, which she was way too good at.

She didn't answer right away. He had to work hard not to glance up and see what *her* face looked like.

"Boyfriend? I guess you could say that. Briefly." She turned back to the stovetop, where the stir-fry was sizzling and popping. She turned the burner down. "But it was a long time ago."

Yeah, she'd already mentioned that, and both times her voice had sounded funny. Sad.

Colin watched her back for a while, wondering. She wasn't too old to be in love, and Jack was handsome. The nurses made a lot of excuses to come into the room when Jack was there.

Jack might even be rich, if the stories about the Killian gold were true. Colin would like to have a rich dad, and he wasn't ashamed to admit it. His mom worked too hard, and there were lots of things they still couldn't do.

And why shouldn't someone rich and handsome fall in love with his mom? She was the best-looking mom of all his friends, everyone said so. She had explained to Colin that she'd become a mother very young, which was unusual, and that made her younger than the other moms.

But she wouldn't explain about his dad. Not yet, she said. When he was older, she'd tell him everything, but for now he would just have to wait.

He was getting tired of waiting. She wouldn't even be specific about how *much* older, and he had a sinking feeling that she was never going to tell him.

His New Year's resolution, at the beginning of this year, had been to solve the puzzle on his own. He hadn't gotten very far because it was a tough puzzle to solve. You couldn't exactly go up to people and say "Hey, are you my real dad?

But he'd tried to approach it scientifically. For starters, he had a list of names in a book that he hid in the floorboards of his bedroom. Names of people who might be his father. Men his mother mentioned a lot of times, or smiled at in a really girlie way. Or maybe someone would tease her about having dated someone in the past, and Colin would add that name, too.

His uncle Ethan was even on the list, though Colin knew Uncle Ethan and his mom were like brother and sister, so he probably hadn't ever been a boyfriend. Once Colin had asked her straight out if she would ever marry Uncle Ethan, and she had laughed as if it were so funny that he knew it couldn't be true.

"Jack's pretty nice," Colin said now. He figured he could use this conversation to fish for more info. "But he's a little bossy. He asks me a lot of questions, like he's checking me out, to see if I'm good enough to hang around with his grandfather or something."

His mother grew very still. "What kind of questions?"

Colin tried to remember. He'd just said that to see how she would react. Jack's questions actually didn't bother him. It was nice to meet someone who didn't always want to talk just about themselves, someone who was interested in Colin for a change.

"Ummm…well, he wanted to know what my birthday is. And where I was born, you know, how long I've lived here and stuff. He likes to hear about you, I think. And he said he thinks Uncle Ethan sounds neat."

She turned around again. "You told him about Uncle Ethan?"

Colin realized she was holding the oven mitt so hard it was crumpling in her hand.

"Yeah," he said, feeling defensive, though he wasn't sure what about, exactly. "Is there something wrong with that? It's not like Uncle Ethan's a secret or anything. Everybody knows about him."

"No." She smiled. "No, of course not. In fact, he's arriving in a couple of days. He says your present is super this year. Now go wash up and change out of those dirty jeans. Dinner's ready."

Colin stood, glad of the excuse to go upstairs. He wanted to get out his book with the list.

There was already one Killian name on it. Sean Killian. Colin had learned about genetics in science class, and he knew you got your eyes and hair and everything from both parents. His mom had blue eyes, so that was okay, but she didn't have hair as dark as his.

Sean Killian did.

Of course, so did Tommy Newton's dad, but he was disgusting. He was fat, and he'd hit Tommy's mother once, for letting the baby fall off the bed. Colin hadn't wanted to put Mr. Newton on the list, but he had to be scientific.

If you wanted to solve a puzzle you had to look at all the clues, even the ones you didn't like.

Besides, if you looked at it logically, how great could his real dad be, if his mom had to keep him a secret? She hadn't married the guy, after all. Probably someday Colin would find out that his dad was a murderer, or a retard, or somebody who hit women, like Mr. Newton.

But just in case…tonight, he was going to add Jack Killian to the list.

WHEN THEY STOPPED TO HAVE LUNCH, using one of the oldest slabs in the Killian graveyard as a picnic table, Jack and Sean had been treasure hunting for almost two hours. The metal detector had led them to four chunky, rusted-out auto parts, two bent golf clubs and a gold box full of antique brass buttons.

No gold. Not even a single, washed-up coin.

To Jack's relief, Sean hadn't seemed to mind. He had been pretty excited about the buttons—his years as a junk dealer had introduced him to people who collected almost anything you could think of, and he said he could unload them for big bucks.

So, even if it was technically a failure, the morning had been a blast. While Sean had wielded the metal detector, Jack had given himself over to rediscovering Sweet Tides.

They'd tramped happily through the silver maples, mossy live oaks and ten-foot-high banks of slumbering azaleas that had been the undisputed kingdom of their youth. They'd laughed and horsed around like kids again, beginning every sentence with "Hey, remember the time…?"

When they'd reached the small, sunny hill on which the earliest Killians had been buried, they'd stopped, as planned, for lunch. Stacy had packed some sandwiches and Thermoses of tea for them, which had made Jack give Sean a quick raised eyebrow. He'd been surprised to see Sean flush.

"These are darn good," Jack said now as he made his way through his second chicken-salad sandwich. "Is there anything your amazing Stacy can't do?"

Sean grumbled. "She's not *my* Stacy," he said. "And stop with the endless winking. It's not like that. You know she's not my type."

True enough. Jack thought about tormenting Sean some more, but decided he was feeling too lazy and full of chicken.

He leaned back against the tombstone behind him. It belonged to Roderick Killian, who'd died in 1790, at twenty-six. Roderick's two-month-old son was buried beside him, but that tiny tombstone had fallen over and broken into three sad pieces more than a hundred years ago.

Roderick was the newest resident of this cemetery, which was partly why the boys had

always liked coming up here to play. All the trage-
dies here, and there were many, had been tamed by
the long, powerful whip of the centuries. Jack and
Sean didn't know the men and women buried here,
and neither did their parents or their parents'
parents.

Since 1800, the Killians had all been buried in
town, at the Presbyterian Church graveyard, where
a large Killian mausoleum still had enough slots for
a half dozen or so more generations.

Yawning, Jack traced the numbers carved on
"baby boy" Killian's marker, the edges of which
had been softened by hundreds of spring rains and
winter storms.

Sean watched him. "Funny how Killians always
have boys, isn't it?"

Jack nodded. He shut his eyes and tilted his face
up to catch the bright sunlight that made the
December chill easier to take. "Guess Killian genes
just don't have any sugar and spice and everything
nice. We're too ornery to make girls."

Sean tore idly at the grass. "It was a girl that time
Mom miscarried, remember? I think that was really
hard for her."

Jack opened one eye and squinted at his brother.
He wasn't going to let this nice afternoon dete-
riorate into a maudlin melodrama.

"I think she really wanted a girl," Sean said.

"Yeah? Is that why she always dolled you up in
those lacy dresses? Not that you didn't look
adorable, but—"

Sean made a growling sound. He flung his sandwich to the side and rolled toward Jack, prepared to pummel him. Jack tensed his abdominal muscles and got ready to fight back, pleased with himself.

A good rough-and-tumble beat a self-pity hanky-fest any day.

"Jack?" The female voice just barely broke through the grunts and laughter. "Jack? I need to talk to you."

Jack held Sean off with one hand—though Sean was two years older, Jack was two inches taller, and that made all the difference—and looked up into the sun.

"Nora?"

Sean's battering stopped instantly. He looked up at the newcomer, too. "Nora?"

"Hi, Sean," she said stiffly. Jack couldn't read her expression because her back was to the sun. But if body language meant anything, she hadn't come in peace. She was as ramrod straight as the wrought-iron rails in the fence that circled the cemetery.

"Stacy told me you'd probably be here, having lunch. I'm sorry to interrupt, but I need to talk to you, and I have a meeting in twenty minutes."

For a split second, Jack tried to picture Nora hiking through the Sweet Tides acres, as they had, pushing aside low evergreen branches and stepping around fallen tree trunks. She definitely wasn't dressed for it. She wore a blue wool suit and low, ladylike pumps.

But then he remembered that most everything west of here had been sold off decades ago. This edge of the property now abutted a two-lane highway that led into town. Just about twenty yards to the west, beyond that stand of birches, cars were rolling by.

"Okay," he said. He didn't stand up, didn't brush the mulchy leaves from his sleeves, though he knew he was covered in them because Sean was. "What do you want to talk about?"

She crossed her arms over her chest, cupping both elbows in the palms of her hands. "Privately."

God, she had developed an autocratic tone. He didn't much like it.

When he didn't answer, she had the nerve to glance impatiently at her watch. That was too much. She'd sought him out, on his own private property, and she dared to cop an attitude?

"This is pretty private," he said with a smile he knew would be irritating. "No one here but me, Sean and bunch of dead Killians who couldn't care less what kind of burr you happen to have under your saddle."

This time she was the one who couldn't think of the right answer. He waited while she made small starts that went nowhere.

"So what is it, Nora? If you've got only twenty minutes, let's don't waste any of them. What do you want to talk about?"

She shifted a little, and the halo around her head disappeared. He could see her features clearly for the first time. If he'd seen that first, he might not have been so obnoxious. Under that arrogant facade, she was as nervous as hell.

"I want to talk about Colin."

Sean made a low noise. Jack covered it by sliding one knee up, scraping his foot across the papery leaves. He rested his elbow on his knee comfortably. "Okay. What about Colin?"

"I understand you have run into him at the nursing home. Several times. He tells me you've been grilling him for information."

Jack smiled again. "Grilling him? You make it sound like a police interrogation."

"I don't care what you call it. I just want you to stop doing it."

"Stop running into him? I'm afraid I can't do that. I haven't seen my grandfather in years. As long as I'm here, I'm going to—"

"No, I meant I want you to stop asking him questions." She moved closer. Her face was very intense—and, damn it, very beautiful. "He's just a child, Jack. In the future, if you have something you want to know about my son, ask me."

Jack stared at her for a minute. "Okay," he said finally. "Here's what I want to know. Who is Colin's father?"

Even Sean inhaled sharply at that one. "Wow," he said softly. "Jack."

To be honest, Jack had expected Nora to flinch. But he'd underestimated her. She stood her ground. Her long blond hair flew around a little in the wind, and her cheeks were pink from the cold, but her expression was steady, her blue eyes unblinking.

"Colin's father is none of your business," she said. "Anything else?"

Finally, he got to his feet. He took a couple of steps closer, so that they were nearly nose to nose. He could smell her perfume, and he knew she'd changed it. She no longer smelled like Confederate jasmine mixed with vanilla—homey and innocent. Now she smelled like sandalwood and spice, more mysterious, harder to understand.

Why did that surprise him? He'd changed over the past twelve years. Had he imagined that he'd left her in some hermetically sealed time capsule? Did he think she'd been floating in a magical preservative made of crushed jasmine petals, sweet red drops from her first glass of wine, and a splash of the salt water he'd kissed from her lips the night they'd gone skinny-dipping in the pond?

Of course not. Life had reshaped her, as it had reshaped him. Their bodies wouldn't fit together anymore, even if they tried.

"Yes," he said. "There's something else."

She waited.

"I don't remember much about my last night in Hawthorn Bay. I was drunk. Really drunk. I asked you to come down, but you said no. I even sent Maggie to ask you. You still said no. After that, I passed out."

He watched for any reaction, but he might as well have been talking to a wax figure in a museum. She barely seemed to be breathing.

"So here's what I want to know. I want to know whether there's anything you'd like to tell me about that night. Anything you think maybe I ought to know. Anything that it might be my *right* to know."

He wasn't even aware of Sean anymore. The moment had narrowed down to this, to the two of them, Nora and Jack, and the question that hung in the frigid air between them.

Finally she smiled, and that smile was colder than any winter day Jack had ever known.

"Yes," she said. "There is one thing I think you should know."

He held his breath.

"You should know," she said, "that I am glad, that I have always been glad, that I didn't come to you that night. And that, if I had to do it over, I wouldn't change a thing. My answer, always and forever, would be *no*."

CHAPTER SEVEN

1880

JOE DIDN'T HAVE MANY breaths left, and each one he took hurt like the wrath of God. He wanted to use them well.

He wanted to use them to tell Angus about the gold.

Still, when the servants brought his son into the bedroom, as he had requested, Joe almost changed his mind. Angus looked too young, too frightened. The boy was only ten, and his mother lay dead in the front parlor, waiting for Joe to join her, so that one funeral would suffice for both corpses.

To this burden of grief, which Angus would carry for the rest of his life, how could Joe add the weight of the gold?

Yet how could he keep silent? If Angus never found the gold, then everything would have been sacrificed in vain.

Angus hesitated just inside the door, hugging his arms against his sides, clearly frightened of the dying man in the bed. They had already dressed the boy in clothes suitable for a funeral—his best jacket and fine breeches, clasped at the knee with silver buckles. Julia had wanted new clothes for her son, in the latest fashions—almost as much as she had wanted those things for herself. She had hated Joe for refusing to dig up enough gold to buy them.

Joe had not realized how virulent her hatred had become, not until she had showed up in his bedroom last night, at the stroke of midnight. He'd been surprised. It had been long since she'd come near him after dark.

This time, she'd brought only two things. Her lover and a gun.

"Come here, son." Joe tried to breathe around the bullet, which seemed to have lodged like a pebble of fire in his lungs. *Not long now, Julia,* he thought.

Angus tiptoed forward, his blue eyes watery, shining in the gaslight. His son looked like him, a sight that pleased Joe even more, now that he knew how easily the child might have resembled someone else.

"Father?" The boy's voice was very small. He sobbed suddenly. "Please don't die. I don't want you to die, too."

Joe's eyes burned as fiercely as the bullet hole, but he refused to cry. "I must," he said. "It's my time."

Angus bent over Joe's outstretched hand. Tears ran down the boy's face and into Joe's palm like rain, the soft rain that fell on Sweet Tides land and brought forth flowers.

"Why?" The boy's voice was high, thin with pain. "Why would anyone shoot you? Why would anyone shoot mother?"

Joe shut his eyes. It was so tempting, the thought of telling him the truth.

It would be Joe's chance to revenge himself on Julia.

Your mother was a faithless woman, he could tell his son now. *She brought her lover here, to steal our gold. She was going to run away with him. She was going to leave us both. But I fought him. For you, for your future, I fought.*

Joe knew the man hadn't intended to shoot. But when the gun had gone off, and Joe had fallen back, Julia's lover had turned to her, the only witness. "I'm sorry," was all he'd said. And then he'd shot her through the heart.

What an irony it was. Her lover had, in his ruthlessness, managed to reunite husband and wife for all eternity.

"He was an evil man," Joe said. "You must pray for his soul."

Angus looked up, his blue eyes bloodshot and swollen. "I won't."

"You must. We will pray together, soon. But now I want to give you something. There is a secret panel above the fireplace. You must open it, and take out what's there."

Angus frowned. "What is it?"

"A map," Joe said, though he had enough breath only to whisper the word. Angus would have to pray for the evil man alone. Joe was praying his last prayer now, asking God to give Angus wisdom—and patience.

It was too soon to dig up the gold—he didn't even dare unearth a few coins, much less the bars. Fifteen years, to these people who had lost everything to the War, was merely a heartbeat of time. Some men still spat on the street when Joe walked by. Others crossed to the other side, to avoid having to speak. One anonymous note, flung through the window of Sweet Tides attached to a stone, had warned him that the gold was cursed.

Perhaps it was. Both Joe and Julia had died for it.

As it stood, all was rumor; nothing was fact. But if a single gold bar, a single stray coin, should surface, they would know he had been a traitor.

They would not hold little Angus to blame, surely. He hadn't even been born when Joe had buried his fortune in the dirt. But they would hate him in their hearts.

And they would confiscate the gold.

"I don't want a map," Angus said, refusing to let go of his father's hand. "A map of what?"

In the doorway now, Joe could see one of the soldiers who had haunted his dreams so long. The soldiers with the golden bones.

He was running out of time. The soldier had come for him.

"A map of what?" his son asked again.

"Sin," Joe said.

My sin, Angus, he tried to say. *Not yours.*

But there was no more breath, and there could be no more words.

THE LANGLEY GROUP HAD DESIGNED upscale developments all over the Carolinas, every one of which had been a financial success. To make their case for the complex they hoped to build on the Sweet Tides property, the president of the company, Jim Samoyan, was putting on quite a show.

He'd invited the members of the Hawthorn Bay city council to visit the nearest Langley Group project, the Blossoms, which had just been completed. The tour had begun with a fantastic lobster-and-wine lunch at the complex's best restaurant.

Nora had insisted that each councilman pay for his own lunch, a gesture of ethical independence that had annoyed Samoyan and made her cousin Tom laugh at her for being a prude. She didn't care. She knew what the rules were, even if Tom wanted to pretend he didn't.

Tom had indulged a bit too freely in the wine, she thought as he climbed into the limousine beside her for the next part of the show, a tour of the office complex. His breath was thick and too sweet.

She turned her head, pretending to look out the window.

It took two limousines to transport them all, but Jim Samoyan rode in theirs. As mayor, Nora technically held a position of importance, and Tom was Langley Group's best friend on the council, the driving force behind their agenda.

"We hired the very best Southern architects," Jim said as he took his seat opposite Nora and Tom.

"I think you'll be impressed with how accurately they've replicated the antebellum look."

"You'd do that for the Sweet Tides complex, as well, wouldn't you?" Tom was feeding Jim the right questions, like a scripted television infomercial.

Jim nodded. "Absolutely. The condominiums would all have Doric columns, as would the office buildings. I promise you they would remain true to the flavor of the Old South."

Tom was an idiot, Nora thought to herself as she continued to stare out the window. Did he really think this was impressing her? She'd heard it all before. She'd seen the blueprints. Lots of square block structures with faux Southern geegaws attached to the facade. It would be kitschy and cheap, and trash in fifty years.

The complex was only about a mile from the restaurant. They could have walked, if Mr. Samoyan hadn't been hell-bent on showing off. The itineraries they'd been given listed four buildings to tour: the Magnolia, the Jasmine, the Gardenia and the Dogwood.

Boy, they were heaping on the Southern syrup with a big ladle. She sighed as the limo braked to a stop, then exited quickly. *Might as well get it over with.*

Once they were inside, a young woman with a Christmas-red hoop skirt and a Scarlett O'Hara accent welcomed them, handing each of them a silk magnolia. Nora accepted hers with a smile. No sense taking out her irritation on this poor girl, who probably thought the whole shtick was just as silly as Nora did.

Nora heard Tom swear under his breath. "What the hell is *he* doing here?"

"Who?"

"Jack Killian." Tom glared out the window. "If that meddling son of a bitch thinks—"

"It *is* his property you're talking about tearing down," Nora said, though she was unnerved, too. She knew how this would look—as if she were part of the whole conspiracy, as if she were letting some businessman buy her vote with lobster and limousines and artificial magnolias.

Jack had caught Jim Samoyan out on the sidewalk. Nora and Tom watched through the window as the two men talked. The other limousine drew up, and the other two councilmen, along with city attorney Bill Freeman, emerged. After a few more minutes of pantomimed discussion, they all began to move toward the building.

Samoyan entered first. He hurried up to Tom. "Mr. Killian would like to join the tour," he said quietly. "I think it's an excellent idea. He can see our quality firsthand."

Tom frowned, but Jack was now within earshot. Samoyan turned to welcome him to the fold. "Come, Mr. Killian. We're delighted to get a chance to make our case face-to-face. I'm sure we'll win you over. To know a Langley Group project is to love it."

Jack's smile was completely neutral.

Samoyan waved his hand. "Do you know everyone?"

"I do," Jack said. "Hello, Dickson. Nora."

Tom nodded. "Killian."

Nora had to admire Tom's restraint. He hated Jack—really hated him. But he was much too smooth to show irritation openly.

Tom's poise used to impress her. About four years older than she was, he'd been blessed with physical grace, silky blond hair, intelligent brown eyes and classic features. What few imperfections he'd been born with—a minor underbite, a slight myopia—had been surgically eliminated.

Their mothers were sisters. When they were kids, Nora had naively believed that blood relatives by definition possessed the same values. And, of course, she'd been young enough to think that beauty and charm were the same thing as goodness and virtue.

Through the years she'd learned that Tom never used his many gifts for anything other than the gratification of his own appetites. Money, women, power, possessions.

And, at least in this one case, revenge.

Jim Samoyan opened his arms expansively. "Shall we go, then?"

Nora had expected the tour to be boring, but that was before Jack had joined it. Jack said almost nothing. He hung in the back, just watching, never once approaching Nora. Still, she saw everything through his eyes, and it wasn't just tacky—it was tragic. Who in his right mind would tear down Sweet Tides to put up these ridiculous boxes?

She watched the other two councilmen, wondering what they were thinking. One of them, Lon Hambrick, looked skeptical. That was a good sign. The fourth councilman, Paul Allingham, was Lon's doubles partner, and the two men frequently voted in tandem.

By the time they reached the penthouse of the Magnolia, which served as a conference room shared by all the tenants, Nora had relaxed a little.

The penthouse was a circular room, kind of like a doughnut, with a support pillar in the center that held the elevators and restrooms. The exterior walls were banks of sparkling windows, which offered a panoramic view of the town.

Everyone oohed and aahed, and then Samoyan pointed out a buffet spread of desserts, including an ice sculpture Christmas tree and petits fours sugared in the shapes of brightly wrapped presents.

The men made a beeline for the table, but Nora couldn't eat another thing. She went to the window and gradually made her way counterclockwise, until she was safely on the far side of the central column.

She could use a minute or two alone.

But she should have known that wasn't possible. When she reached the other side, she saw that Jack was already there. He was staring out the window, looking down at the roofs of houses that dated back to the early 1800s.

Nora paused, wondering if she could sneak away again without being seen.

"It's okay," Jack said without turning his head. "I was avoiding the jackals and blowhards, not you."

She smiled at his description. It couldn't have been more apt.

"Thanks for not including me among the jackals. But how do you know I'm not one of them? How do you know I don't think the Langley Group is the best thing that could possibly happen to Hawthorn Bay?"

He laughed. "Sorry, Nora. You're not a very good actress. Every time Samoyan says the word *functionality* or mentions the *Old South feel* you make a face, as if your lobster is disagreeing with you."

"Maybe it is," she said. "It was pretty rich lobster."

"I'll bet."

She went over and stood at his side, and for a moment they both stared down at the beautiful antebellum houses. She twirled her silk magnolia between her thumb and forefinger. It had been sprayed with something, and it gave off a scent that was disturbingly both flowery and chemical.

She thought about apologizing for coming on so strong the other day, when she accosted him at the Killian cemetery. But she didn't want him to get the idea that she'd changed her mind. She still didn't want him interrogating Colin.

She just wished she'd taken a more civil tone about it.

However, he seemed willing to let it go, so she decided to do the same.

"Samoyan is pretty eloquent about his projects," she said. "But even he can't explain to me why anyone needs to tear down a genuine rice plantation house with three hundred years of history in order to put up a bunch of imitations."

"It's cheaper," Jack said flatly. "Cheaper to build, cheaper to maintain, cheaper to tear down when they want to start over with some new scheme. How do you think conglomerates like Langley get rich enough to put lobster on every table and ice sculptures in every boardroom? Illusion is a hell of a lot cheaper than reality."

"I guess so." She looked at him. "I'm going to vote against it," she said. "I want you to know that. You don't have to worry about, about our past. I won't let my vote be influenced by anything... personal."

"That's more than your cousin can say."

She started to shake her head, but Jack stopped her.

"Come on, Nora. We all know what's behind this. We all know why he's salivating at the very thought of bulldozers on Sweet Tides land."

He was right, of course. Tom's motives were purely personal.

Twelve years ago, Jack Killian had almost killed him.

It had been quite a scandal. For reasons known only to the two of them, Jack had taken Tom out to one of the remote spit islands just off South Carolina's coast, beaten the hell out of him and left him there to die.

Luckily, one of Tom's friends had rescued him, so Jack hadn't quite succeeded in murder. But he had humiliated him, which, in Tom's view, was almost as bad. Jack was three years younger than Tom, and yet Jack had managed to break the older boy's arm, blacken his eyes and plant bruises up and down his torso.

Worst of all, Jack himself had come out virtually unscathed, as if Tom hadn't even managed to land a punch.

Nora had always wondered why Jack had done it. Even now, when she had accepted the truth about what a boor Tom really was, she couldn't quite understand it.

Everyone said the Killians had cruelty in their blood, but Jack had always been so gentle with her….

Of course he was, Maggie had said. *You know what he wanted, and even Killians know that some things are easier to catch with honey.*

Now, Nora realized that anything Maggie had ever said about Jack was suspect, too. Everyone, it seemed, had a hidden agenda. Apparently you had nothing to rely on in life but your own instincts.

And her instincts told her that Jack Killian was dangerous. At least to her. And to Colin.

When she'd learned that Jack didn't remember anything about the night before he'd left for the Army, she'd been so relieved she'd nearly fainted. She couldn't believe her luck, but clearly he didn't have the slightest inkling that he might have slept with Maggie that night.

He didn't remember that he had betrayed Nora.

Of course, not remembering it was not quite the same thing as not doing it in the first place. She thought she understood why he had. She had taken her cousin's side. Nora had been frightened by Jack, disgusted by the unbridled violence. She had believed his father's genes were coming out in him.

And that would be the one betrayal he couldn't endure. It must have hurt him a great deal. He must have wanted to hurt her back.

And he *had* hurt her, terribly. Unfortunately, he'd hurt Maggie, too. And the baby who was the result of that night of rage and pain.

And he had hurt himself, though he didn't know it. He'd denied himself the joy of knowing his wonderful son.

"Actually, I'm surprised you're not voting with Tom on this one," Jack said suddenly.

She started. She'd been lost so far in the past.

"Why? I've always loved Sweet Tides. I love all the old mansions. If I'd been able to go to college, I was going to be a history major, remember?"

"You might still think it would be best for the

town, if you got rid of those dangerous Killians once and for all."

She looked down at her flower, wondering how to answer that. Were the Killians really so bad? Were they any worse than anyone else?

She thought of her arrogant cousin. Once, she'd heard Tom bragging to another businessman that he'd brought a project in under budget by hiring undocumented workers, then refusing to pay them, knowing that they couldn't fight back. The other man had thought it was so clever, as if honesty and fair play were things only fools would bother with.

Was everyone willing to lie and cheat, if the motive was strong enough?

She thought of her own lies, and the child who had her name, but not her blood.

"Sometimes I don't think I know what's right for anyone about anything anymore," she said.

"Don't know what's right?" He laughed. "Well, that doesn't sound like the Nora Carson I used to know."

She tried to laugh, too. She couldn't deny it. She'd been so sure of herself back then, so safe and smug inside her mansion, with her parents barring the door to anything ugly.

So quick to judge him.

"It seems so long ago. Do you think we're even the same people we were back then, Jack?"

He turned away from the window. He looked at her so intensely that she felt little nerve endings twitch beneath her skin.

"In some ways I'm nothing like that boy," he said. "And in some ways, I'm exactly the same."

Without warning, he took hold of her upper arms and pulled her into him. She shivered, feeling her balance shift. She was acutely aware of the sheer drop, ten stories down, through the window just beside her.

But as long as he held on to her, she was safe. She looked up into his eyes. They caught the afternoon light and glowed a hot, neon blue.

"I still want you, Nora," he said. "As much as I ever did."

Was he going to kiss her? She remembered how warm his kisses were. They started at her lips, but the heat didn't stop there. It slid through her, softening and warming every inch of her, inside and out.

She tilted her head back. He was so tall—he would have to bend his head to hers, and she would feel taken over, owned, safer than she'd been in so long....

She shut her eyes and waited.

After a long minute, he touched her chin with the tips of his fingers.

She opened her eyes. The light in his had gone out.

"We should go back," he said, and his voice had turned cold, too. "Before we do something we'll both regret."

CHAPTER EIGHT

COLIN'S MOM WAS FINISHING up a batch of jam, so Colin figured he had about an hour before she came upstairs to check on him. That wasn't enough time, really, but it would have to do.

He eased out of bed so that his springs wouldn't creak. He knelt on the floor and dragged out the cardboard box he'd pushed under it earlier this afternoon.

It was a box of junk that Mr. Killian had given him. Sean and Jack and Colin had all been visiting Mr. Killian at the same time the other day, and suddenly Mr. Killian had gotten super-excited and had begun waving his hand around and trying to talk.

It had sort of scared Colin, but Sean had decided he was talking about music. Apparently Mr. Killian's own father—Colin's mind could hardly imagine anything that far back—had been a songwriter.

"A really bad songwriter," Jack had said with a laugh. "One halfway decent Christmas song, and a bunch of hymns so saccharine you choked just trying to sing them."

Colin wondered if they could really be that bad. Probably not. That was just Jack's way, to make fun. Jack never took anything seriously.

Anyhow, it had turned out that Mr. Killian had wanted Sean and Jack to get this box of music stuff and give it to Colin. That had embarrassed Colin, for two reasons. One, he didn't want it. What the heck could he do with a bunch of smelly old sheet music and some dirty old player-piano rolls? The only player piano he'd ever even seen was at the nursing home, donated by the Killians. And, though his mom had made him take two years of piano, he could just barely read music, so it wasn't as if he could play these songs himself.

Even more importantly, he didn't want anybody to think he was sucking up to Mr. Killian so that he'd get presents. It hadn't even occurred to him that the old guy had anything to give.

He'd thought maybe Sean and Jack would forget about it, but they hadn't. The very next day, they'd brought the box to the nursing home and given it to Colin, which had clearly made Mr. Killian happy.

And then the weirdest thing had happened. Right after Sean and Jack had left, Mr. Killian had motioned Colin over to the bed. He had touched the box with his good hand and tried to say something. He'd tried three times before he'd gotten it right.

And then he said it. "Treasure."

So now Colin was interested. A lot.

He heard a plinking sound at his window.

Good. That meant Brad had been able to sneak out. The Butterfields' house was just three doors down, and once Mr. and Mrs. Butterfield settled into the family room to watch TV for the night, Brad could have invited the entire sixth grade over for a toga party, and no one would have noticed.

Colin went to the window of his room that opened onto the upstairs porch. Brad had already climbed the maple tree and was wriggling himself backward onto the railing. He was wearing his pajamas, a plaid bathrobe and a really dumb-looking pair of bedroom slippers with doggy faces that his mom must have picked out.

Still, he'd agreed to come, in spite of the fact that it was really cold, so Colin decided not to make fun of the shoes. At least not tonight.

Colin pulled his jacket on over the sweatsuit he slept in. Then he wedged the box through the window. When Brad landed on the porch with a soft thud—another plus for the fuzzy sippers—everything was ready and waiting.

"Hey." Brad wiped his hands on his robe to get rid of the bark dust. "Is that it?"

"Yeah." It didn't look like much, Colin knew that. But Brad was Colin's best friend because he had imagination, which most of the other boys didn't. Brad didn't think the only interesting thing in the world was which girl had or hadn't bought a bra yet.

Colin was confident that Brad would appreciate the possibilities here.

"So open it." Brad picked something out of his braces and talked around his fingers. "You said you've only got an hour. Let's get started."

For a second, when Brad saw the moldy old piano rolls, his face fell. But when Colin brought out the sheet music and announced that the great grandfather Killian had actually written the music himself, Brad's eyes lit up again.

"Awesome! Was he the one who buried the gold?"

Colin wasn't completely sure about all that, but he was doing research, and it was beginning to come clear. "I don't think so. This guy, his name was Angus, couldn't have been old enough during the Civil War. It must have been his father. But his father probably told him where he buried the gold, and this guy could have written some clues into the songs, don't you think? Maybe in code or something."

Brad sat back on his heels, staring at one of the hymns. "This is church music," he said doubtfully.

"I know. But there's a normal Christmas song, too. Sean and Jack said it was the old guy's favorite. They said their grandfather used to talk about how Angus made such a big deal about it. He thought his song was great, and it would be a big hit someday."

He stared at Brad, getting excited all over again. "He always said that they better not throw it away, that it was the song that would make the family rich."

Brad looked confused. "Well, then, that's no good. That must be what Mr. Killian meant when he said *treasure* to you, and—"

Colin shook his head. "No, no," he said, trying to remember to keep his voice down even though Brad was being so irritating. "Can't you tell what he really meant? He meant there was a clue in the song. Like a song-map."

Brad stared down at the box, obviously skeptical. "You don't know that," he said. "You dragged me out here when it's, like, fifty below, and it's just a wild goose chase?"

Colin gave Brad a dirty look. "Have a little imagination, butt head. Think. Angus knew the gold was hot. He couldn't admit straight out that they even had it. So he had to plant subtle clues."

Brad was still frowning.

"Anyhow, it's worth a try, right?" Colin raised his eyebrows. "Or would you rather go home and watch PBS with your mom and dad?"

Brad sighed. Colin knew he wouldn't go home. Even when things seemed dull, Brad knew that Colin might at any moment dream up something cool to do, and he didn't want to miss it. Nothing interesting ever, ever happened at Brad's house, and that was just a fact.

"Okay, then. Here it is." Colin pulled out the Christmas song, which was called "The Starry Skies Sang Lullabies."

"First, you should just read it," he said.

Brad's lips moved as he studied the song, which

had three verses. When he finished, he looked up and rolled his eyes.

"Brother," he said. "That's corny."

"Whatever. All songs look corny written down. It's the music that makes them sound right. But anyhow, what do you think? Do you see anything that might be a clue?"

Brad looked again.

"Not really," he said. He clearly was afraid of missing something obvious. "Do you?"

Colin shook his head. "Not right off. I've tried a bunch of stuff. Like working with every first letter of each sentence. But that doesn't spell anything at all. It's like TRALGMAT DOG."

"Dog?" Brad chewed on his fingernail, then had to work to get the sliver of nail out of his braces. "Could that mean something? Do they have a dog?"

Honestly, sometimes Brad was retarded.

"Sure," Colin said sarcastically. "They hid a fortune in gold in the collar of their *two-hundred-year-old* dog."

Brad scowled. "Okay, jerk. You got anything better?"

"I don't know. I wondered if the notes might mean something. You know how every note has a letter name? Like A, B, C? I thought maybe if we translated the notes into their letters, it might spell something."

Brad had been forced to take piano lessons, too, and he'd been even worse than Colin. At least Colin had some musical talent, even if his fingers were clumsy and always hitting the wrong keys. When Brad played, it sounded as if someone had left a drunken monkey alone in a room with a piano and a hammer.

"I guess." Brad stared at the sheet music. "But how many words can you spell with just seven letters? I mean, you can't even spell *gold* with the letters on the scale."

"I know." Colin looked over Brad's shoulder at the music. "I thought of that. And if you were worrying about spelling words instead of writing a nice melody, the song would sound lame, wouldn't it?"

"How about the lyrics?" Brad ran his finger across the words, which had been handwritten by someone with really good penmanship.

"The lyrics?"

"Wouldn't that be the easy way to do it? I mean, look, here he talks about a hill with a tree on it, and he says 'the river sings, while the Christmas bell rings, to the baby asleep in the house dark and deep.' Maybe he's describing something around Sweet Tides."

Colin's growing excitement fought with his envy that Brad had thought of the idea, not him. He was used to being smarter than his friends about puzzles.

Still… It was a really good idea.

"That's great, Brad," he said, deciding he couldn't be mean enough to deny his friend his moment of glory.

Brad narrowed his eyes. "Are you making fun of me?"

"No, really. This is a great idea. You could have found something."

Brad's smile was so wide his braces caught the moonlight and gleamed like diamonds. But he didn't get a chance to wallow in his thrill because just at that moment, the window of Colin's kitchen went black.

That meant his mother was finished with the jam and would be heading their way any minute.

Like soldiers on a dangerous but familiar sortie, they knew what to do. Silently, without even saying goodbye, Brad hoisted himself up on the railing and reached for the low-hanging maple branch. Colin scooped up all the loose sheet music and shoved it back into the box.

Then, as Brad's doggy slippers disappeared into the darkness, Colin climbed over his sill. He closed the window, tossed off his corduroy jacket, slid the Christmas song under his pillow for safekeeping and jumped back into bed.

He didn't mind going to sleep now. He would dream of trees and rivers that sang.

And the look on Mr. Killian's face when Colin was able to tell him that he, eleven-year-old Colin Carson, who lived in a tiny house, got in trouble in math class and didn't even know who his own father was, had found the Killian gold.

THE FIREPLACE IN THE GUN ROOM was about ten feet long, and it made a grand blaze that warmed even this high-ceilinged space. Jack was glad to note that Sean had sold all the old guns that used to be racked here, as well as the animal trophies—early generations of Killians had apparently loved to kill furry things.

The absence of all that death made the room a much more inviting spot, and Jack and Sean had spent a lot of time in it the past few days.

Today, Jack worked on his laptop, and Sean sorted through a small, relatively disappointing stash he'd bought from a local estate.

As the afternoon moved toward sunset, the laptop wasn't able to hold Jack's interest. He found his gaze drifting to the window. The river was like a sparkling ribbon, and the bare trees were black spiderwebs against the amber sky.

"Let's go for a walk," he said. It surprised him, this overwhelming urge to fill his lungs with damp, river air and have his feet touch the ground. He never felt that way in Kansas City. Was it really so different, if the land you walked on was your own?

His brother looked up from a heap of old clothes.

"Can't," he said. "I've got a dealer coming in a few minutes, to take this mess off my hands. I'm not through checking the pockets."

Jack closed his laptop. "For what?"

"You'd be surprised at what people leave in their pockets. Money—not just coins, but bills. Found a hundred-dollar bill one time. Receipts. Letters." He wiggled his eyebrows. "Oh, the love letters I've read. Amazing what people will sign their names to."

Jack laughed. "Anyone we know?"

"Sometimes." Sean tossed a suede coat onto the pile and picked up a black sweater. "Once, when I bought a lot of women's clothes, I found a rental receipt for a one-bedroom apartment over in the raunchy part of Chesterfield. A full year's rent, paid in advance. Clearly a love nest. Guess whose name was on the dotted line?"

"No idea."

"Tom Dickson."

Jack whistled softly. "Is that so?"

"Yep. I kept it nearly a month, dreaming about what I could do with it. Finally I decided, who gives a flip what that jerk does in bed, or who he does it with? I'll bet even his wife doesn't care. I ended up putting the receipt through the shredder."

Sean tossed the sweater aside. "Of course, that was before he started making noises about buying Sweet Tides. It might have come in handy now, as a sort of crude bargaining chip."

"I'm not sure we're going to need one," Jack said. "I saw the faces of those councilmen yesterday, and I think we're going to be okay. Except for Dickson, they didn't seem very enthusiastic. "

"Even Nora?"

"Especially Nora. She hated the Langley Group guy, Samoyan, who is a real sleaze. Definitely not her type. He couldn't sell her ice in hell."

Jack stood up and stretched. He was cramped from hunching over that computer for two hours. He really did want that walk.

"I'm going to prowl around a little." He headed for the door. "If I find any gold, I'll let you know."

Sean snorted impolitely, but Jack ignored him and kept going. He grabbed a windbreaker from the hall tree. It was too cold to stay out long in just the flannel shirt and jeans he wore indoors.

He walked toward the river, which was more muted now that the sun was sinking, but was still alive with light. The water was shallow here, where it ran alongside the back of Sweet Tides, and it burbled peacefully over rocks and fallen logs. The noise filled his mind, so that he didn't have to think at all.

For about fifteen minutes, he might as well have been alone in the world. But then, just as he reached the crest of a small hill, he saw a young boy kneeling on the ground, peering down at something.

The boy had his back to Jack, but Jack recognized the black corduroy jacket that almost matched the scruffy black curls on the bent head. It was Colin Carson.

Jack didn't want to scare the kid, so he was careful to make plenty of noise as he climbed up onto the last few feet.

As the snapping of dry leaves and twigs finally penetrated his concentration, the boy turned his head. His eyes widened, and his mouth went slack.

"Mr. Killian!"

From this angle, Jack could see everything. The heap of dirt to Colin's left, the small silver spade with the red handle, and the three-foot hole in the ground.

Correction. The three-foot *empty* hole in the ground.

Boy, did that look familiar.

"Hi, Colin. Hit gold yet?"

Colin frowned. He chewed his lower lip, clearly wondering if he could spin this scenario any other way.

Jack shook his head. "You've gotta be either digging for treasure, or disposing of a dead body. I don't see a body, so…"

Colin put down his spade. His hands were mottled with dirt, the fingernails little black crescent moons.

"I wasn't going to steal anything," he said. He rubbed his hands against his jeans. "Honestly. Even if I'd found the gold, I would have given it to Mr. Killian."

Jack sat down next to him. Here under the oak, it must be ten degrees colder than it was in the sunshine. Jack looked into the hole, which was tangled with roots and small stones. It was pretty impressive—about three feet deep and two feet wide. Colin must have busted his butt here for hours.

"You did all this work for nothing? You're trying to tell me you don't even want the gold?"

Colin shrugged. "I just want to find it. I know it wouldn't belong to me. I just want to figure out where it is. That's different."

"Yeah," Jack agreed. "It's different, all right. Most people would—" He broke off. "Did you know that my great great grandfather was shot to death by a guy who wanted to steal this gold?"

"No." Colin looked interested. He got off his knees and sat comfortably cross-legged. "Was that Angus?"

"It was Angus's dad. Joseph Killian. He was the one who supposedly buried it in the first place. Years later, he and his wife were both killed by a robber. Everyone assumed the guy had come looking for the gold."

"That was pretty dumb. How are they going to tell him where it is if they're dead?"

Jack laughed. "That's what I always thought. The story doesn't really make sense, does it? But nothing about this gold ever has. That's why I don't believe in it. I think it's about as real as Aladdin's cave, or the pot of gold at the end of the rainbow. Nice story, but mostly baloney."

Colin knocked his spade against the edge of his shoe, dislodging the wedges of dirt. Jack couldn't read his expression because the boy stared unblinkingly into the open hole.

"You really think it's just a fairy tale? You really think there isn't any gold?"

Jack was sorry to be the Grinch who spoiled Christmas, but he knew that the sooner you stopped dreaming hopeless dreams, the better.

"I really do," he said. "There isn't any gold."

This was one tough little kid. Instead of getting

tearful with disappointment, he looked up and stared at Jack a long time, his eyes narrowed. He seemed to be appraising Jack, calculating the odds that he knew what he was talking about.

Finally, he blinked. "Maybe not," he said, squaring his jaw. "But you could be wrong."

"Colin, I'm not wrong."

"You *could* be. You're that type. You don't like to just *believe* in things. Like with your grandfather. I heard you tell Sean that Mr. Killian isn't ever going to get any better. You don't know that, either. He might. You don't like to just hope. You want to be sure, or you don't want to bother."

Jack was speechless. It was an overly simplistic description, but it was pretty damn accurate. This kid was scary smart.

"Look," Jack said. "I don't care if you dig so many holes you turn Sweet Tides into Swiss cheese. If this is your idea of fun, go for it. Just don't make gold-digging your financial plan, okay? If you need money, or if your mother needs money—"

"My mother makes *plenty* of money."

"I know." Jack put out his hand. "I just meant—"

Colin stood. Leaves fell from the sagging bottom of his jeans, which were damp from the wet ground. He stuffed the spade into his back pocket, then ran his dirty hand through his tousled hair.

"I told you, I wasn't going to steal your stupid gold. We're not poor. My mom works really hard.

She is mayor of this town, and she makes the best jam in the world. Everybody buys it."

Jack hadn't been sure about Nora's financial situation—she had been born into one of Hawthorn Bay's big social families, after all. But something about having sold Heron Hill didn't quite jibe. He'd seen the cute but modest little block house they lived in today.

Now he saw that his instincts had been right. The Carson fortune was gone, and Colin knew it. He was instinctively defensive of his mom.

Jack admired that—and, at the same time, felt an ache of empathy. Jack knew what it was like to feel defensive for a mother you loved, but whose problems were bigger than a boy could fix.

Suddenly, Jack really wanted to straighten this out. "Look, I know that. I think what I was trying to say was that, if there's ever *anything* you need, or your mom needs, I would like to help. Not just money. Anything. You see, your mom and I…well, I used to—"

Oh, brother, he was getting in pretty deep.

Colin watched, his blue eyes dark and focused. He was clearly eager to hear the end of the sentence.

"It's just that we—" Jack tried to sound casual "—used to be good friends."

"How come you're not anymore?"

It didn't make sense to lie to the kid. He was intuitive, and he'd know it was a lie. But it also didn't make sense to go into too much detail.

"We had a fight, and we didn't see each other for a long time. But I still want her to be happy, you know? I would like you to feel that you could come to me, if either of you needed anything."

Colin's jaw softened subtly, and the tension in his shoulders subsided a fraction. For a minute, Jack thought maybe the boy was going to ask for a favor.

He wondered what. Money to buy his mom a Christmas present? Jack remembered going to Patrick, one year, asking for the money to buy another of the endless glass unicorns.

Jack wondered what Nora collected. What talismans did she gather around her to ward off loneliness and fear? He wished he could see inside her house. He wondered if he could gauge her happiness by the color of her walls, the length of her curtains, the quantity of her clutter.

Colin chewed his lower lip, obviously debating with himself. He shifted from one foot to the other, and he toyed with the spade handle. He opened his mouth, then shut it.

Jack waited, unsure whether a nudge would be helpful.

"I don't really need anything right now, but—" Colin took a deep breath. "Can I ask you one thing?"

Jack nodded. "Of course. I said *anything*."

"Okay, well, when a grown-up is keeping a secret—a big secret, not just like what you're getting for Christmas, but something major…is it always something bad?"

Jack fought the urge to analyze the question, to second-guess what the boy wanted to hear and then provide it. Once again, he felt the need for honesty.

"Not always. Sometimes the secret might just be something... very complicated. Or they might have promised someone else they wouldn't tell."

"But why would anyone ask you not to tell a good thing? I mean, if I got an A on my math exam, I wouldn't ask my teacher to promise not to tell my mom."

Why indeed? The only vow of silence Jack had ever made was to Amy Grantham.

The kid had a point.

"Sometimes it's complicated. How about what you're doing today? Does your mom know you're here?"

Colin's eyes slid away. This clearly embarrassed him. "No. She thinks I'm at Brad Butterfield's house."

"So you're keeping it a secret, right? But it's not because you're doing something bad."

Colin grimaced. "She'd think it was bad."

"Yeah, but you don't think so. But it's very complicated, so you didn't tell her. See what I mean?"

The boy's grimace turned to a small smile. "Yeah. I guess I see. Okay. Thanks."

He began buttoning his jacket. "I'd better go home now. I rode my bike, and it's getting dark. She's going to call the Butterfields pretty soon, and then I'll be busted for sure."

"How about if I give you a ride?"

"Well…" Colin looked tempted, but uncertain. "Could you let me off at the end of the block, so that she wouldn't see you?"

Jack nodded. "Absolutely. We don't have to tell her about any of this," he said. "Because, after all, it's very—"

Grinning, Colin finished the sentence with him. *"Very complicated."*

CHAPTER NINE

1927

AT MIDNIGHT, ANGUS KILLIAN finished his unsavory task. It was done. He had dug up the gold and hidden it anew, so that the men who came in the night with shovels and barrows and maps could never find it.

He was sure he'd found and moved all the bars, though he'd had to leave some of the coins out there. There was just too much of it, and he was physically exhausted.

Still, he was glad the job was finished. Another generation of Killians might be led to it some day, by God or by greed. But he, Angus Killian, would never have to touch the evil things again.

The townspeople said the gold was cursed, though Angus noticed that didn't stop them from hunting for it. Angus was a religious man, and he didn't believe in curses. But he did believe in evil. He believed that some deeds were so despicable, so hateful in the eyes of the Lord, that He couldn't wait until the hereafter to mete out punishment.

Everyone in Hawthorn Bay knew that, long ago, Angus's father had lied about this gold. Old Joseph had loved money more than his brave brothers who had been fighting for their lives in the Civil War. More than his God, whose commandments expressly demanded truth, no matter what the cost.

Joseph Killian had died for that sin. Angus would always remember the smell of his father's room as he'd lain, a bullet lodged in his heart, struggling for breath.

Blood smelled like gold, Angus had learned that night. Metallic. Hot. Unclean.

He'd smelled the blood on his mother's body, too. And he'd seen her smeared lips, from kissing the man who'd killed her. At only ten, Angus had not understood the details of that terrible night, but he understood the sin had destroyed them both.

It had terrified him, but terror had been his salvation, for he had turned onto the path of the righteous that night. It didn't make the citizens of Hawthorn Bay love the Killians any more—like the hypocrites they were, they despised his virtue as much as they'd despised his father's sin.

Now fifty-seven, Angus had few illusions left. He wasn't an easy man. His wife, Mary, had left him—and their three boys. She'd said he was cold, that he was hardly human, and that no son of his could ever learn kindness or love.

Perhaps she'd been right. James and Mark were at university now, but Angus heard the stories. They were devils. They cheated on exams, seduced maids and waitresses and drank themselves into ugly tempers every night.

And they hated him. He'd accepted that. He'd given up on them, reconciled himself to the fact that they would make a bad end. He was glad, almost, that he wouldn't be here to witness it.

It was too early to tell what Patrick, the youngest, would become. Angus didn't hold much hope. Patrick was only twelve, but he already despised his father—he called him a monster, taking his cue from his rebellious brothers.

No. He wasn't an easy man to love.

Now the doctor told Angus his heart was failing. Angus believed him. The beating lump in his chest felt as heavy as a river rock.

Angus went into the parlor, to the player piano, and sat down. He picked up the music roll. Should he insert it? He ran his hands across the metallic cylinder. He had paid a lot of money to have these rolls made, so that his songs would live after him.

Once, he had thought his music might make his fortune. Now, he could only hope that someday people would listen to his many hymns and his one beautiful Christmas ballad, and finally understand who he was.

For now, they mocked him. Patrick and his friends, those coarse young people from heathen homes, loved the rolls of jazz they had bought. But when Angus began to play his own songs they groaned and ran away. Patrick would be beaten for it later.

Angus set down the roll. He wanted to play the notes himself, though he knew that even the servants would scatter to other parts of the house. He knew what they whispered. They said he grew mad when he played.

But it wasn't madness they heard.

It was his thwarted, terrified humanity, the humanity Mary said he didn't possess, bleeding through his fingers onto the ivory keys and finally becoming melody, becoming beauty, becoming love.

JACK KNEW IT WAS A FOOL'S GAME, this keeping a mental tally of things he noticed about Colin, assigning them to categories: Killian or Not Killian.

But he couldn't seem to stop himself from doing it anyhow. In theory, Jack accepted Nora's absolute denial that she'd come to him that night—primarily because he knew that Nora was a rotten liar. So the kid couldn't be a Killian.

Still, Colin intrigued him, and Jack found himself spending more and more time at the nursing home, where he could observe the boy at leisure.

Every day, though, the mystery just deepened. In addition to his coloring, an obvious match, Colin was a born devil, which fit the Killian profile. But he had a soft heart, and frequently regretted his mischief, which didn't.

He was energetic, athletic, sarcastic and stubborn. *Match.*

But he got great grades at school, apparently, and he had infinite patience with old Patrick's infirmities. *Definitely no match.*

Now, in the cold twilight, Jack settled himself on the steps of Nora's pretty, poinsettia-laden front porch, delighted with this new chance to gather details for his list.

It had been dumb luck, really. Nora, who was running late picking up a friend at the airport, had asked Stacy to bring Colin back from the nursing home. When Stacy had arrived to pick him up, Sean and Jack had been there, too, so they'd decided to tag along.

Jack knew it was pushy. Nora's feathers would definitely be ruffled when she found him here, but…well, as he'd said, Killians were born devils. He wanted a peek at the domestic setup, and he didn't intend to let a few icy glares dissuade him.

Stacy had a key, so she and Sean were already inside, helping out by getting Nora's dinner started. Colin had asked Jack to help him figure out how to play Angus's Christmas song on the guitar, so they'd camped out here, where they wouldn't be in the way.

As Jack watched Colin struggle with the guitar he'd borrowed from his friend Brad's father, he put another big checkmark on the No Match column. This kid couldn't play the guitar worth squat.

All Killians were musical, at least as far back as old Angus, who'd fancied himself a composer, and had bought one of the first player pianos, a big clunky thing they'd sent to the nursing home with Patrick.

After a couple of hopeless attempts to strum the strings, Colin made a frustrated sound. He moved closer to Jack, pushing aside a poinsettia that was in the way. He held out the guitar and the sheet music.

"I can read music, so I know what the notes are. But we don't have a piano anymore, and I can't figure this thing out. It's crazy. It's not like the piano at all."

Jack nodded. "It is hard. Somebody's got to teach you. Patrick taught me. He was really good."

Just holding the guitar reminded Jack of all the summer nights he'd spent on the back porch of Sweet Tides, listening to Patrick play. He could almost smell the Confederate jasmine and wisteria on the air, and hear the crickets sawing away. They'd stop when Patrick began to play, as if they, too, wanted to listen.

Sometimes Jack's dad had joined them, beer in hand, and started to sing along. His father might have been a beast, but he'd sung like an angel. Jack used to hold his breath when the song was over, praying that the beautiful sounds had transformed his father, like magic.

But they never had. After a couple of minutes, Kelly would tilt back his beer, swallow noisily, make some irritable comment about how the goddamn steps needed painting or the weeds needed pulling, and shuffle off to his car.

He wouldn't be seen again until morning.

Jack glanced down at the music, though he didn't really need it. He knew this song. Most of old Angus's music was sanctimonious, droning religious stuff, but this Christmas carol was kind of nice.

"I just want to know what the tune is," Colin said, looking embarrassed. "I know you don't have time to teach me how to play. I was terrible at the piano, anyhow, so I don't think I have any talent."

Jack played a chord. The guitar was so out of tune it was painful to hear. Brad's dad must be tone deaf.

He began to turn the tuning heads. "I'd be happy to teach you, if you want to learn. But I'm rusty. I don't even own a guitar anymore. I haven't played much since high school. I mostly did it to impress the girls."

Colin watched Jack's fingers carefully, as if he thought he could pick it up by osmosis. "Girls like my mom?"

Jack fought to keep his face expressionless. Nora had loved to listen to him play. A sad song with a poignant melody had been the easiest way to melt her resistance, and he'd been selfish enough to exploit it shamelessly. He'd kept his guitar in the back seat of his car for two whole years, just in case.

He decided to change the subject.

"Listen. This is how each of the strings should sound, if they're in tune."

For the next fifteen minutes, he played, and Colin watched. The kid soaked up information like a dry sponge. He might not have native talent, but he had a quick mind. Jack had a feeling that anything Colin chose to learn would get learned in a hurry.

They were so absorbed that Jack, at least, didn't hear Nora's car drive up. His first clue was when Colin turned his head and his face lit up with a toothy smile.

"Uncle Ethan!"

He vaulted off the porch steps as if he had springs in his shoes. He ran across the small plot of grass that was the front yard, and reached the car just as a tall man with brown hair and wire-rimmed glasses stepped out.

"Uncle Ethan!"

The newcomer folded Colin in with a big hug. "Hey there, High C," he said. He held Colin out to look him over. "Darn, boy. What is Nora feeding you—alligators? You're twice as big as you were this summer."

Jack set the guitar aside and stood, watching the scene curiously. "Uncle Ethan" was one of the pieces of Nora's life Jack had been eager to understand a little better. Who exactly was he? How did he fit in?

He certainly seemed to feel at home.

Nora got out, too, and beamed at the two males, clearly pleased at their camaraderie. "Colin, help Ethan with the packages in the trunk, will you? I think he's got—"

That's when she saw Jack.

She looked silly, standing there with little clouds of breath misting from her open mouth, her hand still held out, dangling the car keys toward her son.

Colin took them from her. "Mom, I told Jack and Sean it was okay if they stayed for dinner. It is, isn't it? Stacy said she would make extra pork chops. I wanted them to meet Uncle Ethan." He smiled extra hard. "It's okay, right?"

All that Carson breeding came to her rescue.

"Of course it is," she said, and if Jack hadn't known her so well he wouldn't have heard the stilted quality in her voice. "Ethan, you've never met Jack Killian, have you?"

The serious-faced man glanced at Nora, then turned and smiled at Jack.

"No," he said, moving toward Jack, his hand outstretched, as if nothing could delight him more. "I don't think I have. It's a pleasure."

Jack put out his hand, too. But he had seen the look that had passed between "Uncle Ethan" and Nora. It had been brief, about two seconds of rapid, wordless messages, like a subliminal quick-cut montage in an action film.

Quite an interesting look.

Now Jack just had to figure out what it meant.

NORA WAS ABOUT TO RUIN the salad, her hands were so clumsy. Ethan came up behind her and took the knife out of her hands.

"Let me," he said. "You need to sit down a minute and take a deep breath."

"I'm fine," she said. But she relinquished the knife. He probably needed something to do, to take his mind off…everything.

She and Ethan had shooed everyone else out to the front porch, telling them to work on some carols together, contending that they would cook better alone. But really she'd just wanted time to talk to Ethan privately, to hear what he thought, now that he'd actually seen Jack.

They had a pretty good view of the others from the kitchen window, though they could just barely hear Jack's easy finger-picking as he played every Christmas song Colin, Stacy and Sean could think of, from "Silent Night" to "Jingle Bell Rock."

Nora noticed that Colin didn't seem to be singing. He was watching the others, wide-eyed, admiring. It made her feel skittery inside, to see him look at Jack like that.

"It's damned eerie, isn't it?" Ethan's voice was quiet. They both knew they mustn't be overheard. "When you told me you suspected Jack, I—" He tossed a handful of chopped celery into the salad bowl. "I guess I believed you, but I never thought—"

"They'd be as identical as clones?"

Ethan nodded, his deft doctor's hands dicing tomatoes perfectly, even while he stared out the window.

"Well, Colin seems to like him," he said. "They seem to get along. I guess that's a good thing. I mean, if…if…"

Nora touched his forearm. She knew this was hard for him. In a way, it brought it all back too vividly. He had changed that day, when Maggie had died in his boat, her blood pooling around her, her newborn baby crying in her arms, as if he sensed the great loss that had just come upon him.

Ethan had always been quiet, but after that he'd been painfully serious. He worked too hard and laughed too little. It was as if he lived in fear of making another mistake.

The horror of that day had changed Nora, too. But while Ethan had been alone with his grief and his guilt, Nora had had Colin. Even from infancy, Colin had been special. Rambunctious, funny, dramatic and difficult. Full of affection and warmth. So like Maggie and, Nora now knew, so like Jack, too.

A child like that had gone a long way toward restoring laughter and hope to Nora's life.

"Do you think Jack knows?" Ethan stared at the two males, with their identical dark curls and teasing smiles. He shook his head. "How could he *not* know?"

"He suspected right away. He asked me who Colin's father was. He asked me whether I had come to him that last night, when he was too drunk to remember. That's when I realized he didn't know. However it happened with Maggie that night, he truly didn't remember."

"God," Ethan breathed. "He—she—and then he forgot all about it."

Clearly Ethan couldn't imagine such a thing. He'd kissed Maggie three times, that was all.

"It was lucky that Jack phrased his question that way," she went on. "I was able to say no, I had *not* come to him. It was easier to be convincing, since I didn't have to lie."

They talked so softly they had to stand elbow to elbow in order to hear each other. And still they checked out the window every few seconds, to be sure the caroling continued.

"But how long will that story satisfy him?" Ethan gestured toward the window with the tip of the knife. "Look at the two of them! What if he asks for proof? A paternity test?"

A chill ran down Nora's back, puckering the flesh between her shoulder blades.

"He won't," she said. "He is only staying through Christmas. He'll head back to his other life soon, and he won't think about Hawthorn Bay, or Colin, or any of us, for another twelve years."

"Maybe."

Ethan didn't meet her gaze, but his profile was somber. "Do you ever think we made a mistake, Nora? Handling this the way we did?"

"No."

He put the last of the tomatoes in the salad and turned on the faucet to wash the knife. "I'm not so sure. Maybe we did. Maybe we should have gone through the conventional channels. Arranged for you to legally adopt Colin."

Nora shook her head. She'd tortured herself with

this question a million times. She always came back to the same answer. They had done the only thing they could do.

"Do you really think Maggie's parents would have let me take Colin? You heard Maggie. The only thing she cared about, even when she was dying, was making sure her father couldn't get hold of her baby. We promised we wouldn't let that happen. How could we have broken that promise, Ethan?"

He placed the heels of his hands on the edge of the sink and dropped his head, as if he were tired of trying to untie this emotional knot.

"We couldn't have. But damn it, Nora, my name is on that birth certificate. My father's name is on Maggie's death certificate. *Injuries from a fall*...and I talked him into that. If the truth should come out now—"

"It won't." She squeezed his arm. "I promise. It won't. You helped Maggie, that's all you did. You and your dad, you helped her save her son. And you gave me...everything that matters. Whatever happens, I won't let you suffer for that."

He nodded. They were silent for a moment, and the sweet notes of "O Holy Night" seeped in through the edges of the window. Jack and Sean were harmonizing. The tears, which memories of Maggie always brought close, threatened to spill over.

"I loved her," Ethan said suddenly. "It's ridiculous. I only knew her for four months, and she's been gone eleven years. But I still love her. I can't seem to move beyond it."

"I know." But it startled her to hear the raw pain in his voice. It was as if Maggie had died a few months ago, instead of more than a decade. Ethan had remained a big part of Nora and Colin's lives, but they rarely discussed Maggie this openly.

Maybe he needed to get some help.

Nora blinked away the unshed tears and tried to smile. "Don't you think Maggie would want you to be happy? I know everyone says that, it's such a cliché. But you know what a firecracker Maggie was. She believed in living in the now. She put all her energy into every single minute. She would be very annoyed if she thought you were still pining away."

Nora could just imagine Maggie on the subject. She'd complain about what a waste it was. Ethan was sexy, and smart, and good-hearted—and there were too few men like that. He owed it to the world to get out there and make some living, breathing woman happy.

Ethan smiled. "Yeah, she'd be merciless, I suspect. She hated whiners." He picked up the salad bowl and handed it to Nora. "But while we're on the subject, I don't think she'd be too happy to hear that you're still single, either."

Nora laughed. "Then she'd better send Mr. Right straight to my front door. Because I am way too busy taking care of her little rascal to go man-hunting."

Suddenly there was a knock at the kitchen window. Ethan and Nora both looked up quickly and saw two faces pressed against the glass.

It was Colin and Jack.

"Feed me," Colin mouthed and did a silly pantomime of starving, gripping his stomach and falling into Jack's waiting arms.

Ethan grinned. "Well, how about that. Could Maggie be answering you already? You request delivery of Mr. Right, and voilà!"

Nora shook her head. "No way. Maggie knows, better than anyone, that Jack Killian is Mr. Absolutely Wrong."

CHAPTER TEN

IT WAS CLEARLY TIME for them to go home.

Jack recognized the familiar tired shadows under Nora's eyes that meant she was running on empty. And no wonder. She'd fixed a wonderful dinner, but she had hardly been able to eat it. Her cell phone had never stopped ringing, either with city business or jam business.

In the end, it was Ethan who'd intervened, saying the flight in had been exhausting, and would she mind if he called it a night? Jack decided the guy might be all right.

In the flurry that followed, everyone separated. Sean and Stacy tackled the dishes, Colin showed Ethan to the guest room, and Nora went looking for an extra blanket.

Jack was dispatched to bring in Ethan's luggage, which had been forgotten in the chaos earlier. It didn't amount to much, just one black leather duffle and two professionally wrapped Christmas presents —a small square box for Nora, and a huge rectangular package for Colin. Colin's was heavy and oddly shaped.

Jack had seen that shape before, long ago, under his own Christmas tree. It might well be a guitar. If it was a halfway decent instrument, that was a pretty pricy gift, even for an "uncle."

He decided not to speculate about Nora's gift. It was a jewelry box, but Jack hadn't seen anything tonight that signaled "diamond." There was intimacy between those two, definitely. But not passion. He knew Nora well enough to be sure of that.

In fact, "Uncle Ethan" seemed like the perfect nickname. Ethan might have been Nora's protective big brother.

Jack added Ethan's gifts to the others under the tree, most of which seemed to be addressed to Colin. Then he went back out to gather up the guitar and sheet music, as well as the odd drinks and snack bowls they'd left out there earlier.

"Don't fuss with those," Nora said from the doorway. "I can get them later."

Jack continued stacking the empty glasses.

"It's the least I can do, considering how we crashed your party tonight." He smiled at her. "You were a good sport about it. Your mom would be proud."

She smiled back, the first one she'd given him directly tonight, and walked onto the porch, letting the door shut behind her.

"I hope so," she said. "Although I'm pretty sure she would be appalled at the mismatched napkins."

Jack laughed. He'd liked Angela Carson, who'd

possessed something better than wealth and elegance. She'd had grit. He'd always thought that maybe, beneath the required "official" position that Jack Killian wasn't good enough for her daughter, Angela might have liked him, too.

At least up until the day they'd found Tom Dickson on that island, with Jack's fist marks all over his body.

Nora's dad, on the other hand—well, if Boss Carson hadn't lived in the civilized, modern world, he probably would have taken Jack out beyond the city walls and shot him, just for looking at his baby girl.

"I was sorry to hear you'd lost your dad," he said. "He had a heart attack, I heard. That must have been difficult."

"It was." She stood against the railing and plucked a withered leaf from one of the hanging poinsettias. "But I guess you know all about that. At least I had him until I was grown up and ready to be on my own. And my mother is still only a phone call away. You lost both parents—and you were only nineteen. I don't know how you managed."

"Very badly."

He'd been in the Army, still, when his father had wrapped his car around a tree. He'd been given a furlough, later that same year, to come home when his mother's cancer had finally claimed her. He'd stayed in the next town over, so that he wouldn't have to see Nora.

It wasn't until much later that he'd learned she hadn't been in town, either. She'd been in England, or Ireland, or wherever she'd met the man who'd fathered Colin.

"It's hard, whenever it happens," he said.

She nodded. She seemed softer tonight, and he wondered why. Was she just too tired to keep her antagonism fully stoked? Or was she ready to— maybe not to forgive him, but maybe to hate him a little bit less?

He wanted to say something about how gracious her little house looked tonight, and how her mother must be proud of that, too. She didn't need a mansion like Heron Hill to create grace and warmth. He wanted to tell her how lucky Colin was, to have a mother who knew how to make a home like that.

"You look beautiful tonight," he said.

Where the hell had that come from?

But it was true. Seen through the window, the multicolored lights of her Christmas tree sparkled all around her head, like a halo of rainbows. She wasn't dressed up, but her jeans and green sweater fit her so well it made his mouth water. Her shining curls were springing loose from their red ribbon, into which someone had stuck a small sprig of holly. She wore no makeup, but her cheeks and lips glowed a light, natural pink.

"Thanks," she said awkwardly. She reached up and touched her hair, as if she knew it must be messy, as if she thought he must be joking.

He wanted to touch that hair. It would curl around his fingers like soft satin.

He knew he'd told her it would be a mistake, but damn it...he still wanted to kiss her. He knew he could make those lips burn as red as the poinsettias that bloomed at her feet.

But how could he? The house was built in a U design, with the two wings thrusting forward on either side of the small front porch. It was cozy, protected from the December wind, but it had zero privacy. Behind Jack, the kitchen window overlooked them, and behind Nora, the living room window did the same.

"Nora," he began.

"I want to ask you something," she interrupted.

He paused. "What?"

She took a deep breath. "I don't have any right to ask, I know that, but I'm going to anyway. I want to know why you hurt Tom. Why you left him on that island." She watched him carefully. "Will you tell me?"

A gust of wind came around the corner suddenly. He tightened his shoulders against it.

"No."

She flinched at the curt, unequivocal sound of the syllable. She raised her chin. "Is it because I waited too long to ask? If I had agreed to come to you that night, would you have told me then?"

He put his hands in his pockets. "No."

She stared at him a minute. Then she turned and moved toward the door.

"I see," she said.

"No, damn it, you *don't* see."

He caught her just as she reached for the knob. Grabbing her hand, he pulled her into the only square foot of darkness on the porch, in the corner formed where the front wall met the kitchen.

She gasped softly, but the sound didn't get far. He closed his lips around it, swallowing the sweet, warm cloud of her breath. She resisted for an instant, and then, as he pressed her against the wall, she yielded.

She was soft, and molded easily to him. Their bodies met at all points, from lips to feet, and created just one urgently shifting shadow.

In their private darkness, he deepened the kiss, using his tongue to coax her lips open. She moaned, and moved her hips, as if they, too, wanted to part and let him in.

It was almost more than he could bear. Every part of him throbbed, and reached mindlessly for her.

He slid his hand between her legs. Even through the denim, he could feel the heat of her response. He rubbed the thick seam of her jeans, frustrated, wanting to tear it away, wanting to reach the hot silk of the skin below.

But they could make only small, intense movements, as if the porch light were poison, as if they'd die if any part of their body left the cocoon of darkness.

She shifted again, tossing her head silently against the wall. He felt the ribbon come free and spill to the ground. She arched, straining, and he wondered if she might come for him, might surrender here, against his hand.

He wanted that more than he'd ever wanted anything, more than he wanted his own release.

But he should have known it wouldn't be that easy. It had never been easy, not with her. Without warning, her movements changed, and her hands, which had briefly wrapped around his neck, now pushed at his chest.

"No," she said. "Stop."

Her breath was ragged. Even in the darkness, he could see her eyes shining, glazed with the desire she tried to repress.

He stepped back. Oh, this was viciously familiar.

But, in spite of how Neanderthal he'd just been, he was a thoroughly civilized man. He understood every part of the word *no*.

"I'm sorry," she said, her voice almost a whisper. "I should have stopped you sooner."

He smiled. "Not at all," he said, arching one brow. "If I recall correctly, you stopped me right on schedule."

THE NEXT MORNING WAS CLEAR, but so cold the sky seemed to be made of blue ice. Nora got out her woolen coat and made her way to the Hawthorn Executive Air Field.

She'd heard Tom say he was going flying today, but if she got there before ten, she'd probably still find him on the ground.

At first, as she parked her car in the front lot, she wondered if she could ever find anyone in this big, grassy field dotted with small planes that looked like an unruly flock of white birds.

But a young man at the front desk pointed her in the right direction, and she started walking. She was glad she'd worn sensible shoes because Tom's plane was all the way at the back.

The man must have called ahead, or else Tom recognized her as she hiked toward him, because, when she finally reached him, he didn't look at all surprised.

"I'm heading up in about ten minutes," he said, bustling around his airplane officiously, checking this and that. The plane didn't seem much larger up close, and she hoped it was safer than it looked. "Is this urgent, or can we do it when I come down?"

"It won't take long," she said.

Tom frowned. He had an annoying way of implying that his schedules were twice as important as anyone else's. Perhaps it was true—as a property developer, city councilman and amateur pilot, he stayed pretty busy. His trophy wife Jill frequently lamented that she never saw her husband. But the rumor was that Jill consoled herself with extra tennis lessons from her sexy pro, so maybe the arrangement worked.

"So?" Tom brushed his silky blond hair out of his eyes and looked down at his watch. "What can I do for you, Nora? If it's about the eminent domain—"

"It isn't." She was wearing gloves, but out here on the open field the wind cut right through the leather, so she stuffed her hands in her coat pockets. "It's about the day you said Jack Killian tried to kill you."

Tom's brows dug together like silver knives. "For God's sake, Nora. You came all the way out here to ask me about that old—"

"Yes, I did. I want to know the truth, Tom. I want to know what really happened that day. And I want to know why."

"You know what happened. Your thug of a boyfriend decided to beat the crap out of me. He said he didn't intend to kill me, but if Buster hadn't come along and found me, that's exactly what would have happened."

"Yeah, that's the story I've always heard," she said. "But now I want the real story. Start with the *why*. Why would Jack go to all that trouble? What had you done to make him angry enough to beat you up?"

Tom shrugged. "Who knows? Maybe I'd just pissed him off by being richer, smarter, better looking. Better *period*. Whatever."

"That's a load of bull, and you know it. No one in Hawthorn Bay is better looking than the Killians, not even you, Tom. And why would he beat you up for being rich? Killians don't care about things like that."

He laughed. "Oh, yeah? What do Killians care about? I hope you aren't going to say *love*, honey, because I think that ship has sailed. I didn't notice *love* bringing that boy back to Hawthorn Bay much over the past twelve years."

She stared at her cousin, wondering exactly when their childhood friendship had withered away, leaving only the official blood tie behind. Perhaps it had been the day she'd begun to see through his surface beauty, down to the base metal beneath. After that, perhaps it had seemed a waste of time to try to charm her.

Or maybe, if she were to be even more cynical, maybe it had been when she'd sold Heron Hill. Tom respected money, and little else. A rich cousin was one thing. A poor relation quite another.

"Damn it, Tom. You're not going to bully me into backing off. I want you to be honest with me."

"You want honesty?" He came closer, and his eyes bored into hers. "Okay, sweetheart, here comes a big, sour dose of honesty. The Killians are bad people. They're coarse, and they're violent, and they don't give a damn about anybody but themselves. And if you're out here asking me questions because you've fallen for that scum again, I feel mighty sorry for you."

She looked into his eyes a long time. He didn't back down. He meant the nose-to-nose defiance to be intimidating, but suddenly she remembered how, as a child, he'd always been the most belligerent when he had something to hide.

"You're lying," she said slowly. "You did something, something so bad Jack couldn't let it go. And I'm going to find out what."

Tom shook his head. "Listen to yourself, Nora. He's getting to you all over again. Did he plant that ridiculous idea in your pretty little head? Even if that were true, would that make it right? If I did something bad, it's okay for him to break my arm and leave me for dead?"

"No, but it makes it—"

She stopped. She wasn't sure what it would change.

"It makes it less—" She tucked her coat around her chin. "Why should he take all the blame? Why should you get off scot-free?"

"The truth? Because I am a respectable member of this community. And he's a dirty son of a drunk."

She stepped back, finally. "God, Tom. When did you get to be such a snob?"

Tom pulled on his gloves, as if to say that her ten minutes were up.

"Listen, Nora. I'd leave it alone, if I were you. I don't go digging around into your past, do I? I don't go snooping around trying to find out who knocked my pretty cousin up and left her with a black-haired, blue-eyed, bad-tempered brat. And do you know why?"

She wanted to hit him. If she'd been a man, she might have. "Because it's none of your goddamn business?"

"That's right," he said. He motioned to an attendant standing a few yards away. The man came running. "And now that we're clear on that, sweetheart, I have a plane to catch."

CHAPTER ELEVEN

1936

THEY HAD NAMED THE baby Lily Rose, and so naturally the funeral had been awash in lilies and roses. Even people who hated Patrick, who hated all Killians because they'd been raised to it, sent flowers. The first Killian daughter in a hundred and fifty years, born dead.

The sickeningly sweet scent had filled Patrick's nose, clogged his lungs, while the minister had droned on and on. For the rest of Patrick's life, if he smelled one of these flowers, he knew he'd have to fight back a surge of vomit and tears.

He and Virginia had been married only a year, but he had already sent her roses three times—for her birthday, for their anniversary and for Easter.

Never again. He would send daisies, or chocolate, or simply cover her in kisses.

If only God would give him the chance…

If only He would let Ginny live to see another birthday.

Please God, Patrick prayed, for once not caring

whether he sounded like his father. *Please. I can't bury them both in the same week.*

"I want to die," Ginny had said as they'd walked together, stiff-backed, heavy-limbed, from the cemetery. He had nodded, assuming that she was searching for words to express the enormity of the pain.

He hadn't imagined that she was being quite literal. When they'd returned to Sweet Tides, he'd let her go into the bathroom alone. He'd even been glad of the freedom to cry privately for a while himself.

It hadn't been until the thin line of liquid had begun to snake its way under the door that he'd grown anxious. For a confused moment, he'd tried to identify it. It was very dark, but in the light it had shone a dull red, like a rose petal long past its prime.

Now he walked back and forth outside Ginny's door, waiting for the doctor to come out. Waiting for him to tell Patrick whether enough of the rose-petal blood had remained in her body to keep her heart beating.

Her broken heart.

It didn't seem fair to pray that she should have to live, when she clearly had wanted to be released. But Ginny was only nineteen. Patrick himself was only twenty-one. There would be another baby, another little girl whose blue eyes would open, and laugh, and make her parents whole again.

Even if there were no more babies, Patrick needed Ginny. He *needed* her.

The doctor opened the door quietly. His face was somber, but he met Patrick's eyes, which gave Patrick hope.

"She'll live," he said. "But she's weak. And her mind is not well. She will need a lot of help."

"Anything," Patrick said. "Tell me what to do. The stitches—"

"The nurse will see to her stitches." The doctor looked uncomfortable. "That's not what worries me. It's her mind. She is depressed, to the point of unbalance. I can't be sure she won't try something like this again."

"I won't let her," Patrick said. "I will never leave her alone. Not for a minute."

But the doctor made him see that such a thing was not possible. Ginny didn't need a keeper to prevent her from harming herself. She needed a psychiatrist, to stop her from wanting to.

She needed professional help. It would take a long time. It would cost a lot of money.

The doctor said the last with a heavy sigh. Everyone knew that, though the Killians were not paupers, they had very little money to spare.

What there was, Patrick had inherited, as his older brothers had lived wild and died young. James had fallen from a bad-tempered horse who hadn't liked the drunken, heavy-spurred rider. Matt had tumbled out of the sky, in an airplane he couldn't afford and had barely known how to fly.

Patrick had been much younger than his reckless brothers, and in some ways had hardly known them. But the deaths had seemed to break Patrick's father, Angus. The old tyrant had died last year, leaving the house, a little money in bonds, but no real fortune.

So Patrick had the inheritance, and the little he earned from his new career as a junior accountant. That was all. Not nearly enough to pay for round-the-clock care of an invalid wife.

When the doctor left, Patrick looked in at Ginny, who was sleeping, her soft hair spread out on the pillowcase. The gauzy cuffs around her wrists looked innocent, like a child's lacy nightgown.

Patrick shut the door quietly. He went into the library and took down the box of his father's music from the upper shelf where he'd stashed it after Angus's death.

After his first heart attack, Angus had told Patrick about the gold, about how he had dug it up and hidden it here, in the house. The key, Angus had said, was in the music. If God decided that Patrick should have the gold, he should have it. But he would have to come to it the dutiful and virtuous way—by honoring his father's creations.

How angry Patrick had been that day. Another of his father's mad lectures about the Almighty. Another of his father's egotistical power ploys, designed to bring Patrick to heel.

He didn't want the goddamn gold, he'd said. He didn't need it. He'd make his own fortune, and if he didn't, Ginny wouldn't care. She loved him, something Angus could never understand.

Angus had slapped him, for arrogance, for dishonoring his father, for taking the Lord's name in vain. For refusing to come to heel.

"I'm here now, Father," Patrick told the empty room. His voice broke, and the cracked sound echoed off the high, molded ceilings. "I'll do whatever you want. I'll sing your songs from every rooftop in Hawthorn Bay. Just give me the goddamn gold."

HAWTHORN BAY DIDN'T HAVE ITS own shopping mall, but it shared one with the next town over. The developers had split the distance, hoping that two small towns could combine to create one viable market, and the strategy had paid off.

Today, just five days from Christmas, it seemed to Jack that all shoppers from both towns were here, trying to find the perfect gift they should have bought a month ago.

He was as guilty of procrastination as any of them. He spent an hour at a jewelry store picking out trinkets for the three or four women he dated most frequently, and another hour at the perfume counter, choosing pretty bottles for the paralegals, secretaries and file clerks. The other partners would get wine. His postman, housekeeper, paper delivery-man and condo doorman would have to make do with cash.

"Man, you need to work at a smaller law firm," Sean said as they finally gave up and grabbed chairs at the food court. It was time for a sandwich break. "You must have bought a hundred presents this morning."

Jack refrained from pointing out that if Sean hadn't insisted that he stay in Hawthorn Bay, all this would have been accomplished with much less fuss back in Kansas City two weeks ago. And it would have saved him a small fortune in overnight shipping.

Besides, Sean had put a pretty serious dent in the mall's inventory today, himself. Jack was surprised to discover how many friends his brother had. At least twenty pals had made Santa Sean's list, in addition to the obligatory business-related gifts.

Twenty friends. That must be a world record for any Killian living in Hawthorn Bay.

"If I worked at a smaller firm, I wouldn't have the luxury to just skip out for a month," Jack observed mildly as he checked out the food court's offerings. Luckily, he wasn't a prissy eater. Hamburgers, tacos, sub sandwiches, they all sounded fine to him. He'd eaten a lot worse in the Army, and even during that last year at home, when his mother had been too sick to cook, and his father had been too drunk.

At the Desserts Galore marquee, he paused. He cocked his head. "What's the hell is a boggy bottom pie?"

"It's like a big brownie pancake, with ice cream and berries on top." Sean laughed. "It tastes a lot better than it sounds."

"It would almost have to." As Jack scanned the

booths, he noticed a thin redhead standing in the pickup line at the Italian Eaterie, holding half a dozen shopping bags.

"Hey, isn't that Amy Grantham over there at the pizza place?"

Sean was studying the Burger Box menu. "You think you see Amy Grantham buying food? You gotta be hallucinating." He looked up. "Well, I'll be damned. It is Amy Grantham."

"Order me something big and greasy, okay? Extra onions." Jack patted Sean's shoulder. "I'm going to see if she wants to join us."

Sean chuckled. "Not once she hears about the onions, she won't."

But Jack was already halfway across the food court. When he reached Amy, she had just picked up her tray.

Two pieces of cheese pizza. Good for her.

"Jack!" She smiled at him. "Wow. You must have heard me thinking about you. I was just reminding myself to call you when I got home."

"Well, now you won't have to. Sean and I are getting burgers. Come sit with us."

Sean and Jack had snagged the only empty table in the whole place, so she couldn't have said no even if she wanted to. Jack watched as Amy arranged her bags. She looked good. Still too thin, still too tired, but…

He couldn't put his finger on it. She just looked more normal. More relaxed.

"Sorry about all the bags," she said, tucking one

under her chair so that Jack would have enough leg room. "I've been on a real spree. That's one of the things I wanted to tell you."

"Actually, I think it's Eddie you'd better tell. It's a joint credit card, right?"

"He won't care this time," she said. She blushed a little, then ducked down and dug through one of the bags. "See?"

At first, Jack had no idea what he was looking at. Then he realized she held one of the smallest white cotton undershirts he'd ever seen in his life.

"You're—"

"Yeah." Her thin, freckled face lit up like a flashlight. "I'm going to have a baby."

He hugged her hard. "Fantastic," he said, and meant it.

"I've wanted this for so long. You remember?"

He remembered. Motherhood had been her dream for years, since way back in the Al-Anon days. But then Tom Dickson had come along and derailed all dreams.

And then the anorexia. He wondered whether that had made it difficult to conceive.

She might have been thinking the same thing. She picked up a slice of pizza and, with an air of determination, took a large bite.

"Is this why you were going to call me? To tell me about the baby?"

She nodded, chewing deliberately. "Partly." She swallowed, and then smiled at him as if she'd done something miraculous. Which, he supposed, she had.

"But that's not all I wanted to tell you." She glanced over toward the Burger Box, where Sean was still waiting in a ridiculously long line. "I wanted to tell you that Tom Dickson came to see me yesterday."

Jack felt his shoulders tighten. "Why the hell would he do that?"

"I'm not sure. He seemed upset. Someone had clearly stirred his juices. Got him pretty riled. I thought maybe it had been you."

Jack smiled grimly. "Oh, I do hope so."

"Anyhow, I told him to get the hell out of my house before Eddie got home. But he said that he was only there to give me a warning. He said that if he ever heard that I'd been spreading lies about him, if I started saying he'd done anything nasty back in high school, he'd sue me for slander."

"What a bastard. He wouldn't dream of making it all public like that, and you know it."

"Yeah, well, he also said that if he heard I'd been talking, he'd give Eddie such an earful that he would never touch me again unless he was wearing rubber gloves."

A spurt of adrenaline shot through Jack so hard and fast he almost had to push his chair back and sprint out of the mall. Somehow, he managed not to be such an idiot. But his heart pounded in a caveman fury.

Fight or flight, my ass.

Just fight.

"Don't look like that," she said, putting her hand over his arm. "I'm not asking you to go smash him up for me."

He tried to smile. "It wouldn't be for you, Amy. It would be for the good of the planet."

"Men," she said. She took another bite of pizza. "You are so loaded up with testosterone that you can't even hear what I'm trying to tell you. I don't care about Tom Dickson anymore. When he left, I did some hard thinking. I decided that, if I'm going to be a mother, I've got to start being brave. So I sat Eddie down, and I told him everything."

Jack stared at her. "You did?"

"Yep. And you know what? He doesn't care. He said nothing that happened before he met me matters."

"He did?"

She laughed, and Jack realized that Amy's laugh was something he had heard only a very few times in his life.

"Yes, he did. So that's why I was going to call you, Jack. Because I wanted you to know how happy I am."

She folded the little white shirt carefully and returned it to the shopping bag. She didn't seem to be able to stop smiling. It made her look ten years younger.

"And here's the most important thing. In the past twenty-four hours, I've become quite a fan of honesty. So I hereby release you from your vow of silence, Jack. If you want to tell anyone what really happened that day, it's perfectly fine with me."

She squeezed his arm. "I suggest you start with Nora."

THIS WOULD BE THE LAST CITY council meeting before Christmas, and Nora expected it to be a circus. Hostility seemed inevitable. She only hoped it wouldn't come to name-calling and flying fists.

The final item on the agenda was Tom's request to raise the offer for Sweet Tides, as a last resort before filing an eminent domain claim.

The audience was crowded, unusual for any meeting, much less one held just four days before Christmas. Jack and Sean Killian were there, as was Jim Samoyan from the Langley Group. Several reporters had shown up—from the local paper, of course, but others, too, from as far away as Columbia.

The mood was restless. It was strange, Nora thought, scanning the edgy, unfriendly faces. On this issue, for once, the locals seemed to be rooting for the Killians.

Perhaps the old "traitor's gold" legend was finally losing its potency. It was about time, she thought wryly. Most of the people around here today couldn't tell you six accurate facts about the Civil War if their lives depended on it.

Or perhaps the little people of Hawthorn Bay

just didn't like the idea that the city council could decide to confiscate a person's property at will.

Today the Killians…but tomorrow perhaps any one of them?

She braced herself. If the vote went for Tom, the Killian camp looked prepared to wage war. And, of course, if the vote went against Tom, he certainly knew how to make a scene.

They moved through the short agenda quickly, and finally the moment arrived.

In a bold voice, Tom moved that the council allocate the funds necessary to double the offer for the Sweet Tides property, and to set up a committee to investigate eminent domain proceedings, should the bid be rejected.

It seemed as if the entire room held its breath.

But, to Nora's amazement, the anticipated chaos never came.

The motion simply lay there.

Nora waited, then officially called for a second.

Nothing. She glanced quickly at Tom. He leaned forward, looking at his fellow councilmen one by one.

His face was ruddy with anger, his glare intimidating.

But still no one seconded the motion.

Finally Nora cleared her throat and spoke the formal words that declared the issue dead. "Since there is no second, the motion is not before this meeting."

The room broke into loud, spontaneous applause.

Obviously Nora wasn't the only person who was sick of Tom Dickson's bullying. That pleased her. It made the world feel a little less lopsided.

Tom sat back in his seat, clearly stunned.

Nora glanced at Jack. He was probably getting a special kick out of seeing Tom ambushed so thoroughly—and so publicly.

But she got another surprise. Jack hardly seemed aware of his victory. He was deep in conversation with a woman Nora didn't know, a super-thin redhead who looked sweet, but just slightly downtrodden.

Oh, well, it was none of her business, obviously. And after what had happened the other night, when he'd kissed her on the porch, she'd be smarter to avoid him, anyhow. Clearly she still had very little willpower where Jack Killian was concerned.

When the meeting adjourned, she gave a couple of quick comments to the reporters, then headed to her car. She had to pick Colin up from Stacy's house. She'd promised they'd go out for fried chicken before he went to the nursing home at three.

She'd parked out back, by the river, as usual. It made for an easier exit. But today that choice had been a mistake. In the slot right next to her sensible sedan was Jack Killian's Jaguar.

And leaning against the car's sleek, feline nose was Jack himself.

She refused to skip a beat. She moved down the sidewalk at her natural brisk pace, fishing her keys out of her purse as she walked. When she reached the cars, she smiled politely.

"I thought you'd be inside, giving interviews," she said.

"Nope. Sean's on interview duty. He's the homeboy, so it makes sense. The visiting brother doesn't really have any human-interest value."

"You don't? I would have thought the old attempted-murder story would provide extra helpings of human interest. *Bad blood, payback is hell,* don't reporters love stuff like that?"

He raised one shoulder. "They might, if they knew about it. The little girl from the local paper was probably just learning to ride a bike when all that happened. The gal from the Columbia paper isn't much older, and she's not local, so she doesn't have a clue. It's ancient history, Nora. Nobody cares anymore."

Ancient history…

Was it? Sometimes it seemed as if it had all happened yesterday. Sometimes, she felt as if she could reach back into the past and fiddle with the words. Rewrite the story.

In the new, improved version of her life, she would throw on some clothes and run down to the park, where Jack would be waiting. She would let him make love to her, and the baby born nine months later would be her own.

Really, truly, biologically. Morally and legally her own.

But Jack was right. Twelve years was a long

time. And the past was written in indelible ink. She couldn't even go back twelve minutes and change that chilly tone she'd used to greet him just now.

Oh, what was wrong with her? Surely they could be civil, couldn't they? After all these years? If she kept being so illogically hostile, he'd suspect that she had something to hide.

"Jack, about the other night—"

"Forget it. It was a mistake. My mistake. I'm sorry."

"I'm the one who's sorry," she said. "I know better than to get into a—compromising position like that. Colin was right upstairs, for heaven's sake. He could have looked out the window at any minute."

Jack smiled. "Well, I don't have children, so maybe I don't understand the rules. Does a kid turn to stone if he sees his mother kissing somebody?"

She felt herself flushing. "No, but—" She shifted her purse under her arm. "That was more than a kiss, Jack."

"Was it? Okay, then what would you call it? What exactly was happening between us?"

"Nothing." When he raised his eyebrow, she bit her lip and tried again. "Nothing significant, I mean. We've always had a lot of problems, but a lack of chemistry was never one of them. I guess the chemistry still works, but that doesn't mean anything. It's like a light burning in an empty house."

She'd pulled the image out of the air, but the

minute she spoke the words she knew how true they were. Ever since Jack had left, one part of her heart had been like an empty room, hollow, and helplessly waiting.

But not for him.

Someday, she hoped, someone would fill that emptiness, but it could never be Jack. Their sins against one another were too profound.

His jaw seemed to grow subtly more square, which she recognized as a sign that he was very angry.

"Clever simile," he said. "In other words, I can come knocking, but there won't be anyone at home?"

She didn't answer. His blue eyes were glassy in the winter sunshine, and looked like ice.

"Don't worry, Nora. I don't intend to stand out there all night, banging at the door. I did that once before, remember? I learned about that cold, empty place where your heart should be, and I learned the hard way. Believe me, I've long since given up any idea of fighting my way in."

"Okay," she said numbly. She fumbled for the button to open her door. She suddenly wanted to get away. "Okay, that's fine. We understand each other, then."

"Perfectly," he said.

She struggled to get the door open. Her fingers were nearly frozen.

Then she felt him take hold of her arm. For a minute she wondered if he planned to yank her up against him again in another unstoppable kiss. Her heart skittered, frightened—and perversely excited, too.

But he didn't pull her in. He didn't want a kiss. He just held on, while his eyes bored into hers.

"There's one more thing I want to say," he said. "It's about Colin."

She couldn't breathe. She looked at him, wondering how his hand could be so hot when his eyes were so cold.

"You have to tell him the truth," he said. "About his father. The kid is going crazy, trying to figure it out."

"That's ridiculous—"

"No, it isn't. I see him almost every day. I hear things. He keeps a list, did you know that?"

She shook her head.

"I saw him scribbling in it, at the nursing home. I'm on that list, Nora. Sean is on it, too. So are Ethan, and his friend Brad's dad, and probably every man he's ever heard you mention."

"Oh, my God."

"Yeah." Jack's jaw tightened. "So tell him, damn it. I don't care how embarrassing the truth is. I don't care if his father lives in San Quentin or an insane asylum, or an igloo on the moon. I don't even care if his father could be any one of a dozen nameless black-haired boys in a Dublin pub."

He let go of her arm. She fell against the car, looking for support.

"Just tell him. He deserves to know."

CHAPTER TWELVE

EVERY CHRISTMAS, NORA DELIVERED baskets of jam, preserves, cookies and tea to their friends and neighbors. She tried to get it done at least a week before Christmas, but this year it seemed as if everything, from Colin's behavior to the eminent domain fiasco, had conspired against her.

So here she was, in her kitchen, just three days from the big event, scrambling to put the baskets together. Colin was supposed to be helping, but he couldn't tear himself away from the guitar Ethan had given him for Christmas.

Luckily, both Ethan and Stacy were pitching in, so she might make it in time. Ethan had a doctor's gift for organization and detail. Stacy had a flair for arranging the items and tying dazzling bows.

"I've got to leave early tonight," Stacy said. "Sean's entering a boat in the Christmas parade. He's asked me to help him decorate it."

Ethan and Colin both made immature *woo-hoo* noises. Even Nora grinned at Stacy, who frowned.

"Hey, I'm good at decorating." She held up a bow. "I'm helping you, too. It doesn't *mean* anything."

The males both laughed, but Nora put out her hand, calling for quiet. "You're right," she said. "All it means is that Sean's boat will be the best-looking boat in the parade."

Stacy wrinkled her nose. "I'm not sure about that. It's an ancient junker he bought in some estate sale. He's just in it for the fun. He doesn't expect to win."

He was probably right. The annual Christmas Boat Parade, which would take place tomorrow night, was an elaborate affair. Local businesses and organizations all entered fancy boats, and so did the local bigwigs.

Nora used to joke that the prizes were always awarded based on sheer wattage. They certainly didn't judge on good taste or beauty.

Nora would have to ride on the City of Hawthorn Bay boat, which meant three stultifying hours with her cousin Tom, and the other councilmen. She wasn't looking forward to it.

Ethan held up a jar of blackberry jam. "This is the one for Bill Freeman, right?" He twisted it, checking for the small tick mark Nora had added to it earlier. "He's the one who gets the sugar-free version without the sugar-free label?"

"Right." Nora reached over and pulled a box of cookies out of one of the baskets. "No, no, no! Farley Hastert never, ever gets the rum cookies."

"Oh, sorry. He's the lush?"

Colin looked up from the guitar. "Who's a lush?"

"Get back to practicing," Ethan said. "You still sound terrible."

For answer, Colin strummed the strings roughly. "Give me a break," he said. "I just got it an hour ago."

Nora smiled to herself. Colin had badgered her until she'd finally given in and allowed him to open the present early. Ethan had joined in the petition because he would be flying out again first thing in the morning, and he was eager to see whether the present had scored a hit or not.

It had.

For a whole minute, Colin had been speechless. He had picked the guitar up as gingerly as if it had been made of sugar. Then he'd simply held it, following the lovely wood grain with his fingertip, not making a sound.

That hadn't lasted long, unfortunately. The minute he touched the strings, he'd been hooked.

For the past hour, Colin had either been practicing his scales or informing them that this was how Jack had told him you should make an open G. It wasn't enough to simply murmur "um-hmm." He insisted that you look, to see how hard the finger placement was.

He seemed to be working on that Killian Christmas song, the one he and Jack had practiced the other night. But Nora couldn't be sure. For every chord he formed correctly, there were at least three dreadful ear-busters.

"Okay, out!" Nora pointed toward the living room. "We need to work in peace. Come back when you don't sound like someone strangling a cat."

Colin trotted out, clearly just as happy to be

released. "Come on, Uncle Ethan," he said. "Let's go."

With a shrug to apologize for abandoning ship, Ethan tagged along. He was clearly bored with the bows and baskets, and besides, this visit had been too short, and Nora knew he wanted to spend more time with Colin.

"Do you think Colin looks tired?" She turned to Stacy when they were alone. "I wonder if he's putting in too many hours at the nursing home."

Stacy bent over a sparkling gold bow, fluffing out its many loops.

"Yeah, he looks a little tired," she said. "But if you think you can pry him away from the nursing home, think again. I hear it's become quite the *in* place this Christmas. With the Killians, anyhow."

Nora waited. An odd tone in Stacy's voice told her this was leading somewhere.

As if stalling, Stacy stepped back to judge her bow. It looked perfect, of course, and even she seemed satisfied. She placed the basket on the "finished" counter and finally gave Nora her full attention.

"Nora, look…you know I don't like to give other people advice. Heck, I've messed up my own life so bad no one would listen to me anyhow. But I'm just wondering…do you really think it's such a good idea for him to be spending so much time there?"

Naturally, Nora had already thought of that. She'd even told Colin that his punishment was over, that he was free to spend the rest of his Christmas vacation having fun. But he'd said he liked reading to the old people and they'd be disappointed if he stopped coming.

Short of forbidding him to go, which would have looked very suspicious, there wasn't much she could do.

Except…hope that Jack had believed her when she'd told him that his "lost" night had not been spent with her—and thus, couldn't have resulted in Colin.

But these were private fears, fears no one guessed at but Ethan. At least she'd thought they were.

She'd never talked about any of it with Stacy. The only person, other than Ethan, who knew the truth about Colin was Nora's mother, Angela. Nora just hadn't been able to lie to her. With her customary serenity and courage, Angela Carson had supported her daughter completely, and made sure that the entire town did the same.

Nora looked at Stacy and tried not to let her anxiety show. "Why do you say that? Why would it be a bad idea?"

Stacy was a fiddler at the best of times, and when she was nervous it was compulsive. She didn't have her glasses with her, so she toyed with a length of red ribbon flecked with metallic gold threads, wrapping it around and around her index finger.

"This is so awkward," she said. "It's just that—"

She glanced toward the living room and lowered

her voice. "I've been going through old papers and things at Sweet Tides. I'm almost finished—I'll probably start writing my thesis after the new year. Anyhow, I've run across a lot of pictures."

"Pictures of what?"

"Of Killians. Killian children. Killian sons, to be precise, considering that's all they seem to have."

"Oh."

"Yeah. Anyhow, these boys. Jack, Sean. Their dad. Their granddad, and both of his brothers, too. They have a certain look, all of them." She took a deep breath. "Colin has that look."

Nora's heart was beating too fast. Obviously, this wasn't the first time she'd heard someone speculate about Colin's coloring. But usually it was some rude busybody, and she didn't mind being a little rude in response. This was her best friend. Tact was required.

Still, from the beginning, Nora had set boundaries. Some subjects were off limits.

"Yeah, well," she said. She tried a wry smile and a shrug, shooting for amused indifference. "I guess I've always had a weakness for boys with dark hair and blue eyes."

Stacy hesitated a second.

Then she nodded. "Yeah. Yeah, I know. Me, too. Zach, and now—"

She cut herself off, but Nora knew what she'd been going to say. *Zach, and now Sean Killian.*

Stacy picked up another spool of ribbon, a lovely green velvet, and rolled off a couple of yards.

Had Nora dodged the bullet? She hoped so. This conversation was a no-win situation. She couldn't be honest with Stacy, and she didn't want to hurt her friend's feelings.

Stacy started looping the bow, her head bent over her work. She looked stiff.

Darn. Were her feelings hurt?

Nora picked up a tray of freshly baked Toll House cookies and busied herself sliding them off onto a plate.

"I guess it's just a preference, like anything else," she said lightly, trying to smooth things over. "Like plain M&Ms or peanut."

"Guess so. Except more dangerous. M&M's can't break your heart." Stacy paused. "Or leave you pregnant."

Nora glanced up. "Stacy," she began, with a warning in her voice.

"I'm sorry. I know I'm over the line. You don't have to tell me anything."

"Look, I don't want you to think that—"

"It doesn't matter what I think." Stacy lowered her voice. "But you can't just ignore it forever, Nora. You've got to ask yourself the important question."

"Which is?"

"What does *Colin* think?"

JACK HAD ALWAYS LOVED TO SIT on the front porch on a cold December night. The grounds spreading out before him weren't as well-tended as they used to be, but Sweet Tides in winter was still one of the most peaceful places on earth.

The sky was black and starry, the air clean and still. The river slid like liquid glass over its muddy bed. Now and then an owl would hoot-hoot from its branch high in the black cypress, but mostly everything was as silent as an oil painting.

He was tired, but still he lingered, moving the porch swing with one foot and listening to the rusty hinges creak and echo down the hollow night.

Truth was, with Sean still out at the marina with Stacy, Jack had no enthusiasm for going inside.

The rooms were too crowded with memories. His bedroom was the worst. He had lain in that same bedroom a thousand nights as a boy, listening for the sound of his mother's weeping.

Once, when he'd been about six, the crying had sounded so heartbroken that he'd crawled out of bed and headed to her room, to see what was wrong.

But she hadn't been there. He could still remember the cold terror that had washed through him as he'd stood there, staring at the empty bed.

When she'd come home, an hour later, she'd found him standing, half-frozen, in the hall. She'd assumed he must have been sleepwalking, and had forced Kelly to put a motion-sensor alarm at his bedroom door. Jack had welcomed it. If he couldn't get out, he reasoned, then no one could get in.

By the time he'd turned seven, he'd toughened up. He'd told himself he'd just been dreaming that night. There was no such thing as ghosts. The lights that played tricks in the room were merely slivers of moonlight glinting off mirrors and silver candlesticks. The restless, cracking sounds weren't bones walking toward him down the hall—they were the weary settling of a very old house. The moans and whispers were just the wind.

All that was still true.

Besides, it was getting cold out here, and he was too old to fall prey to his own imagination. He stood, stretched, yawned and headed inside. He was exhausted. The spectral weepers and moaners would have to get a megaphone if they wanted to wake him up tonight.

He thought about leaving the front door unlocked, but surely Sean had brought along his key, in case his charisma failed him at the eleventh hour.

But thirty seconds after Jack had checked every room on the first floor and started climbing the dark, twisted stairs, he heard a knock at the front door.

Great. Perfect timing.

He about-faced and headed back down. "I ought to leave you out in the cold, you lame-brain," he called out.

He threw the dead bolt and hauled the big door open. "So, Romeo strikes out, huh?"

But it wasn't Sean. Jack had to drop his gaze about a foot and a half to see the boy standing there.

It was Colin. His face was smudged with dirt,

and his curly hair popped out in all directions, like crazy springs. His expression was one of barely contained panic.

"Jack?" They'd moved past the "Mr. Killian" stage days ago. "Jack, can you help me? It's an emergency."

"Of course."

It didn't occur to Jack to hedge, or to ask first what the hell the boy was doing here in the middle of the night. The mud on Colin's cheeks looked tear-streaked, and Jack knew this wasn't a wimpy kid. "What can I do?"

"I need a flashlight," Colin said. "The biggest one you have."

He held up his hands to show the size, and in the hall light Jack thought he saw blood. He took Colin's fingers. "Hey, you've cut yourself."

Colin looked at it, too. "Yeah. It's no big deal. There was a broken bottle, and I didn't see it. My flashlight sucks."

"We need to clean that hand up."

"Later," Colin said, his voice tense. "I've got to get back out there. I lost something really important, and I have to find it."

But the more Jack looked at the cut, the less he liked it. The pad of Colin's palm, just under his thumb, had been ripped open. The edges of the skin were jagged and pulled loose. The open wound was caked with dirt.

"No," Jack said. "Now. We've got to wash this and put something over it."

Colin's brows drew together, and for a minute Jack was afraid that he'd just turn and bolt back into the night.

"It won't take long," he assured the boy. "And as soon as it's clean, I promise I'll help you find your stuff. I've got a couple of lanterns so bright they look like the headlights of the mother ship. We could find a termite hiding in a tree trunk in Tennessee."

Colin smiled, finally.

"Thanks," he said. "That would be great."

As Jack walked Colin back to the kitchen, where the first-aid supplies had always been kept, he noticed that the boy's head kept swiveling, left to right, taking in everything he saw with wide eyes.

"I've never been inside this house before," Colin said. "It's awesome. I can't believe how big it is."

Jack laughed. "Sometimes it's too big," he said. "Especially when you're alone. To tell you the truth, I'm glad you showed up. Sean's not here."

"I know. He and Stacy are working on his boat. She likes him, I think."

"Yeah. I had figured that out."

They made slow progress, as Colin stopped to gawk—the high ceilings, the carved cornices and the heavy drapes that trailed along the marble floors all clearly intrigued him.

"It's awful dark," he announced finally. "That's why it feels creepy. Maybe you should break out your mother-ship flashlights."

Jack laughed. "Maybe."

"Really, I'm serious. When we lived at Heron Hill, it was big, too, but it felt nice because it was all lit up. You should get some new stuff, too. Fun stuff, like a big-screen TV and video games and those chairs that let you lie back and be all sloppy and relaxed. Invite your friends over. Then it would be fine."

Jack tried to imagine Sweet Tides like that. Lamps and friends and a Barca lounger. Would that really be enough to banish the memories?

He flicked on the kitchen lights, which were pleasantly bright. Bright enough to show Jack just what a mess Colin really was. His jeans looked black, and he left a trail of dirty sneaker prints wherever he walked.

Had the dumb kid been digging for gold all night?

Colin hopped onto the bar stool Jack dragged up to the edge of the sink. While Jack waited for the water to get hot enough to kill whatever germs had been lurking in that cold, moldy soil, Colin poked curiously at his wound.

Jack was glad to see that it didn't seem to dismay the kid too much, though it looked awful.

"Is it going to hurt?" Colin didn't sound frightened. He actually seemed to have relaxed ever since Jack had assured him they had a good flashlight.

Jack decided on honesty. "Probably. We're going to have to scrub the heck out of it before we can put on a bandage. Want me to give you a bullet to bite on?"

All Southern boys knew the Civil War stories about wounded Rebels having to undergo surgery without anesthetic. Colin smiled devilishly. "No, sir, but maybe a little whiskey would dull the pain."

"In your dreams, soldier."

He was a brave kid. He watched everything Jack did, as if he needed to store the information for the next big battle. He hissed a couple of times, when the soap stung his skin, but overall he made remarkably little fuss.

By bandage time, he was pale under the dirt, but ready to go.

"Okay," Jack said. "Now that I know you'll live, I've got some questions. First, tell me where your mom thinks you are."

"At Brad's house." Colin looked sheepish. "I'm supposed to be spending the night there. I am spending the night there, later, when I'm through here. Brad can let me back in through the window."

"So I don't need to call her? She's not likely to be having a heart attack, wondering where you are?"

"No." Colin's panic returned. "No, and even if she was, you couldn't call her until we find my ring."

"Your ring?" Jack's imagination had conjured up about a dozen things that Colin might have lost out there, from the key to his bike lock to his favorite baseball card.

A ring had not been on that list.

"Yeah." Colin frowned defensively. "It sounds

girlie, but it's not. And I didn't steal it, so don't think that. It's mine, but my mom keeps it in her jewelry box. She says I'm not old enough to take care of it, so I can't have it yet."

Jack raised his eyebrow.

"I know," Colin said. "But it's mine, damn it."

Jack raised his eyebrow another inch.

"Sorry," Colin muttered. "I know I shouldn't have taken it. But, ever since I was little, she's told me how special it is. And it really is cool. I think it must have belonged to my dad. So I thought it might help to have it with me. It might make me lucky."

"Lucky about the gold?"

Colin nodded. "You think that's dumb, don't you? But there is gold out there."

He dug in his jeans pocket with his good hand and pulled out two small, ornate gold discs. Jack had seen enough of these through the years to recognize them instantly. Two pieces of Confederate gold. The same siren's lure that had kept so many men digging on Sweet Tides property for two hundred years.

Poor kid. He didn't realize that these two pieces of gold were probably all he would ever see of the Killian gold.

"See? I found these last time," Colin said. He was excited. "I figured out the gold is buried under that tree, on the little hill by the river. The clue is in the words to the Christmas song Angus wrote."

"'The Starry Skies?'"

"Yeah. I'm going to give these to Mr. Killian for Christmas, but I was hoping to find the whole thing first. He'll be really excited. Remember when he gave me that old sheet music? I think he was trying to tell me about the clue in the song."

Jack started to laugh, but he wondered...

Could that be true?

Jack knew that Patrick's speech center had been damaged, but no one was sure how much mental clarity was still left behind the garbled words. Was it possible that Patrick had enlisted this boy to do the searching for him? Was it possible that, even from his hospital bed, Patrick was still worrying about the legendary family fortune?

Colin jumped down from the stool. He held out his hand, urging Jack to hurry. "Can you get your flashlight now? We should hurry, before anything happens to my ring."

"Okay," Jack said, trying to forget that just a few minutes ago he'd been exhausted enough to bunk down with ghosts.

He'd made a promise, and he intended to keep it.

Enough things had been lost in the past two hundred years, as people had searched for this imaginary gold. Even if it came from a gum-ball machine, Colin's lucky ring was not going to be added to that list.

THEY FOUND IT HALF AN HOUR LATER.

Just when they'd begun to lose hope, Jack's

mother-ship torchlight picked up a tiny glint of gold in the black dirt. Colin dove for it with a cry of joy.

"You found it!" He dropped his torch, the beam shooting crazily through the trees and settling on a live oak ten yards away. He knelt on the ground, brushing the earth from the ring, then shoved it on the middle finger of his right hand.

It was too big, even there.

"Thank you, Jack," he said breathlessly. He clambered to his feet and impulsively hugged Jack around the waist. "Thank you. You're the best."

Jack wanted to hug him back. It was so strong, the urge to kneel down and take the boy into his arms. But everybody knew that you couldn't get that close to other people's kids. In today's uptight world, anything could be misconstrued.

Somehow, Jack confined his reaction to a polite pat on Colin's bony shoulder.

"Well? Don't I get to see the ring? After all this tramping around hunting for it?"

Colin laughed, obviously light-headed with relief. "Sure!" He pulled it off and handed it to Jack. "It's still dirty, but you can see. It's a guy's ring. It has some Latin words carved into it."

Jack almost dropped it. All of a sudden, he couldn't feel his fingers. All the blood had rushed to his chest and set off a small, hot explosion behind his ribs.

It couldn't be.

But the weight, the color, the shape of the ring

were all so familiar. He knew, without even looking, that he could take it and slide it onto his finger. It would fit perfectly.

It had been his mother's father's ring, and her grandfather's before that.

Jack's mother had given it to him, the night before he'd left for the Army. She'd meant to give it to Sean, as the firstborn. But Sean had been at college—hardly a dangerous place. Jack had needed it more.

It would keep him safe, she'd said, while he was away.

She'd said he was ready. If he was mature enough to be a soldier, he was mature enough to inherit the ring.

But she had been wrong. He had thrown this ring away, that same night, in a fit of drunken disappointment and self-pity. What did he care about being safe, if Nora didn't love him?

The next afternoon, when he'd finally pieced together enough of the night to remember what he'd done with the ring, he'd gone back to retrieve it. He'd had only about ten minutes, before his flight out of town.

But it had been gone.

He'd been miserable. The guilt was terrible because it should have been Sean's ring. He'd confessed everything to his brother, calling him at college from a pay phone on the basic-training base. He'd tried to explain. Someone must have seen it, he'd said, glimpsed it lying abandoned under the hedges. Someone must have picked it up, feeling incredibly lucky, and kept it.

Now he finally knew who that someone was.

"I can't read Latin," Colin went on, oblivious to anything but his own relief. "But my mom told me what it says. It says—"

Jack spoke the words in his head, the words that suddenly held such a terrible, indisputable irony.

It said *Fideli Certa Merces.*

Riches to the faithful.

CHAPTER THIRTEEN

THE CITY OF HAWTHORN BAY'S fifty-two-foot vintage mahogany sloop, which had looked so beautiful starting out, with its tall sails transformed into Christmas trees by rows of colored lights and prancing reindeer leaping and blinking off the point of the bow, was in trouble.

They'd been gliding along on motor power, the sails purely decorative tonight, when suddenly the motor began to grind and squeal. The air on deck filled with the grimy smell of dirty oil, which made the expensive champagne feel slimy in your mouth and gave the canapés a peculiar flavor.

"What?"

"What's happening?"

The elegant hum of conversation rose to a nervous buzz. The boat slowed. Smaller craft began to pass them, the plebeians in tiny day sailors and catamarans laughing and waving their beer cans at the stuffy, overdressed, becalmed politicians.

And then, just about at the halfway point of the parade, the impressive boat carrying Hawthorn Bay's elite humiliatingly came to a dead stop.

Bill Freeman, who had joined Nora along the railing to avoid the more insufferable snobs collected by the bar, sighed heavily. He peered over the side of the boat.

"Know how to swim?"

An image of Maggie, giving Ethan one last, irritated look before she dove into the green Maine water, filled Nora's mental vision. With effort, she shook it off before it could bring tears.

"Not well enough," she said with a smile. "I'm afraid we're stuck."

She looked around the deck. Several people were already on their cell phones, protesting the indignity to anyone who would listen.

As mayor, she probably ought to go mingle, assure people that everything would be fine. The city had hired a captain, and Nora was sure the man was already working on the motor, but patience was not one of the virtues this crowd possessed.

Oh, let them stew, she thought. They liked little glitches—it gave them a chance to feel superior. Tom was about twenty feet away, holding forth to some poor woman about the shoddy workmanship you found everywhere these days. Funny, Nora thought, how that bothered him only when it inconvenienced him personally. He didn't seem to mind building cheap housing and office space for other people.

She took another sip of champagne. To heck with the responsibility of being mayor. It didn't involve babysitting a bunch of spoiled grown-ups.

"I'm going to get another drink." Bill held up his empty plastic flute. "Want one?"

Nora shook her head. "No, thanks. I think I'll just enjoy the show."

And it was quite a show.

They'd lucked out with the weather. It was a cold night, but beautiful, as if the sky had decked itself out in strings of sparkling white stars for the occasion. The river, rocked by the slow wakes of a hundred boats, gave back rippling reflections of thousands of red and green and yellow and blue lights.

Even the shoreline was alive with color. The stores and houses along the river had joined in the festivity, setting out extra displays. Every roofline, gable, chimney and door was outlined in lights. On the lawns, glowing red Santas waved, white fairy-light reindeer nodded their antlers, and silver angels blew golden trumpets.

She wondered where the Butterfields' boat was. Brad's dad loved to fish, and he had a nice little cabin cruiser that they'd decorated like a giant Christmas present with a huge red bow. Colin was riding with them and would spend the night at the Butterfields' house afterward.

That would make the third night this week. She wondered whether that might account for Colin's yawns and shadowed eyes. Maybe the boys were staying up too late, playing video games.

The Butterfields were nice people, but they

tended to sit in front of their TV all night and lose track of everything else.

"Hey, Nora!"

She looked around. No one on the boat seemed to be paying any attention to her. Had she imagined it?

"Hey! Mayor lady!"

Then she understood. The call had come up to her from the water below. She leaned over the railing and found Sean Killian's boat.

The small Boston whaler had obviously seen better days, but its decorations had the signature Stacy Holtsinger touch. She'd used only a few scallops of tiny blue lights, shaped like waves, to outline the boat. Then, attached to the tip of the mast, one huge white Christmas star.

Simple, but it made the other boats look tacky and overdone.

Stacy stood up and waved at Nora, smiling. "What's up with the bigwig boat? You guys run out of gas, or what?"

Sean's craft rocked, as a bigger boat went by. Sean, who was sitting on Stacy's left, reached up to steady her. Jack, who was behind the wheel, just kept watching Nora.

He looked beautiful by starlight, she thought stupidly. Even artificial starlight washed lovingly over him, dropping silver sparkles into his black curls and flattering his classic profile. She could imagine what it would do to his eyes.

No, she didn't have to imagine. She could remember.

"Our motor died," she said, forcing her thoughts back into line. "They're working on it now, but who knows?"

"Bummer," Jack said. He gave her that slow grin that had always made her stomach tingle. "Want a ride?"

She opened her mouth, surprised. Then she cast a furtive glance toward the other people on her boat. It was a crazy suggestion. She was the mayor. She couldn't just ditch the rest of the city government crowd.

Could she?

She looked back at Jack, and she knew by his saucy raised eyebrow that her indecision must be written all over her face.

"Yeah! Come on, Nora," Stacy said, laughing. "Do it. It'll be fun."

"I can't," she said, but even she could tell she didn't sound as if she meant it. The little boat looked so cozy, so simple and free. Just a few friends, a cooler of cola and the stars in your eyes...

"I can't."

"Yes, you can," Jack said. He handed the wheel to Sean, who was already standing, ready to take over. He moved to the side of the boat as Sean steered them alongside the city's yacht.

"There's a ladder right beneath you." Jack stretched out his hand, as if to show her how close they were, how easy it would be. "Make a break for it."

She put her hand down and found the first rung

of the ladder. She looked at the water, which was cold and full of colors. "What if I fall in?"

Jack laughed softly. "You won't," he said. "I'm right here."

She glanced one more time at the crowd behind her. No one was looking her way.

"Come on, Nora," Jack said. He held her gaze. "Surprise me."

She couldn't really be considering it. It was absurd. Knowing it would be cold, she had worn her red-velvet Christmas dress, which was the worst possible outfit for indulging in impulsive prison breaks that required climbing ladders, jumping onto moving boats and other physical insanity.

But she did it anyhow.

She kicked off her high heels, held them by the tips of her fingers, then threw one leg over the side of the boat.

"By God, she's coming!" Stacy sounded shocked, which annoyed Nora. Was she really that prissy and predictable?

She tucked her long, full skirt into her belt, then carefully made her way down the ladder, one bare foot after the other.

She felt ridiculous. Even worse, she felt nervous, as if she actually were an escaping prisoner, as if someone might at any moment turn a spotlight onto the side of the boat, pinning her there for all the world to see.

The bottom of the ladder was still about three feet higher than the deck of Sean's boat, a distance she hadn't appreciated from above. She hesitated, acutely aware of the movement of both boats as they reacted to the shifting water.

"This dress is velvet," she said, as if that made any difference. "It'll weigh a ton if it gets wet. If I fall in, I'll sink right to the bottom."

"Nora." She felt Jack's hands circle her waist. "Shut up and jump."

His touch was light, but it was the security she needed.

She saw Bill Freeman walking toward the spot where he'd left her, a fresh champagne flute in his hands. Their eyes met over the rim of the boat. At first Bill looked shocked, but, slowly, as the situation sank in, he began to smile.

He winked. Then he raised his hand to his forehead and gave her a crisp goodbye salute.

Okay, there was no going back now.

She shut her eyes, then pushed off gently. She dropped, landing with her back against Jack's chest. The boat dipped and wobbled under her weight, but Jack held her steady.

Stacy and Sean began to clap and whistle their approval. Nora laughed, suddenly breathless. Her head fell back against Jack's shoulder.

She felt his lips at her temple. She could tell that he was smiling.

"Welcome aboard," he said.

TWO HOURS LATER, THEIR OWN MOTOR died, but by then they'd had so much fun none of them really cared, least of all Jack.

The parade was over, and they had almost made it back to Sweet Tides anyhow. They could see the outline of the house from the river, its columns gleaming under the stars.

Jack was glad to see that Sean had at least possessed the foresight to bring oars. He wouldn't have relished the idea of jumping into the freezing water and towing the boat to shore.

Rowing wasn't difficult—the river was calm and fairly narrow here—but when they finally felt the bump as the bow hit the riverbank, the women applauded. That was how much the mood had mellowed. Even Nora seemed relaxed.

"Tell you what," Sean said as he jumped out, then held up a hand to help Stacy out, too. "Why don't you and Nora wait here with the boat, and Stacy and I can go get the tool kit?"

Nora's laid-back attitude vanished so fast it was almost laughable. She stood awkwardly, holding on to the gunwale as the boat rocked.

"It's okay," she said. "I don't mind walking. We can all go together."

Stacy turned her back on the men and looked at Nora, but not before Jack glimpsed the intense glare in her eyes.

"No, Nora," she said with slow emphasis on each word. "You two should stay here. You don't have the right shoes for walking that far."

There followed a brief battle of wills. Jack could see only Nora's end of it, but clearly there was quite a dialogue going on with their eyes. Nora must have been very fond of Stacy because, in the end, her gaze dropped first.

She apparently had decided to sacrifice herself so that Stacy could have some private time with Sean.

"Okay," she said. She plopped back onto the cushioned seat and tried to smile, though her jaw was tight. "Take your time. We'll be fine."

They both watched as Sean and Stacy disappeared into the trees. It was probably a ten-minute walk to the stables, where Sean kept his tools, and a ten-minute walk back. But Jack had a feeling Sean wouldn't be coming back at all. When a decent interval had elapsed, Jack's cell phone would probably ring, and Sean would say that he didn't have the right tools after all, Jack should just take Nora home, they'd fix the boat tomorrow.

But in the meantime, Jack had been handed the chance he'd been waiting for. He needed to talk to Nora alone, and, for the moment at least, she was essentially a captive audience.

He didn't climb back aboard the boat. She might be more comfortable if she had at least that symbolic separation. He leaned over the gunwale and pulled another cola from the cooler.

He tilted it toward Nora. "Want one?"

She shook her head. "No, thanks," she said politely. "I've reached my limit."

He chuckled and closed the lid. "You may be over your limit, actually," he said. "I'm not sure you would have sung 'A Hundred Bottles of Eggnog on the Wall' with us if you'd been stone-cold sober."

"Probably not," she agreed. This time her smile was more natural. "But you two do sound fantastic together. That's one thing the Killian men sure can do. They can sing."

"Why, thank you, Mayor."

He leaned against the boat, the cola open and fizzing pleasantly. This was nice. Starlight floated on the water like silver paint, and the night wind made soft sounds in the trees. He almost wished he didn't have to bring up anything serious. He would have liked to stay like this all night, just a boy and a girl flirting by the river.

But that innocent time was long gone. They were grown-ups now, and they had to start dealing with their issues maturely. Facing them squarely.

There were things that had to be said.

"I'm glad we stayed behind," he said. "I've been wanting to talk to you about something."

Funny. Now that he knew exactly what she was hiding, he could read her so much better. He knew that the slight recoil wasn't about him personally. It wasn't fear that she'd been abandoned on a dark night with a semi-homicidal Killian. It wasn't even fear that she might be unable to resist his seductions.

It was, instead, terror that he might force open her Pandora's box of secrets, and let all the dangerous truths fly into the air, changing absolutely everything.

In one way, he wondered why he didn't hate her.

If everything he believed was true, she had stolen eleven years of fatherhood from him.

But he had hated Nora Carson only once in his life—the night he'd lain there, drunk, angry, believing she had abandoned him. He never wanted to feel like that again.

So how did he feel? He wasn't sure. In the twenty-four hours since he'd seen his ring on Colin's finger, Jack's emotions had seesawed up and down, from shock to fury, from disbelief to confusion, and then to something that he couldn't quite identify.

It might have been the tentative, bewildered first stirrings of joy.

He was completely sure of only one thing. He wanted her to tell him about Colin. He wanted her to trust him enough for that.

And that meant he had to help her. He had to open the dialogue, clear the path for honesty by offering honesty of his own.

"You asked me to tell you what really happened with Tom that day," he said. "I couldn't do it then, but I'd like to tell you now."

She sat very still, her hands folded in her lap. Her blond hair caught the starlight and shone like a halo. The soft folds of her wine-velvet skirt draped around her gracefully. She might have been the Lady of Shallot, frightened as she sailed into the world outside her protected tower.

"Why now?"

"I'm not the only person involved in this story," he said. "I had given my word that I'd never tell.

But the other person is ready to tell the truth. She's tired of hiding from the past."

Nora's head tilted. "She? The other person is a woman?"

He nodded.

"I always thought there might be someone else. I—" She twined her fingers together. "I thought it might be Sean."

"No. Sean wasn't part of this. In fact, he doesn't know the whole story, either."

She looked surprised. "You didn't even tell your own brother?"

"I had promised," he said simply. "Sean didn't need to know. He trusted me."

He heard how it sounded. Sean had trusted him—Nora hadn't. But it was the truth. And tonight they were dealing only in truths.

"Anyhow, the woman involved was Amy Grantham. You probably don't know her. She still lives here, but on the wrong side of the tracks. She's just a girl I knew, a couple of years younger than we were. She was only sixteen at the time."

"No, I don't think I've ever heard of her," Nora said. "How did you—how did you know her? You must have been close, if she could make you take a vow of silence."

"We met at a meeting for children of alcoholic parents. She'd had a rough life. Their family didn't have any money—her dad drank it all, the same way mine did."

Nora nodded. "Okay." She swallowed. "Were you lovers?"

"No. But we were very close, for a while. It's the kind of thing that accelerates intimacy. You learn things about each other, things other people don't know. It's like being members of a secret family. Yes, that's how it was. She was like my secret sister."

"All right," she said. Her voice gave nothing away.

"Anyhow, she was pretty, or could have been. She had beautiful red hair, a good figure and an open, pleasant face. She had an eating disorder back then, so she was too thin, but…"

He stopped, remembering Amy chewing that pizza the way a sick person might take medicine. She'd come such a long way. He said a quick prayer that she would win the fight.

"She was mixed up, but she was a good person, deep down. The problem was, she'd fallen hard for your cousin Tom."

Nora's inhale told him she realized how dangerous that could be.

"It was kind of pathetic, everyone knew he'd never take a girl like her seriously. Everyone but Amy. She was hooked. Tom was slick as hell, you know that. I'm sure he flattered her just enough to keep her addicted, to keep her hoping."

"I can believe that," Nora said. "Every female in school thought he was gorgeous. They used to come to me, asking me to get them a date with him."

"Well, I hope you didn't do it," Jack said, "because your cousin Tom was a real sick dude."

"What do you mean?"

"I mean he was a sick son of a bitch. He started sleeping with Amy, on the sly. He'd come to her house late at night, after he took his real girlfriends home, and get her to sneak out. That went on for about a month."

Nora looked down at her hands. "I'm so sorry," she said. "Poor Amy."

"But he got bored, I guess, because then he wanted more. He told Amy that he wanted to do a threesome, with her pretty little sister as number three."

Nora lifted her head. Her wide eyes gleamed in the starlight.

"Yeah. The kicker was that her sister was only fourteen. I told you, Tom was one sick man. Anyhow, this is the part Amy was really ashamed of. This is the part she couldn't bear to let anyone know about. She agreed to bring her sister out to the spit island one day after school. She couldn't stand the thought of losing him, so she said she'd do it."

"Oh, my God. Did she?"

"No. At the last minute, she chickened out. She went to the island herself, hoping she could placate him, doing God only knows what, so that he wouldn't be so angry. But he was angry. He made her do—"

He stopped. Apparently it didn't matter how

many years had elapsed. His heart still pounded with the need to teach Thomas Dickson a lesson.

"He made her do every sick, humiliating thing he could think of. He knocked her around. And then he left her there. Alone, on that island, with no way to get home except to swim. If I hadn't gone out looking for her—"

"Jack." The word was full of real horror. "Oh, Jack."

"So the next day I stole a boat and I took Tom out to that same island. I beat the hell out of him. I told him that if he ever laid another hand on Amy or her sister, I'd kill him. And I left him there."

She didn't respond, which didn't really surprise him. This story didn't exonerate him. The fact that Tom was a psycho didn't justify Jack being a thug. But she had to know the truth. Though he had no idea what the future held for them, he knew it couldn't begin with lies and secrets.

"I'll admit I was glad to do it. In a way, I was doing it for myself, too, and for all the people Tom Dickson treated like trash because they weren't as blessed or as rich as he was. But I swear to you, Nora. I had no idea I'd broken his arm. It was only about a hundred yards to shore. He was the athletic type. I assumed he'd swim home and maybe, just maybe, stop being such an asshole for a while."

Nora opened her mouth, as if she were about to speak, but she closed it again without making a sound.

She took a deep breath. And then, moving carefully so that the boat wouldn't wobble, she stood.

"Jack, I—" She paused. "Can you help me out?"

She made her way gingerly to the bow. He set his drink on the ground and met her there. He held out his arms, and she moved toward them. She put her hands on his shoulders—and though the touch was gentle it went through him like electricity.

As he lifted her above the gunwale and onto dry ground, his fingers circled her waist, pressing into the smooth velvet. Her soft hair fell forward, into his face, teasing at his lips, and it smelled of that mysterious new perfume, the dusky sandalwood and spice.

Though her balance was steady now, he found himself holding on to her. He could feel the warmth of her fragile body beneath the wine-red velvet, and it made him shiver, wanting more.

"I can't make myself let go, Nora," he said, his voice a rough whisper. "I've wanted to hold you for so long."

He felt her startled intake of breath, but she didn't pull away. She hadn't removed her hands from his shoulders, although now that they both stood on firm ground she had to lift her arms to reach him.

Her breath came shallowly, as his thumbs began to move, drifting along the lower edge of her rib cage.

"I remember you so well," he said. "I remember the shape, the feel of every inch of you."

He watched her eyes, which glistened in the starlight. If those eyes had turned cold, if she had whispered even the faintest *no,* he would have stopped.

But she didn't. She panted lightly, as if she were trying to control a primitive fear. But even when his hands rose all the way to the curve of her breasts, she didn't tell him to stop.

He cupped the graceful swell, stroked and pressed against the pebbling tips. Though the velvet was rich and thick, he could feel her heartbeat through it. He knew when its rhythm began to race.

Her hands tightened on his shoulders. She shifted, angling her body toward him. The soft warmth between her legs met the hard fire between his. He groaned, his heart a jackhammer, his whole body pounding with desire.

He could have taken her right there, in the boat, or in the river, or on the cold, hard ground. For himself, he was beyond caring how it happened, as long as it did, finally, happen. He was burning up, and he needed to quench the fire.

But somehow, for her sake, he held back. If she would let him make love to her, he wanted this time to be better.

He wanted it to be more than a drunken coupling in the scratchy winter grass. He wanted it to be soft sheets and soft words, and long stretches of foreplay that ended in explosions of pleasure. He wanted to soothe her to sleep afterward, and lie together, spooned in safety, with all the time in the world.

He wanted to offer her all the things she had always deserved, but had never been given—at least not by him.

He bent his head toward her breast.

"Jack," she whispered. "Jack, I need you to—"

His heart froze. He could feel her pulling away.

"Don't say it, Nora. *Please*. I don't think I can stand it if you tell me to stop."

She tilted her head back, so that she could look at him. The starlight found a fevered flush along her cheek and a fast-throbbing pulse in her slender neck. She threaded her hands into his hair, the way she used to do. It made him shiver now, just as it had done all those years ago.

"You didn't let me finish," she said. He heard the undercurrent of husky desire in her voice, and his heart came back to life with thick, hungry beats. "I was going to ask you to hurry."

CHAPTER FOURTEEN

HOURS LATER, NORA LAY beside Jack on the soft four-poster bed, trying to commit the entire room to memory.

The corner rosettes on the cornice above the door, the elegant tidal marsh landscape over the mantel. The ornate Chinese rug, though she could only guess at the colors in the dimness.

The slant-top desk by the window—she wondered if he'd done his homework there, as a teenager. She wondered if he had found it hard to concentrate on world history, thinking instead of her.

And of course the beautiful mahogany bed. The carved headboard she had reached up and gripped, clinging to her last shred of control. The rumpled white sheets frosted with moonlight. Soft pillows that spilled, forgotten, onto the floor.

She wanted to learn it by heart, so that for the rest of her life she could close her eyes and see him lying here, wet skin shining, black hair tossed against white cotton, eyes closed in exhausted, dreamless sleep.

As for the rest of it…

The kisses, the touches, the feel of his body, finally, *finally* inside her…

She didn't have to make a special effort to imprint those memories. They would be part of her forever.

She held her breath as he stirred in his sleep. She'd promised herself that she would stay only a few more minutes, only until he moved. If he let go of her, that would be her sign it was time to leave.

When they had finally collapsed, shaking from the fading tremors of their last amazing climax, she had tried to roll away. But with a sleepy murmur he had reached out and pulled her up against his chest, her bottom against his belly. Settling his head above hers on the pillow, he had wrapped his arm around her waist, reaching up to cup her breast in his warm palm.

He'd fallen asleep almost instantly. His hand softened. His legs, braided with hers, relaxed heavily, and his breathing grew deep and even.

It was strange how comfortable such a tangled position could be. She'd even slept a little, herself.

He shifted again, murmuring something that might have been her name, and finally turned away, unwinding his legs.

Immediately her thighs and calves felt cold, deprived of his warmth. The large house had central heating, but the rooms were cavernous, and the chill had never completely vanished.

Except when she was in his arms.

She eased off the bed by inches, praying that he wouldn't wake. If he did, if he looked at her with eyes full of starlight and held open his strong arms, she knew she would fall right back into them. And then how would she ever find the courage to leave?

She bent and gathered her clothes from the Oriental carpet. They were scattered all the way from the door to the bed, as Jack had pulled them free. The red velvet dress had been the first to go. It was halfway out in the hall.

The bathroom was the next door down the corridor. She knew where it was because he had gone there to get the condoms, and again later, to get more. She walked softly, her bare feet silent on the glossy hardwood floor.

Before she dressed, she pulled her cell phone out of her dress pocket and called for a taxi. If the request was already placed, she'd be more likely to stick to it, even if he tried to persuade her to stay.

She tried to whisper her request, but the dispatcher sounded annoyed. "Did you say Sweet Rides? Where is that? Don't you have a regular street address?"

She finally made herself understood. Then she turned her attention to dressing. Her fair skin was pink in places, where his attentions had been concentrated. The heavy velvet felt rough against her skin, much rougher than Jack's hands had been.

She clasped her belt. Looking in the mirror, she ran her fingers through her hair to work out the worst knots, and finally just gave up. The taxi driver would assume the worst, but so what? He'd be right.

When she heard footsteps coming down the hallway, she took a deep breath and rushed to put on her last shoe. She had to be suited up and ready to go, so that nothing he said could dissuade her.

But to her surprise the footsteps seemed to be coming from the other direction. And they didn't pause at the bathroom. They went farther, stopping instead at Jack's bedroom door.

Nora peeked out. It was Sean.

She felt irrationally embarrassed. Paralyzed, the way she used to feel when she was eighteen and her dad came out to see why it was taking Nora and Jack so long to say good night.

What should she do? Announce herself?

"You sleeping alone, too? Guess we both struck out."

She stuck her head out of the bathroom cautiously. Sean stood in the bedroom doorway. He wasn't facing Jack. He had his back to the door frame, and seemed to be sliding up and down, scratching his shoulder blades on it while he talked.

He hadn't drawn a breath, even talking around a loud yawn. If Jack had tried to interrupt him, it wasn't getting through.

"And you know tonight was your last chance," he went on, "because tomorrow, when she finds out you hired a lawyer, she's more likely to shoot you than scre—"

"Sean!" Jack's voice finally pierced Sean's sleepy self-absorption. "For God's sake, shut up."

"Why?" Sean scratched his head and yawned again. "It's true. Hiring Harry is the kiss of death—"

Nora came out of the bathroom.

Sean's jaw dropped. His mouth was open wide enough to catch a baseball, and he didn't even seem aware of it. He stared at Nora with round, trapped-animal eyes.

"Holy shit," he said.

"Hi, Sean," she said. "Hired Harry for what?"

Jack must have found his clothes because suddenly he appeared in the doorway, too. He wore jeans, still unbuttoned at the waist, and nothing else.

"Nora," Jack said. "Nora, I swear. I was going to tell you."

She transferred her gaze to him. "Hired Harry for what?"

Sean cleared his throat. "Tell you what, maybe I'll just slide on out of here, just run on to bed, what do you think?" He looked at Jack. "Good idea?"

"Excellent idea."

Sean sidled by Nora as carefully as if she were a ticking bomb. "Don't pay any attention to me," he said. "I'm an idiot. I'm sorry."

"Get out of here, Sean," Jack said. Sean nodded. He rounded the corner quickly and disappeared down the stairs.

Nora turned back to Jack and asked her question for the third time. "Hired Harry for what?"

Jack held out his hand. "Come back in, Nora. Let's sit down. We can talk this over privately, and be more comfortable."

"It's too late for privacy. And I don't want to be comfortable. I want to be answered. *Hired Harry for what?*"

Jack ran his hand through his hair, which was as big a mess as hers. "To advise me about Colin."

Suddenly she wished she had accepted his offer of a place to sit. She wasn't sure her knees would lock firmly enough to hold her up.

"Why?" She steadied her voice. "Why would you need legal advice about my son?"

"Because he's my son, too."

She started to voice some mindless, instinctive protest, but he cut her off.

"Don't," he said. "Don't lie to me anymore. I know the truth, Nora. *I know.*"

She shoved her hands in the warm, velvet pockets of her dress—not because she was cold, but so that he wouldn't see how badly they were shaking. She lifted her chin and forced her voice to come out frigid and firm.

"What exactly do you think you know?"

"I know that, somehow, later that night, you changed your mind. You came down to say goodbye to me, and we made love."

She made a dismissive noise. "You've already admitted that you were so drunk that night that you don't remember anything. Are you saying you've had a sudden, convenient recall?"

He looked as if he were wrestling with both anger and sadness.

"No, I still don't remember. I wish I did, Nora. I wish I knew what I did that night. I was drunk, and I was angry with you for not trusting me. Did I say something unforgivable? Did I do something—" He frowned sharply. "God, did I force myself on you?"

"Of course not," she said. "Don't be ridiculous. You saw how it was, just now, between us. Do you really think that, if I had come to you that night, you would have needed to *force* me to make love to you?"

"I don't know." He shook his head. "I don't know anything. All I know is that I've been a father for eleven years, and I missed every single second of it."

"Jack, there's no—"

He put up his hands. "Don't. I'm not on a fishing expedition here. I'm not trying to trick you into incriminating yourself. I tell you I *know*."

"But how could you?"

"I saw the ring. Colin's ring."

She couldn't breathe. He couldn't be making this up. He really must have seen Colin's ring, somehow. No one even knew it existed except Colin, Ethan and Nora herself.

"That doesn't prove any—"

"Yes, it does. I know that ring, Nora. It was mine."

She frowned. "That's ridiculous. I never saw—"

"You wouldn't have. My mother gave it to me on my last night at home. She'd kept it hidden for years, so that my father wouldn't sell it. It was mine for only one night. *That night.*"

He waited, as if he expected her to protest again, but she couldn't think of anything to say.

"When Maggie came down to tell me that you weren't coming, I was so angry I got pretty wild. She was scared to death of me—she drove off so fast I'm surprised she didn't wreck the car. When she was gone, the last thing I remember doing was taking off that ring and hurling it into the bushes."

She still couldn't speak, though he paused to give her a chance. How had he seen it? Had he asked Colin to steal it, and show it to him?

"And now Colin has the ring." He shook his head. "You tell me, Nora. What else can that possibly mean?"

Nora knew she must be as pale as the waning moon outside. No blood was able to make its way to her face. It was all pooling miserably in her stomach, and sinking through her legs. She felt as if she might be sick.

Maggie had worn that ring, on a gold chain around her neck, every single day. Nora had caught her sometimes, just sitting, staring out the window, with one hand on her belly and the other hand wrapped around the little gold circle.

Maggie's last conscious action had been to take the ring off and give it to Nora. "For Colin," she'd said.

Her last words.

The thought of Maggie gave her courage. Nora wasn't the bad guy here. She had just spent the past eleven years trying to set straight a horrible, hopeless situation that Jack and Maggie had created.

"Why didn't you tell me about this sooner, Jack?"

She looked at his naked chest and remembered her hands there, exploring him while he did the same to her.

"Why didn't you tell me…before? Before we…"

His eyes were very dark. "I was going to," he said. "But I wanted you. I needed you. And I knew you wouldn't have—"

"You're darn right I wouldn't have." She fisted her hands inside her pockets. "Well played, Jack. A little strategic timing, and you think maybe you can walk off with everything. The woman. The child… everything. Very slick."

"Damn it, Nora. It wasn't strategy. The truth was, I couldn't think about anything but you. You were just as lost. We both forgot everything else, for a little while."

He was right. She'd certainly forgotten what a danger this man posed to her heart, her happiness, her family.

"And, frankly," he said, his voice cold, "if we're going to start accusing one another of keeping secrets…"

Her stomach tightened. She felt bruised, pummeled by her own fear and the accusations in Jack's eyes. She had to get out of here. She had to go home, where maybe she could clear her head.

She'd call Bill Freeman. He'd help her think what to do.

She heard a horn outside. It sounded like the prize-fight bell, sounding the end of this punishing round. She turned, eager to stagger to her corner, praying she could buy enough time to regroup before the match started up again, this time in earnest.

"That's my taxi," she said. "I have to go."

He grabbed her arm. "No. Stay."

She stared down at his hand, willing him to let go.

Reluctantly, he did. But he held her with his gaze. "Nora, you can't just run away. You know we need to talk."

"No, we don't," she said. "You've hired someone to represent you. I'll do the same. If there's any more talking to be done, we'll leave it to the lawyers."

CHAPTER FIFTEEN

1980

IT WAS NO KIND OF DAY to be outside. The sun was so hot it raised blisters on Kelly Killian's neck. But he hated this goddamn gazebo, and he was going to tear every last board of it down before sunset, even if it killed him.

He used the claw end of his hammer to pry out another piece of wall. How many hours had Bridey wasted out here? She said she liked the fresh air, and the roses, and the corner of the river you could glimpse behind the cedars.

But he knew what she really did out here.

She escaped. She daydreamed. She pretended that she didn't really live at Sweet Tides, that she wasn't really married to Kelly, and that she didn't really have two sons who, though they were only four and six, already looked just like their father.

Maybe she even pretended that she wasn't pregnant again, with another Killian boy.

She wanted a girl this time; she made no bones about that. She longed for a daughter, who would play Barbie dolls and unicorns with her all day long, while her sons went hungry for attention.

Just like Kelly did himself.

Just like Kelly had *always* done.

He'd grown up with a crazy mother who couldn't think about anything but the little girl baby who'd died. As if her living, breathing son was just a piece of chopped liver.

And then he'd married a crazy wife who sat around eating her heart out over not getting a daughter, too.

Well, tough. Killians didn't have girls. If Bridey wanted daughters, maybe she should have married that milksop architect she had been so in love with, back when Kelly had first met her.

He smiled as he swung his hammer. *Oh, that's right.* Mr. Milksop hadn't *wanted* to marry Bridey. He hadn't loved her. That's why, in the end, she'd settled for Kelly.

And no amount of mooning and daydreaming out here in the gazebo could change that.

Kelly ripped a board off so roughly it slapped him in the face. One of the nails gouged a hole in his cheek, missing his eye by about an inch.

"Damn it." He sat down on the gazebo bench and wiped his palm across his face. Then he wiped the blood on his jeans.

Everything was quiet out here today. Though it must be ten miles away, he could hear a train going by. He wondered where it was headed.

Now that the walls were half-gone, he could see

the house. It looked like hell, and why not? It used to take a plantation full of servants to keep this monstrosity going. He had five people living with him—his whining wife, his lecturing father, his crazy mother and his two lazy sons. Not one of them would lift a finger to help him.

If only he could find that gold.

He leaned back, crossing his arms behind his head. Bridey would be surprised to learn that she wasn't the only one who daydreamed. He thought about the gold all the time these days. If he found it, he'd be on a train to Anywhere Else so fast he'd leave his own shadow behind.

No one would miss him, and he wouldn't miss them, either. He was only forty-three, and he was so damn tired.

Tired of trying to be good enough to earn somebody's love. Tired of coming in second. Second with his own mother. Second with his own wife. Hell, even his sons, just little kids who should have idolized their dad, preferred their grandfather.

Sometimes Kelly dreamed of trains, fast-moving freight cars piled high with lumps of gold instead of coal. In the dream he was always running, running so hard his heart nearly exploded, trying to catch the handle and jump on.

He never could.

He wondered sometimes whether his father knew where the gold was, and just didn't think Kelly could be trusted with it. Patrick didn't approve of Kelly. Didn't like Kelly's drinking, he said.

Well, news flash. Kelly didn't like it, either. But no one had been able to suggest any other way to deal with a life so disappointing you couldn't hear a train go by without wanting to jump on it and run.

"Kelly? Kelly, where are you?"

It was Bridey. Come out to whine about the gazebo, no doubt. He pulled his hat down over his eyes and pretended to be asleep.

"Kelly, something's wrong. I need you to call the doctor."

Kelly heaved a long-suffering sigh. This woman had more aches and pains than a whole wing of a hospital. Ordinarily, she conveniently got them just about the time he came to bed, so that only a brute would insist on having sex.

"What is it now?" He tilted his hat back and looked at her through the gaping hole in the gazebo.

She stared back at him helplessly.

"I don't know," she said. "I think it's the baby. I'm bleeding…"

She dropped her arms down, stiffly, palms out, to show him. He rose slowly, trying to process what he saw.

Between her hands, her light blue cotton skirt was brightly stained with blood.

So much blood.

She was losing the baby, and he had no idea in hell how to stop it. He could call 911—he was starting even now for the house, but he could tell it was too late. It would be just one more failure that would somehow end up being his fault.

Poor Bridey, every one would say. No one would stop to think that Kelly had lost a baby, too.

No baby. No gold. No love.

No nothing.

Bridey began to cry.

And somewhere in the distance, Kelly heard the mournful sound of another swiftly moving train.

"NORA, SIT DOWN AND TRY TO RELAX." Bill Freeman looked up from the papers he'd spread out on the coffee table in Nora's living room. "Better yet, go upstairs and let me handle this."

Nora shook her head. "I can't. If I refuse to talk to him personally, it will just antagonize him even more. I panicked the other night, but I'm calmer now, and—"

"If this is calmer," Bill broke in, "I would hate to see what agitated looks like."

She tried to smile. "Yeah. You would."

The doorbell rang. It might as well have been electrically wired to her heart, which responded by pumping frantically in her chest.

Bill was right. She wasn't anything close to calm.

Thank goodness she'd found an excuse to get Colin out of the house. One of the big Christmas blockbuster movies had opened this week. Ordinarily, she made him wait until after the holiday—it seemed more in keeping with the season to focus on home, family and giving. He'd been ecstatic when she'd announced that, this one time, he could go early.

He never went anywhere without Brad, so Nora had recruited Stacy to take the two boys, and had asked her to make a day of it. Lunch, movie, maybe even a stop at the video arcade. Anything that would ensure they didn't come home before dark.

Stacy had accepted her mission without any questions, but her expression had been extremely curious. In a way, that was a relief. Nora wasn't sure how close Sean and Stacy had become. She'd wondered whether Sean might have spilled the gossip during pillow talk.

But apparently, bless his heart, he hadn't.

The bell rang again.

Bill stood up, adjusted his belt over his paunch and shrugged into his jacket. He looked like a teddy bear, but underneath that Southern charm she knew he was a very shrewd lawyer.

On the other hand, with a case like this, she might need a miracle worker, not an attorney. The facts simply weren't on her side.

"Ready?" Bill smiled at her. "Okay. Deep breath, and—" he put his hand on the doorknob "—showtime!"

The introductions and handshakes were a blur. Nora noticed only general impressions. Jack was blank-faced and cold. His lawyer, Harry…Harry something, she had missed his last name…was young, with smart, sharp eyes and a prominent nose that gave a rather intimidating hawkish look.

Next to this guy, Bill Freeman looked sloppy, sleepy and halfway over the hill.

Somehow they all found chairs. Bill and Harry claimed opposite sides of the coffee table. Nora sat stiff-backed in her chair, as if she were made of iron stakes instead of bones. She noticed that Jack took the seat farthest away from her.

"This shouldn't take long," Harry began politely. He seemed comfortable taking the lead, though he was on enemy ground. "In fact, I think it would be better if we don't try to get too far ahead of ourselves here. Clearly the first move is simply to arrange a paternity test."

Nora clutched the arms of her chair so hard her elbows hurt. Bill had advised her to keep quiet until he asked her to speak. That was just as well. She was so frightened, she wasn't sure she could get a word out through her iron-tight throat.

"A paternity test won't be necessary," Bill said. "Ms. Carson is willing to stipulate that Mr. Killian is the father."

Nora felt Jack's gaze whip to her, but she couldn't meet it. She kept her eyes locked on Bill, as if he were the life rope she must cling to or sink.

With a groan as he bent over his protruding belly, Bill lifted a sheaf of legal papers from the coffee table and handed it to the other lawyer. "I've drawn up a document to that effect. I think you'll find that it's all in order."

Harry leafed through the papers without comment, without even a twitch of reaction in his face. He handed them to Jack, who scanned them quickly, as well.

Too quickly. Even Nora could tell that the men weren't really reading the document. Her heart tightened and started to drag down, down, in her chest.

"As you see," Bill said, "we've covered all contingencies. Ms. Carson—"

"I'm sorry," Harry broke in. "I'm afraid we must insist on the paternity test. In fact, Mr. Killian has arranged an appointment with a laboratory nearby, and—"

"Mr. Mathieson," Bill said genially, "I understand that you want to exercise every caution. But I assure you, Ms. Carson will not retract her admission, and even if she did—"

"No," the other lawyer said without so much as a smile to soften the categorical refusal. Nora wondered if it was always like this with lawyers, that no one let anyone else complete a sentence. "My client deserves to know definitively whether or not he's the boy's father. Surely you can appreciate that he would prefer not merely to take Ms. Carson's word for something that has such far-reaching implications."

Nora flushed. In other words, Ms. Carson had already proven herself a liar. Why would anyone believe her now?

Bill chuckled. "Come on, Mr. Mathieson. Your client is the one who told my client that he was one-hundred-percent certain the child was his. Now she agrees. Where's the problem? If we don't contest it—"

"He has moral certainty," Harry Mathieson said. Nora wondered if the man knew how to smile. "Before Mr. Killian goes any further, he would like medical certainty, as well. Surely your client can have no objection to that. It's a simple blood test. We will, of course, assume all costs."

Bill looked at Nora, and she knew what he was asking her. This was a reasonable request. Did she want him to keep fighting a losing cause?

"We've scheduled a trio test," Harry went on, clearly sensing a weakening of defenses and leaping into the breach. "Therefore, the reports would establish, both medically and legally, that your client and mine have equal rights to the child. It would protect them both, Mr. Freeman. Your client does not stand to lose by this procedure."

Bill still looked at Nora, waiting for a sign.

Harry Mathieson seemed baffled. "I'm not sure what the objection is. We can get a court order to compel the testing, but my client was hoping that wouldn't be necessary. Surely, at this preliminary stage—"

Nora finally looked at Jack.

"Don't do this to Colin," she said. Her voice was thin, threading through the unyielding column of her throat. "I will agree to any reasonable custody terms you offer. Please. Don't put him through this."

Jack hesitated. He glanced at his lawyer, who imperceptibly shook his head.

"Ms. Carson," Harry said smoothly, sounding

warm and concerned, which angered her. A minute ago he hadn't even been willing to give her a name—she had been merely "your client."

"Ms. Carson, we don't have to tell the child just yet, if you would prefer to wait for the reports. The lab will be discreet. Colin doesn't have to know what we're looking for."

Jack turned to Nora suddenly, and she was surprised to see how cold his eyes were.

"Why are you fighting this, Nora? You know this won't *put him through* anything. What a joke. He'll be relieved to know that he is finally going to get an answer. That he is finally going to get *the truth.* He certainly hasn't been able to get it from you."

"Jack—" Harry Mathieson put out one well-manicured hand.

Jack shook his head. "No. I'm through dancing around this with legalese." He stood. "The test is scheduled for the day after Christmas. At 10:00 a.m., Harry will call Bill and give him the address and the details. Be there."

She stood, too. Their gazes locked. "If you do this, Jack, I'll never forgive you."

Jack laughed. It might have been the harshest sound ever uttered in her little living room.

"Well, at least you're consistent, Nora. But you know what? I think I'll live."

CHAPTER SIXTEEN

COLIN WAS SO NERVOUS HIS palms were sweating, and he had to wipe them on his pants. Good thing they were corduroy because they could absorb a lot of sweat without showing it.

It was his turn, any minute now. As soon as Jack got the mechanical roll loaded properly into the player piano, Colin would have to go on.

It wasn't the singing that scared him. He knew he had a pretty good voice, and he had learned the Killian Christmas song super well. He'd practiced it endlessly on his new guitar.

What freaked him out was the thought of all these people sitting around, listening to him. There must be fifty people here. He'd never sung in front of a big audience before.

Brad had reminded him that most of the old people at the nursing home were deaf anyhow, but that didn't help. Jack and Sean were here, too. And they weren't deaf. They sang really well, and they'd know if he messed up.

His mom smiled at him from her chair in the

front row. She'd been really nice to him all day, the way she was when he was sick.

In fact, when he'd asked her if he could wear his lucky ring, he hadn't even really paid attention to her answer, he'd been so sure she was going to say no, like always.

But she'd said yes, shocking the heck out of him. He'd had to ask her to repeat it, just to be sure.

"Why not," she'd said, her voice sounding strangely sad. Colin figured it might be because she had to accept that he was growing up.

Or maybe it reminded her that someday soon she'd have to tell him the truth about his dad.

She still didn't look very happy, even though she was smiling at him in that encouraging way mothers always did. Colin wondered why she wasn't sitting with Sean and Jack and Patrick. She hadn't even spoken to them when they'd come in. Colin wondered if they were having a fight.

He hoped not. He had been planning to ask her if Jack and Sean could come over after the nursing-home party, for the marshmallow roast and games and stuff they always did on Christmas eve.

Right now, she didn't look like that would be okay with her at all.

He kept clearing his throat, trying to stay ready to sing, but Jack was taking forever with the piano.

"You've gotta baby an old lady like this, Colin," Jack said with a wink, "if you want her to do anything for you."

Colin felt his throat going dry. He looked around, trying not to let his nerves get to him.

The big recreation room at the nursing home looked really pretty, with red flowers on every table, colored lights at the windows and a huge Christmas tree in the corner, twice as big as Colin's tree at home. All the residents looked nice, too. They had dressed up special, because it was Christmas Eve and this was like a party.

Some of the girls who volunteered regularly had just sung a medley of Christmas music, and, even though they didn't sound that great, the old people had clapped like crazy.

Maybe Brad was right. Maybe they were all stone deaf.

"Finally! This roll is as old as time, and Lord only knows how long it'll last, but I think it might just see us through." Jack frowned at the piano, and he didn't look very confident. He patted the piano, as if for luck. "All we can do is try. You ready, Colin?"

Colin nodded. He glanced out at Mr. Killian, also in the front row, next to Sean. Mr. Killian raised his good hand. That was the "yes" symbol, which made Colin feel better.

Yes, Mr. Killian, was saying. *Yes, this is what I wanted. You can do it.*

"I'm ready," Colin said.

Jack sat down and started the piano. He pumped the pedals slowly, and the tinny, old-fashioned music swelled out into the room.

"When the world lay in tears, men imprisoned by fears," Colin began. It was a nice melody, and it was just right for his voice, not too high and not too low. He thought he sounded pretty good. Mr. Killian was smiling, even though he could do it with only one side of his mouth.

"An angel flew down, with a star in her crown." That note was pretty high, but Colin hit it perfectly. Out of the corner of his eye, he saw that Jack was staring at him, as if it surprised him to hear Colin singing so well.

Colin's heart got big with confidence and sudden pride. See? He might be crummy at the guitar, but he wasn't a total loser.

"And promised a new joy to come."

There was a pause here, while the player piano did a beautiful trilly thing. Colin wished he could have met Angus Killian, who'd written this song. He wondered what kind of man could write music that was both sweet and sad at the same time.

Colin sang the next verse even better, now that he wasn't afraid. He stood up straighter, which made his lungs get more air, and he could hold the long notes practically forever.

When he got to the chorus, with the title line "The starry skies sang lullabies," he saw Mr. Killian's eyes fill up with tears. Colin frowned, worried, but then Mr. Killian raised his hand again and nodded, just a little.

It was okay. Mr. Killian wasn't crying, at least not sad crying. He was just happy. Embarrassingly,

Colin felt a stinging behind his own eyes. He took a deep breath and started to tackle the last verses.

Suddenly something terrible happened.

The player piano, which had been doing fine so far, began to make a disgusting noise. It was as if it was playing all kinds of wrong notes, all at the same time. It sounded crazy, really loud and mixed up, like a room full of cats screeching together.

Jack immediately stopped moving the pedals, to silence the awful noise. He looked at the roll.

"Oops," he said. "The thing must have decayed more than we thought." He turned to the audience. "I'm sorry, folks. Guess that's the end of the song."

Several people groaned their disappointment. Colin's mom looked sad, but it was Mr. Killian who reacted the most violently. He began to writhe in his wheelchair, moving every muscle that was still under his control. He began to make that babbling noise that was the only speaking he could do.

Sean stood up and tried to calm his grandfather.

"Grandfather, don't be upset," he said. "The roll is just too old. We'll get it fixed."

But Mr. Killian kept shaking his head. He seemed to be staring only at Colin, and he kept raising his hand over and over.

Colin thought he knew what the old man meant.

"It's okay, Mr. Killian," he said. "I know the song by heart. I can finish it."

He began to sing again, this time all alone.

He sang straight to Mr. Killian, as if he were the

only person in the room. He sang clearly, and with all the heart he could find. He and Mr. Killian locked gazes, and gradually, as the notes rolled over him, the old man's stiff, clumsy muscles seemed to relax.

Colin wondered why he had never before realized how sad this song was. The burning behind his eyes got worse.

On the last stanza, Colin almost lost his voice. He faltered, unsure what to do. But suddenly Jack was standing beside him. He put his hand on Colin's shoulder, and then, strong again, they sang the last lines together.

"For the lost and forlorn, a promise was born. And peace flew in on angel wings, bringing joy this Christmas morn."

When the last note died away, practically everyone was crying, including Colin.

But that was okay. Because, standing here with Jack Killian's warm hand on his shoulder, for the first time in his life Colin felt completely at peace.

ALL THE COOKIES WERE BAKED, the presents bought and wrapped, the house glowing with lights. Tomorrow's turkey was thawing in the refrigerator and the potatoes were cut and ready to mash.

Colin was finally asleep. He'd insisted on taking the Christmas song's flawed piano roll with him. He might be dreaming of that song now, of his victory today, when his voice had moved the room to tears.

But Nora hoped his dreams had brought him home again. Perhaps he was dreaming about what lay inside the colorful boxes under the tree.

It should have been the perfect Christmas eve. She should have been crawling into bed herself, exhausted but satisfied that she'd done everything she could to make tomorrow a success.

Instead, Nora sat on the edge of her bed, fully dressed, staring at the floor, fighting panic.

She had twenty-four hours to stop Jack Killian from tearing apart her life.

What could she do? How could she stop him?

She lifted her head, letting out a small gasp.

Yes. That was it.

She could run away.

She could pull out her suitcase, pack her clothes, then go into Colin's room and do the same for him. She could wake him gently and tell him they were going to Maine to surprise Uncle Ethan, to celebrate Christmas with snowmen and icicles and sleigh rides.

Later, much later, she would break it to him that they were never coming back to Hawthorn Bay.

It was possible. Of course, she would miss it all—her little house, her friends, even the nonsense involved in being the mayor of this tidal marsh town. But she could start over. She'd lost things before. She'd lost Maggie and her father, and Heron Hill.

And Jack.

She knew how to recover. She knew how to bounce back.

She'd teach Colin how to do that, too. She'd teach him that home wasn't a town or a house. It was people. It was family.

It was love.

Love.

As the word echoed in her mind, she put her head in her hands and bit back a sob of despair.

Because she couldn't run away.

For Colin, all those important things—people, family, love—were right here, in Hawthorn Bay.

She'd seen it today, when Jack and Colin had stood together, singing. Their voices had blended perfectly, and those two blue-eyed, handsome faces had matched like mirror images.

But even those touching things were merely superficial connections. Much deeper, much more important, was the glow on Colin's face.

He belonged there.

He was a Killian.

She was almost ashamed to realize how little she'd understood the meaning of those words, until today. She'd thought of being a Killian as some kind of formula, some DNA code that mattered on paper, or in a courtroom, but nowhere else.

She'd believed that, because Colin's whole life had been spent in her care, he had become a Carson.

How wrong she was! He loved her, yes. And he had learned a lot of things from her—to love animals, to play games and play fair, to laugh a lot, to eat good food straight from the earth.

But his soul was pure Killian.

From the beginning, he'd responded to Jack's affection as instinctively as a plant turned toward the light. It wasn't just that he was starved for male attention. He soaked up Ethan's friendship, too, but there was a difference.

He liked Ethan. Ethan made him smile.

But he *needed* Jack. Jack made him whole.

It wasn't exactly *love,* which was too pat and conventional a word. It was more like—*belonging*.

Finally, the panic subsided. In fact, to her surprise she felt strangely calm.

She picked up the phone and dialed Stacy's number.

"I'm sorry to ask this on Christmas eve," she said. "But could you come over and sit with Colin for a little while?"

She paused, feeling the one last frisson of fear that came right before the leap into the empty air. Right before the long, bottomless fall. "There's something I have to do."

COLIN HEARD HIS MOM WHISPERING TO Stacy. He didn't sit up because she might hear him and realize he was awake, but he listened as hard as he could, hoping to make out even a few words.

He couldn't get much. She must really be trying to keep her activities secret.

He wondered if she was heading out to pick up that cool, bright blue fourteen-speed bike he'd asked for.

Momentarily, his hopes rose, but they dropped again immediately. He didn't really think so. It was too late for the stores to be open, and besides, she had told him they couldn't afford it.

She usually didn't lie about things like that. She wasn't the kind of mom who liked to tease you, make you worry, and then pop a big surprise at the last minute.

Brad's mom did all that, and Colin had always thought it was mean. Brad went through a lot of disappointment for nothing. And by the time Brad actually got whatever he used to want, he'd talked himself out of wanting it.

Colin listened some more. This didn't actually feel like Christmas whispering, somehow. That was always happy-sounding, with giggles. This sounded...

He couldn't think of the right word.

It sounded worried. Only worse.

He thought about getting up and going out there. What would happen, he wondered, if he just came right out and asked?

But some prickly kind of instinct told him to stay put. He heard the front door close, and then the car door. He knew it wasn't Stacy leaving because he heard the muffled thrum of his mom's engine start up, then stall, as it always did when it was super cold.

She started it again.

And then everything was silent.

After a couple of minutes, he heard Stacy's

footsteps on the stairs. She came to the doorway of his room and looked in. He lay as still as he could and pretended he was asleep.

Deep in, slow out. A little snort for good measure.

"You faker," Stacy said. She sounded as if she was trying not to laugh. "You are so not sleeping."

He was busted, and he knew it. He sat up in bed and smiled at her sheepishly.

"I was trying to sleep," he said. He reached out and turned on his beside lamp. "I just can't."

She came in and sat on the edge of his bed. "Nobody can sleep on Christmas eve," she said. "Not with a room full of presents downstairs, calling your name."

That wasn't really why he couldn't sleep, but he didn't say so. He was excited about the presents, of course. But mostly he was just still wired up from today.

After the singing, after they'd gotten Mr. Killian back into bed, Colin had given the old man his present, the two pieces of gold Colin had found under the tree, all wrapped up in a special box and a shiny green ribbon.

They had been the only two in the room. Colin's mother had been waiting out by the car, and Jack and Sean had been in the recreation room, helping clean up.

"I'm sorry it's only two pieces," Colin had said as he'd taken the ribbon off. Mr. Killian couldn't do it himself, of course. "I really wanted to find the real treasure. I looked for clues in the song, like you told me, but this was all I could find."

Mr. Killian had raised his hand, as if to say it was okay, he wasn't disappointed. But then he pointed to the piano roll and sheet music, which Jack had placed on the bedside table. Mr. Killian grunted.

"I know," Colin said. "I'm sorry. I guess it got broken, through the years."

Mr. Killian shook his hand sideways.

"I don't understand." Colin picked up the music, and then the roll, and suddenly Mr. Killian moved his hand up and down again.

Yes, his hand said impatiently. *Yes. Yes.*

"You want me to take this?"

Yes.

"Did I understand you right before? Do you think this has something to do with the gold? This song?"

Yes.

The nurse came in then and told Colin it was time for him to leave. Colin knew that sometimes Mr. Killian needed privacy, like for baths and the bed pan and everything, so he didn't argue. He put the piano roll under his arm, folded the sheet music into his pocket and smiled at the old man in the bed.

"Merry Christmas, Mr. Killian," Colin said. "And don't worry. I'll keep looking."

All night long, while he and his mom had played Scrabble, and had roasted marshmallows and listened to Christmas CDs, he'd really been thinking about Mr. Killian's song.

He'd promised he would keep looking, but what else could he do? He'd gone over and over every word of the song, until his head hurt. He'd already tried every kind of code he could think of.

Morse code, cryptograms, anagrams, code wheels. He'd even ironed the sheet music, like in the movies, to see if an invisible message would appear.

He'd researched codes on the Internet for so many hours that his mother had gotten nervous and had given him a lecture about visiting inappropriate sites and exchanging e-mails with strangers— a lecture she'd already given him years ago. Like he'd be that dumb.

Still, nothing panned out.

The truth was, Colin was getting tired of beating against a door that wouldn't open. Even if he found the gold, he wouldn't get any of it himself.

And neither would Mr. Killian, really. He was an old man. What difference would it make to him if they found the gold now? He couldn't go out and buy a cool new car, or fancy clothes, or a fast boat.

But for whatever reason, Mr. Killian did seem to care. And Colin hated to let him down. What if he went to the nursing home tomorrow, or the next day, and Mr. Killian had died?

Wouldn't he feel bad then, if he'd given up looking?

He frowned over at Stacy. She was nice, but he wasn't sure how good she was with puzzles. His mom would be better—except that Colin's instincts told him his mom wouldn't like it if she found out what he'd been up to.

He guessed Stacy was better than nothing. She liked history, especially Killian history. Maybe she would bring new ideas.

Maybe she'd think of something Colin had overlooked.

He reached under the covers and pulled out the piano roll and the crumpled piece of sheet music.

"Stacy," he said slowly. "Can you keep a secret?"

CHAPTER SEVENTEEN

2006

PATRICK STOOD IN THE Sweet Tides drawing room and laughed like a demon. He laughed until his chest ached, until the casement windows shimmied and threw trembling prisms onto the walls.

He was ninety years old, and he'd seen a lot of Fate's best and cruelest tricks. He'd seen the beautiful things that appeared out of nowhere, and disappeared the same way. He'd seen the vanishing money trick, the loaded dice trick, the keep-away shell game, the helpless woman who endured being sawed in half, then sawed in half again.

But this trick beat them all. This, he had to admit, was the pièce de résistance.

He looked down at the thick bar of gold bullion he held in his hands. It gleamed, as splendid as the day it had been minted. The years, which had turned Patrick's hands into weak, knot-knuckled old man's claws, had meant nothing to this bar of gold.

Six months ago, when Ginny had still been

alive, when he could have bought her something beautiful to make her smile, or traveled to the Tibetan mountains to seek a magic doctor to make her mind whole again, he would have killed to find this gold.

Now it meant less than nothing.

That was Fate's final trick. Now that Patrick no longer gave a damn about it, Fate had pulled this golden rabbit out of its top hat and flourished it in his face.

And, like all the best tricks, the answer had been right in front of his eyes all the time. Right there, in his father's music. He remembered the day his father had warned him not to mock his creations, for they held the key to the family fortune.

Oh, so clever, the words that said everything— and nothing.

Angus had been Fate's smiling assistant.

Look over here, no, over there. Look until your heart breaks. Look until it's too late.

Patrick laughed again. He laughed until he cried.

He felt tired, too tired to hold the heavy bar. He set it carefully back into its secret niche, then sat down himself, in one of the silk-covered drawing room chairs. He felt dizzy suddenly, from the shock, no doubt.

And his head hurt. His laughter had been too wild, too unrestrained.

He needed to settle down. He needed to think what he should do next.

Perhaps he should tell Sean and Jack. They

were good boys. When they were little, all three generations of the family had lived together at Sweet Tides. The boys had loved him. They'd sought him out, to play and laugh and cuddle. It had meant everything to him.

But Kelly had hated it. He hadn't wanted to share his sons with their grandfather. And Kelly hadn't wanted his crazy mother to be around the boys, either, though he must have known full well that Ginny had been a danger only to herself.

Still, that's what Kelly had called her, "my crazy mother."

Patrick couldn't stay after that.

It had been time to go, anyhow. Sweet Tides and the legend of the treasure had begun to dominate Ginny's nightmares. She'd imagined that there were ghosts here, ghosts of the slaves who'd worked this plantation two hundred years ago, creating the fortune in the first place. And ghosts of the Confederate soldiers who had died, needing guns and boots, for want of the Killian gold.

So he had taken her away, to a dull, safe house fifty miles inland, where she'd seemed a little better. Over the decades, even science had made strides. Patrick had found a doctor who knew about bipolar disorder, and who knew which medications to prescribe. As long as Patrick had made sure she'd taken them, things hadn't been so bad.

She'd been eighty-eight when she'd died. He'd seen her through, he'd taken care of her till the end. That was one trick he had refused to let Fate play.

He had refused to let anything separate him from the gentle, beautiful girl he'd always loved.

A pain stabbed through his skull, as sharp as a blade. He felt confused. Was he dreaming the pain? He had been talking about magic tricks, and now he felt like the man in the cabinet, with the magician shoving knives into his head.

Or was there one of the ghosts in the room right now? Had he summoned it, by finally finding the gold?

Maybe Ginny hadn't been as crazy as everyone had said. Maybe she'd been the only sane one. The only one who'd known that the gold had cursed them all, right from the beginning.

Yes, he'd better tell Sean and Jack where the gold was hidden. They were good boys. They'd know what to do.

They would be back soon. He hoped they would hurry.

Patrick put his head in his hands and cried out from the pain.

He couldn't remember where the boys had gone. Maybe out hunting for tadpoles, or riding their bikes down the long, tree-lined drive.

But he knew they'd come for him. He tilted forward and felt himself hit the floor.

They would come. They were good boys.

Maybe they'd even come in time.

IT WAS AFTER ELEVEN O'CLOCK when Nora climbed the steps of the front porch at Sweet Tides and knocked on the door.

The Christmas moon silvered the big columns that flanked her, and winked here and there at a window, but otherwise the house looked completely dark.

Maybe Jack wasn't at home.

Surely Fate wouldn't be that cruel. Now that she'd finally found the courage to come…

She shivered and knocked again.

Finally she heard movement inside, and then the sound of a lock being turned. With a creak, the door opened.

"Nora?" Jack stood at the threshold, illuminated by a beam of moonlight. Cavernous black-and-gray shadows stretched out behind him. "What are you doing here?"

"I'm sorry to come so late," she said. "But I need to talk to you."

He hesitated, his hand on the edge of the door. He looked like a charcoal drawing, in this colorless light. His white turtleneck sweater, his black hair, his dark jeans, the silver glint as his eyes moved over her. It was all slightly unreal.

"It's cold, Jack. May I come in?"

For a second, she thought he might refuse. But he stepped away from the door and held out a hand, waving her in.

He shut the door behind her and flicked on the overhead chandelier. The hallway burst into brilliant light. She blinked, trying to adjust.

"Are you sure this is a good idea?" He leaned against the brick archway that led to the drawing room, looking darkly amused. "Wouldn't Bill Freeman have a stroke if he knew you were here?"

"Probably."

She wished Jack didn't look so distant and cynical. It made him seem like a different person, a person she barely knew at all.

"But it doesn't matter what Bill Freeman wants. I have something I need to tell you."

He shrugged. "Okay." He put out his hands. "Let me take your coat."

She turned around and let him ease the black wool coat from her shoulders. Underneath, she still wore the cheerful red skirt and sweater she'd put on for the nursing-home party. She even still wore the same dangling, tinkling earrings shaped like colorful ornaments.

She wished she'd taken those off. They were inappropriately festive, considering the story she had come here to tell.

"Do you want to sit down? There are some comfortable chairs in here. Sean's upstairs, probably asleep. We won't be disturbed."

He reached around the brick arch and found the light plate. Again, a crystal chandelier flared, and the silent gray drawing room came to life.

It was a beautiful space, she observed with some surprise—elegant and spare and well cared for.

She'd never been inside this house, until Jack had brought her here the other night—and that had hardly been a time for sightseeing. She had been entirely focused on the physical burn that had been threatening to consume them both.

Back when they were in high school, he had never invited her to Sweet Tides. She'd understood—his home life was not the kind you'd want others to witness.

He'd described it vividly enough. She could picture what Jack found here when he got home from school. More often than not, Kelly Killian would be drunk, passed out in the gun room. Bridey, Jack's mother, would be sitting alone in this drawing room, rearranging her glass unicorns, or perhaps upstairs in her bed, softly crying.

In Nora's imagination, the interior of Sweet Tides had always looked tragic, shattered, dirty and lost. But the room she saw before her now, framed by this graceful arch, was lovely, with gorgeous plasterwork around the ceiling, doorways and windows. It had only a few pieces of furniture, but each one was a thing of beauty.

She was especially struck by how peaceful the room felt. A yellow-gold silk upholstery covered the chairs, and a warm green-and-blue theme was carried out in the rugs, drapes and paintings.

He led her to one of the gold chairs. She sat obediently, though she noticed he remained standing, maintaining the dominant position.

The strategy didn't bother her. Just by coming here, she had relinquished any claim to power. And the minute she opened her mouth, Jack would realize that he held complete control of the situation in his own hands.

The question that paralyzed her with fear was a simple one.

What would he do with that power?

He seemed content to wait for her to find the words to begin. He stood by the mantel and watched her with a hooded gaze.

She began simply, as she'd promised herself she would.

"I need to tell you the truth about Colin," she said.

His brows flicked together, his first sign of impatience. "I already know the truth about Colin."

"Not all of it." She folded her hands in her lap and commanded herself not to betray her fear by wringing them, or braiding them together with white knuckles, or letting them tremble. "It's true, Colin is your son."

"Yes," he said. "I know."

"But he isn't mine."

As she'd known it would, that statement rocked him.

He stood up straighter. His frown deepened, slowly digging a heavy line between his brows as he stared at her.

He didn't say anything at all. It was as if she'd robbed him of the power to think, much less speak.

"I know you thought I was just playing games when I asked you not to schedule a paternity test. I could tell that your lawyer was suspicious, and assumed that we were pulling some kind of trick. But I wasn't. I knew that, if you let the test go forward, you would discover that there's no way Colin could be my natural child."

"That's insane," he said finally. "How could I be the father if you're not—"

"Maggie Nicholson is Colin's mother." She had to say it quickly. She had to get it out. "Maggie. Not me."

He shook his head. "That's impossible."

"No. It's true. Maggie is his mother. She *was* his mother, I mean. She died giving birth to him. As she was dying, she asked me to take him. She was desperately afraid that her family would find out and try to get hold of him. Apparently her father—"

She broke off, swallowing hard. "Her father was abusive. I never knew that, until it was too late. But she feared for Colin's safety, if he ended up with her parents. She begged me to make sure that didn't happen. And I promised her I'd protect him. I promised her I'd bring him up as my own."

Jack moved away from the mantel. He crossed the room and stood next to her chair. He towered over her.

"What you're saying is impossible. If Maggie is Colin's mother, then I cannot be the father. I never in my life laid a hand on Maggie Nicholson."

She shook her head sadly. "Are you sure about that, Jack?"

"Of course I'm—"

But finally the truth pierced the armor of his disbelief. In the middle of his denial, his face went slack, and his eyes lost their focus as they returned, in his mind, to that night.

"Oh, my God," he said.

He reached out and grabbed the back of her chair, as if he had stumbled on something that almost brought him to his knees. "That night. It was… I made love to Maggie?"

"Yes," she said. "She and I went together to England, shortly after you left town. When we were there, she told me she was pregnant, but she always refused to discuss the father. Before we left Hawthorn Bay, she'd been seeing a married man, so I assumed he must be the one. It explained why she didn't want to tell me, so I didn't push. I never once considered the possibility that she—that you…"

She couldn't finish the sentence. Even now, years after the gut-wrenching blow of the truth, she could hardly believe it had happened.

Apparently Jack couldn't believe it, either. His eyes had narrowed.

"Nora, you're not lying to me, are you? I can't imagine how you'd think this could help your case, but… You're not making this up?"

"I wish I were, Jack. You don't know how many times I've wished I could go back and change what happened that night. If I had come down to say goodbye, I truly believe that you— you and Maggie—"

She stopped herself because she was on the edge of tears. She had vowed that she wouldn't cry while she told this story. It was melodramatic enough as it was.

And besides, in the end it wasn't her tragedy. It was Maggie's.

And it was Colin's tragedy, too. He'd lost both mother and father that terrible day.

"My god, how you must have hated me," he said. "When you realized what I'd done…" He ran his hand through his hair. "No wonder you didn't try to get in touch with me. No wonder you didn't tell me."

"No, that wasn't because I hated you—"

"Nora." Jack looked at her with dark eyes. "We're beyond lying, aren't we? Even to ourselves?"

She held her breath. It was true, she saw that now. Deep inside, she didn't believe he deserved to have this child, not after what he'd done. He had exploited Maggie, betrayed Nora, and then he had simply disappeared. He hadn't even called.

"All right, it's true," she admitted. "I was very angry. You see, I thought you knew what you'd done. I thought it was unforgivable that you hadn't even checked on her. I understood why you didn't call me. But I thought you should have phoned Maggie. Just to be sure she was all right. Just to be sure she wasn't…"

"Yes," he said. "You believed that, because I was a two-timing heel, I had no right to know about my son."

He sounded so cold. It took her breath away.

"I didn't know he was yours at first, Jack. You have to believe that. I suspected everyone on this earth but you. I even called the man Maggie had a relationship with before, the married man. He said it couldn't be his, that he and Maggie had broken it off, and the timing just made it impossible."

"And then?"

"And then I assumed I was safe. It was years before Colin grew so like the Killians that I finally had to face the truth. By the time I did, I...I had been his mother for so long I couldn't bear the thought of losing him."

He started walking again, toward the mantel, but it was an aimless journey. He had no purpose there—it was merely as if he was too upset to stand still.

When he got to the fireplace, he turned.

"God, what a mess," he said. "What a terrible mess."

"Yes," she said. She lifted her chin. "But it's not my mess alone, Jack. I think it took both of us to create this tangle. And it's going to take both of us to make it right."

He didn't answer. He had put up his hand and was pressing his temples hard with thumb and forefinger.

She stood. She'd done all she could do. She'd told the truth. People always told you that the truth would set you free, but that sure wasn't how it felt right now.

She felt bruised, and tired, and so vulnerable it terrified her.

She might have lost everything that mattered in her life.

The man she'd never stopped loving, and the son who was, quite simply, her heart and soul.

In the deep distance, she heard church bells ringing.

It must be midnight.

It must be Christmas.

"I'm going to go home now," she said. "Colin will be up early, eager to open his presents."

Still Jack didn't say a word.

"I know you're angry," she said. "And I don't blame you. We've hurt each other so much."

He laughed. "Is that how you'd describe it? Hurt each other? It's something of an understatement, wouldn't you say?"

"I suppose so." She tried to steady her breathing, which felt hot, with ragged edges. "But I know you, Jack. You're not a cruel person, no matter what people say. I'm not sure any of the Killians ever were as bad as people say. Sometimes human beings just get caught in situations where there's no way to keep from hurting somebody."

She moved toward the front door, pulling her keys out of her pocket. At the archway, she turned.

"Please, Jack. I know how you must hate me right now. I know how easy it would be to seize this chance for revenge. But please, please remember, I'm the only mother Colin has ever known. Don't break his heart just for the pleasure of breaking mine."

CHAPTER EIGHTEEN

JACK CAME TO WITH a flash of adrenaline that ran through his veins like fire along a fuse.

Nora was leaving.

And he hadn't lifted a finger to stop her. Was he insane? Was he going to let the only woman he'd ever loved walk out of this house?

He covered the drawing room in five steps, the hall in three. He caught her just as she pulled open the door.

"Nora, wait!"

She turned, and he saw that her cheeks were wet with tears.

"Oh, God, Nora," he said. He pulled her into his arms. "Don't cry, sweetheart."

Her body was stiff. She held herself away from him as if she were afraid of him, as if she wanted to run. He was such a fool, such a slow-witted fool! He'd let himself get so lost in his own bewildered thoughts that he hadn't paid attention to her anguish.

"Nora, listen to me," he said. "I don't know what to say. I don't even know what to think. I can't wrap my mind around all of this yet, but if you say Maggie is Colin's mother, then I believe you."

"It's true," she said wearily. "I've told you everything. Do the paternity test if you want it in black and white. I won't fight you."

He shook his head. "I told you, I believe you. The only question we have now is, what are we going to do about it?"

The tears started to flow again.

"Damn it," she said, brushing at the shining tracks. "I hate being so weak. I'm not weak, really. It's just that…if I lose Colin—"

"Weak?" He smiled. "After what I've just learned, I'd say you're the strongest woman I ever knew. You found out that the man you loved betrayed you with your best friend, and yet you took the child of that union and brought him up as your own. You brought him up in a home filled with love and happiness and loyalty. Not weak, Nora. Not hardly."

She frowned, as if he weren't making sense.

"What are you saying, Jack?" She blinked hard, to press away the tears. "Are you saying you can possibly forgive me for not telling you?"

"Forgive *you?*" He wiped the dampness from her cheeks gently. "Nora, listen to how absurd that is. I'm the one who sinned here. Not you. No, my love, I'm asking if you can ever forgive me."

She seemed lost, as confused as if he were speaking another language. But on some subconscious level she must have understood him because he felt her relax, just a little.

The air out here was freezing, but he was hardly aware of it. He felt only the vulnerable warmth of her body. He wanted to bring her closer, to wrap his arms around her and protect her from the cold. To protect her from everything.

But she wasn't ready for that yet.

She was still afraid of him. She was afraid of his blood tie to Colin, of what that might mean in a courtroom.

He had so much to tell her first, so many promises to make.

He needed to make her feel safe again.

"Nora, I love you. We'll make this work, I promise. We'll find a way."

She looked hard into his eyes, her own gaze still cautious and afraid. "I need to know, Jack. Are you going to try to take him away from me?"

He shook his head slowly. "Never. How could I? It doesn't matter what the DNA says. You're his mother."

"I've tried to be," she said in a quiet voice. "I couldn't have loved him more, even if he had been my own."

"I know," he said. "Anyone can see that. So stop crying, sweetheart. You have nothing to fear from me. You are his mother, and nothing will ever change that. All I can do is ask if you'll allow me to be his father."

She caught her breath, trying to hold back a sob. "You are his father."

"Not in any way that counts. I need your

permission to become his real father. Will you let me do that? Will you let me become a part of his family? Of your family?"

She nodded. Her lips trembled, but he saw that she was struggling to prevent any more tears from falling.

"Of course I will," she said. "He needs you. When I saw you singing together today, I knew. He doesn't understand it himself yet, but he knows you make him happy. You make him complete."

The enormity of it all swept over him. That spunky, amazing little boy was his own son. And he *needed* Jack.

What if he couldn't fill those needs?

What if, because he knew nothing, absolutely nothing, about being a good father, he ended up disappointing him?

It was damned terrifying.

"I don't know what to do—how to be a father," he said. "You know how rotten my role model was. My own father was just about the worst there is."

"That doesn't matter," she said. "You're nothing like your father, Jack."

"I hope you're right," he said. The confidence he saw in her eyes gave him courage. "Maybe that's a place to begin. I'll give him what I didn't get. I know what I longed for, so I can start there. Bedtime stories and baseball games and laughter and hugs. I'll be there to listen when he's sad, and I'll be there to believe in his dreams."

"Yes," she said. "That's all he needs. Just be there. Just love him."

"I will." Jack pulled Nora closer. "And, if she'll let me, I'll love his mother. I'll make my son's wonderful mother so happy she'll never regret giving me a second chance."

The relief in her face was so bright it seemed to have its own warmth, like a sun inside her.

"Never," she said softly.

"And if you will say you love me, too, Nora, that will be all I need. I'll change. I'll become the best Killian who ever walked on this earth."

She smiled, and a hint of the old, confident Nora peeked through. "According to the folks around here, that wouldn't be very hard."

He grabbed her up and swung her around. He had too much joy to stand still.

"Say it," he demanded, holding her feet just above the ground. "I know you love me. I've never deserved it, but I've always known you did. That's my miracle. That's why I won't be my father."

But she didn't get the chance to answer. Just as she looked up at him, her lips parted, a car came tearing down the drive, honking furiously.

Someone was hanging out of the window, waving and hollering.

Jack set Nora down and moved to stand in front of her. He had no idea who this was, but anyone who drove up to a stranger's house like that on Christmas eve at midnight was either drunk, or crazy, or both.

When the car screeched to a halt just in front of the steps, he finally recognized it. It was Stacy Holtsinger's blue sedan.

Nora raced down the stairs to meet them. "Stacy! Is Colin all right?"

He certainly seemed to be. His was the hollering body hanging out of the passenger's side window. He wiggled himself free and plopped onto the ground without ever opening the door.

"Mom!" He was practically screaming. He clutched a disorderly snarl of paper to his chest. "Mom, I know where the gold is!"

"Keep it down, Sherlock," Stacy said as she got out the other side, much more sedately. But Jack could tell that she, too, was excited. "You're going to wake up the entire city."

"Jack!" Ignoring Stacy, Colin raced up the porch steps, holding out the tangle of papers. "It's so cool! You won't believe it! The answer was here all along! All that digging was just a waste of time. It was in the Christmas song!"

Nora followed, as if they were tethered. Perhaps they were, Jack thought. At the heart.

She bent down and ran her fingers through her son's tousled hair. "Colin, what are you talking about?"

Jack intervened. "Umm—Colin and I have a few things we need to confess to you, too. Apparently Patrick asked Colin to help him try to find the gold. He's been working on it…ummmm…" He looked at Colin. "In his off hours."

Nora stood and gave him a stern look. "His off hours?"

"Mom!" Colin tugged at her sleeve. "You can

lecture us later. Right now we have to go inside and get the gold!"

"He's not kidding," Stacy said as she joined them on the porch. "I know it sounds crazy, but I think the kid has found an honest-to-God clue."

A light went on in one of the windows above them.

"That's one rowdy party you're having down there," Sean said, sticking his head out to grin at them. "How come I wasn't invited?"

Colin craned his neck to see Sean over the upstairs balcony. "Sean! Come down quick! We know where the gold is!"

"You do?" Sean laughed. "Hang on. I'll be right down."

Colin refused to explain anything until he had everyone gathered around. Jack had to laugh at the boy's flair for drama. Colin knew he had the grown-ups' attention, and he planned to milk it.

Jack only hoped that it didn't end in crashing disappointment.

Finally, after what seemed to Colin forever, Sean made it downstairs. He must have known that Stacy was here because, gold or no gold, he'd taken time to brush his hair and splash on some cologne.

When Sean stood next to him, Jack sniffed dramatically and rolled his eyes.

"What?" Sean grinned. "The bottle fell over when I was getting dressed. So what?"

"Hey," Colin said, scowling at the two brothers to hush them up. "Okay. First I'm going to tell you how I figured it out."

He glanced at Stacy. "I mean how *we* figured it out. Stacy helped."

Stacy curtseyed with a smile. "I just figured out how to open the music roll. The genius was all yours, Mr. Holmes."

Colin laughed. "So here's what happened. Mr. Killian gave me this box of his dad's music. He seemed really riled up about it. And when we were alone, he kept trying to say something. It sounded like the word *treasure*."

"You could understand something Patrick said?" Sean sounded incredulous.

"Yeah," Colin insisted, his chin squaring. "If you listen, you can get a lot of the words. He's getting better, whether you guys believe it or not."

Sean glanced at Jack, then subsided. They both knew how Colin clung to the hope that Patrick would recover from this stroke. He didn't seem to recognize that, at ninety-one years old, recovery was a long shot.

"So I started trying to figure out what the music could have to do with the treasure. I tried all kinds of codes and secret messages and invisible ink and stuff like that, but I got nothing. Once, I thought I found a clue in the lyrics, so I went out to Sweet Tides and started digging—"

Nora made a sound, but Jack grabbed her hand and squeezed it reassuringly.

"Later," he promised. She gave him a quick look, but she said nothing else.

"But I still didn't find anything," Colin

continued. "I was pretty discouraged. But then today, when we were singing the song at the nursing home, it began to sound really weird, really messed up. Remember, Jack?"

Jack nodded. "Absolutely. Nearly blew out my eardrums."

"Mr. Killian seemed all upset, and he nearly had a fit until I agreed to take the music home with me again. That's what made me figure out where I'd been making my mistake. You see, I'd been studying the sheet music. But really the clue was here—"

He held up the crazy wad of papers he'd been clutching. "In the roll from the player piano."

"What?" Sean sounded confused. "How?"

For the first time in his whole life, Jack felt a frisson of hope. This actually might be leading somewhere…somewhere besides the usual dead end.

The player-piano roll was about ten inches wide and, once it was unspooled, maybe about seventy-five feet long. Colin gripped one end of it and let the rest fall to the floor.

"I'll show you," he said with a flourish.

He held up the first few inches. "See how there are these little open places, these little rectangles that have been punched out of the paper? That's what makes the notes play. When the right places are cut out, the song sounds right. But if the *wrong* places are cut out…"

He paused for dramatic effect. He fed the paper

through his fingers, searching for the perfect spot. He found it, about halfway through the roll.

"If the wrong pieces are cut out, it's going to sound all messed up and nasty, the way it did today. So I began to wonder, what if someone had cut out the wrong pieces deliberately? What if they did it to leave us a clue?"

They waited, transfixed.

Colin beamed, delighted at the effect he was having on his audience.

"A clue," he said, "like this!"

He lifted the paper and held it up toward the chandelier, so that the bright light from the hundreds of bulbs and crystals shone through the paper.

You couldn't miss it. For a few lines, the punched-out rectangles were sparse, and seemingly random. Then, suddenly, they came close together and clearly spelled out words.

THE GOLD
IS IN
THE ARCH

"Oh, my God," Sean said.

Stacy applauded. Nora was silent, as if she still couldn't believe what was happening.

Jack met Colin's happy smile with one of his own.

"Way to go, kiddo," he said.

"Thanks." Colin dropped the piano roll onto the floor. "Now *you* guys have to do some thinking. Where do you have an arch?"

Jack laughed. He took Colin by the shoulders and turned him around slowly, until he was facing the one and only arch in the entire mansion.

After that it was a free-for-all. With the evidence of the piano roll staring them in the face, no one doubted that the gold had been here once—and much more recently than the Civil War.

But was it here still?

Everyone poked and prodded and knocked and tugged at the bricks, hoping to find something, anything, that would indicate that the gold had not been moved from this resting place.

Jack let Colin sit on his shoulders to explore the highest bricks. Soon Colin would grow too tall, and it wouldn't be possible to do this much longer.

He smiled to himself, realizing how lucky he was that he'd found his son just in time to make this little memory.

"Darn it," Stacy said after about five minutes. "I was so sure it would be here."

"Hey, don't lose hope already," Colin called down from his perch. "Remember what my ring says. Riches go to the faithful!"

Sean had been squatting, working on the bricks nearest the floor, but at that he glanced up, surprise in his eyes.

Jack raised one brow and shrugged. "It's a long story," he said.

Sean's gaze flicked to Colin, then back to Jack. "Can't wait to hear it," he said with a smile.

Jack had been braced for ear-piercing shrieking

and screaming, if anyone should actually get lucky enough to find anything.

But when the miracle happened, it came so quietly he almost missed it.

All he knew was that suddenly, every muscle in Colin's skinny legs went taut.

"Jack," he whispered. "Jack, this one is loose."

"Okay." He held Colin's knees as the boy reached way, way up. "Be cool. Go slowly."

Jack held his breath while Colin dug around. Sure enough, one of the bricks from near the top of the arch came cleanly away in his hands.

The tiny opening was dark and deep. Like many arches of the period, it was actually several bricks thick, so that the feature would fit neatly into the thick walls.

Colin's hands were small, so he worked with excruciating slowness. He handed one brick to Jack, and then another.

"Oh," Colin said, the sound soft and awestruck.

Jack looked up. The chandelier's light finally made its way inside the empty places.

Behind the painted bricks that Colin had removed was another row of bricks.

The only difference was this row was made of gold.

CHAPTER NINETEEN

The Next Year

JACK KILLIAN WAS EXHAUSTED.

Three hours of sleep just wasn't enough, not to face a houseful of people, presents, feasting and general Killian mayhem so early on a cold Christmas morning.

But darn it, the assembly instructions for Colin's bright blue, fourteen-speed bike had been written in some kind of diabolical Martian code. Jack and Sean had still been up, cussing and banging the wrench around, when the grandfather clock in the front hall of Sweet Tides had chimed three.

And then, wouldn't you know it? Jack's head had barely hit the pillow when Virginia Lily Margaret Killian had woken up and started whimpering.

"I'll be fine. You sleep," Nora had whispered, touching his shoulder.

Yeah, right. As if he would dream of passing up the chance to watch his beautiful wife breast-feed their daughter.

Ginny wasn't, to be perfectly honest, as beautiful as her mommy yet, with her scrunched-up red face and her patchy wisps of silky black hair. She was only two months old. But when the baby opened her blue eyes and stared dreamily up at Nora while she nursed, Jack saw what was to come.

She would be lovely and smart and stubborn and sweet. And, if Jack Killian could possibly manage it, she would be the happiest little girl who ever lived.

"Dad, you're zoning out! Come on, open it! It's from Uncle Ethan!"

Jack rallied, blinking away the sleepy haze. Colin had just tossed a present in his lap, a small box covered in shiny blue paper. He peeled away the wrapping.

"Guitar picks?" He grinned up at Ethan. "You sure these aren't for Colin?"

Ethan shook his head. "Nope. They're to go with…" He reached around behind his armchair and pulled out a beautiful honey-pine acoustic guitar. "This! I figured you and Colin could start a band."

Laughing, Jack accepted the guitar and immediately began plunking out a few god-awful chords. Everyone groaned.

"I'm serious," Ethan said, pretending to be offended. "You'll become superstars, and then you can replenish the Killian coffers, which definitely need it, since you were fools enough to give the gold away."

"Not fools," Patrick said carefully. His speech was improving every day, but he still had to work at some sounds. "Smart. The gold was cursed."

Sean, who was sitting next to his grandfather, patted his shoulder approvingly. Then Sean caught Jack's eye and smiled.

They'd spent a whole lot of time trying to decide what to do with the three hundred bars of gold bullion they'd found stashed inside that arch. At first, they'd been caught up with the usual day-dreams—yachts, mansions, trips around the world. Jack wanted rubies and diamonds for Nora. Sean wanted a doctorate for Stacy. They all wanted a college fund for Colin.

But in the end they'd realized they didn't need any of that. They all made decent money in their careers, and Nora had already provided a trust fund for Colin from the sale of Heron Hill.

With the help of Stacy's research, they'd pieced together the full history of the Killian men, and decided that, though there probably was no such thing as a curse, there definitely was such a thing as obsession.

And they didn't want any part of it.

They'd each kept one bar, to make one small dream come true, and they'd given the rest to charity. Everyone involved—Colin, Jack, Sean, Patrick, Nora and Stacy—had each picked their favorite cause, and the money had been divided equally among them.

Ethan, who had returned to Hawthorn Bay so

that he could give away Nora at the wedding, had immediately pronounced it the dumbest move anyone had ever made. But they'd laughed at him, too happy to care what anyone thought.

Maybe the curse was just a myth, but there was no denying that Sweet Tides seemed lighter and healthier since the gold was gone.

Of course, that might have had something to do with the life that filled it to overflowing. Nora and Jack and Colin lived there, and so did Sean and Patrick, and the round-the-clock nurses hired to help Patrick with his therapy.

The walls rang with the noise of a big family, with singing and music and laughter. The kitchen bubbled with Nora's jams. The stables had been remodeled into a duplex that housed both Sean's estate sales and Jack's new law office—all with the unanimous permission of the Hawthorn Bay city council.

Nora fell in love with the gardens, and in the spring she'd coaxed new life out of the old wisteria and jasmine and gardenias. In the summer, the house had exploded with roses.

And in late October, when the first Killian daughter in more than two hundred years had been born, yowling her importance and waving her perfectly formed fingers and toes, even Jack had had to admit that the Killian luck had changed.

Ginny had more presents today than anyone— except maybe Colin, who had definitely cleaned up. Sean had given her a drum set and six sets of earplugs, for when the family couldn't stand the noise. Patrick had given her a framed picture of her great grandmother, for whom she'd been named. Ethan, ever practical, had given her a certificate of deposit.

Colin had taken a long time to decide what his gift to his new baby sister should be. He and Jack had spent hours at the toy store together this past week, but it had been time well spent. Not because the final choice—a musical mobile that twirled pink-spangled ballerinas above Ginny's crib—was so inspired, but because of what Jack had learned by watching his son.

He'd learned that the damage their crazy situation had done to Colin's sense of security had not been permanent. He was going to be okay.

It hadn't been easy, this past year. Colin had been shocked when he'd learned the truth about his biological parents. He'd been ready for a new father—but the idea that Nora was not his "real" mother had unsettled him terribly.

Nora had been amazing, so patient with the boy, even through his tears and his tempers. She understood why Colin felt frightened, and she never pushed him. She just stood by, ready to resume their intimacy whenever he was.

Over the months, things had gradually calmed down. But still, Jack had secretly worried. Would the trauma leave permanent scars? Would it affect Colin's ability to trust? To love?

And would he resent the little baby girl whose

entrance into the Killian fold was so uncompli-
cated? Would he envy Ginny's pure blood connection to Nora, and feel robbed of his mother even
more?

But the tender care Colin had given the choice
of Ginny's Christmas present, and the excitement
with which he anticipated the family's holiday get-
together had eased Jack's mind. Nora's whole-
hearted loving had worked its magic once again.
This was a little boy who knew he was adored.

Jack had come home that night and told Nora all
about it. For the first time since she'd told Colin the
truth, she'd allowed herself the luxury of tears.

"Well, Daddy," she said now with a playful smile.
"Don't you have anything for your little girl?"

Jack reached into his pocket and took out a small
blue velvet box. He handed it to his wife, stealing
a small kiss as he bent toward her. She smelled of
baby powder.

Nora opened the present for the baby, who was
sound asleep. Ginny seemed to have her rhythm down
pat. Nap peacefully when the grown-ups were awake,
scream bloody murder when they were trying to
sleep.

It was a tiny golden unicorn on a thin gold chain,
made from the one bar Jack had kept for himself.

Nora lifted the necklace out of the box. "Oh,"
she said, obviously enchanted. "It's beautiful."

He stroked his daughter's rose-petal cheek with
the back of his index finger. "I hope she'll like it.
Her grandmother loved unicorns."

Funny. Now that he had a daughter, Bridey's glass unicorn collection didn't seem silly at all.

He hoped Ginny loved things like that, things that stood for beauty and hope and mystery and dreams that don't ever die even though they don't ever come true.

After all the presents were open, and a heap of colorful paper and bows stood two-feet deep on the carpet, Colin asked for permission to leave.

He had his new video games to play, new sneakers to try on, a new MP3 player to load up. But what he wanted to do first of all was ride his bike, which had been the hit of the morning.

He raced out the minute he was released.

Laughing, and stepping over boxes and bows, everyone else moved the party into the kitchen, so that they could get the feast going.

Jack and Nora got there first. Ethan was bringing Ginny's basket, and he dawdled, talking baby talk to her in a ridiculously stilted way.

"That man needs a kid of his own," Jack said.

Nora laughed. "You're not going to be one of those guys, are you? Now that you've discovered the joys of fatherhood, you can't wait to recruit everyone else into your new club?"

"You bet I am," he said, unrepentant. He kissed her on the nose. "I think I'll start with Sean. Heck, if Stacy hadn't gone off to North Carolina to get her PhD, I might have had a nephew on the way by now."

"Or niece," Nora reminded him. "But I think

you're wrong about that. Sean is absolutely not ready to settle down."

She glanced toward the drawing room, where Sean lingered with Patrick and the extremely pretty young nurse.

"Stacy hasn't been gone six months," Nora said. "And he's already flirting with every female who walks through the door."

Jack heard the young woman giggle as they strolled toward the kitchen. At one of Sean's favorite stock jokes, no doubt. Sean did love a fresh audience for his old routines.

Jack chuckled. "Okay. You're right. He's going to need some more work before he gets to join the club."

"What club?" Sean came through the doorway. The nurse was right behind, still smiling as she rolled Patrick along.

Jack picked up a sweet potato and tossed it at his brother. "Potato Peelers Anonymous," he said.

Sean caught it one-handed. "Not what I'd hoped, but okay. I'm in."

Jack tossed him another. "Of course you're in. You know the rules. If you plan to eat, you'd better plan to peel."

With everyone pitching in, the work went fast. They finally got everything into the oven and sat down for a few minutes of rest before the next wave of duties.

Patrick had dozed off, and Jack, who felt about ninety-one years old himself right this minute, wondered if he might get a chance to do the same.

But the kitchen door swung open with a loud bang, and Colin came tearing in. He was absolutely filthy, his hair standing out in all directions, and smears of dirt on both cheeks.

He was holding up something long and white that looked a little like...

"Is that a *bone?*" Nora looked horrified.

"Yep!" Colin waved it around triumphantly, as if he'd done something wonderful. Little clumps of dirt fell from the white stick as it flew.

Nora held out her hand. "Get that thing away from the food! In fact, get it out of the house, period."

"I can't, Mom," Colin said apologetically. "I've got to investigate it."

"What?"

"Investigate it. You know, find out whose bone it is, and then see if I can figure out who killed them. I'd better call Brad. I'll bet there are millions of old bones on this property. I'll just have to figure out where to look."

Nora put her head in her hands.

Sean and Jack started laughing.

Just in time to catch Colin's last statement, Ethan wandered in, dangling Ginny's basket from one hand.

"That's not a human bone," he said, in his most unequivocal doctor's voice. "That's the thigh bone from some small animal. Probably a dog."

"No way." Colin stared at Ethan, then stared at the bone. "How can you be so sure?"

"I know bones," Ethan said. He picked up a

deviled egg, stuffed it into his mouth all in one piece and spoke around it. "Definitely not human."

Colin scowled ferociously. At that moment, he looked exactly like his great grandfather.

Jack looked at Patrick, to see if he'd noticed. He had. Jack and Patrick exchanged a smile and a satisfied wink.

Colin turned to Jack, appealing the unwelcome verdict. "Dad? Is he right?"

Jack couldn't help it. It still gave him a little electric thrill every time the boy called him *Dad*.

"Of course he's right," Jack said. "Uncle Ethan knows his bones."

Colin's face fell.

"Rats." He stuck the bone in the hip pocket of his jeans and headed back out the door.

In the silence left behind, Sean began to chuckle softly. Jack joined him, then Patrick. Pretty soon the kitchen was ringing with laughter.

"It's not funny," Nora said, wiping her eyes. "Ever since he found the gold, he thinks he's Indiana Jones. He's going to keep digging and hunting, and God knows what he'll find next."

"Maybe a human skull," Ethan said around another deviled egg. "With a mysterious bullet hole between the eyes."

"Or a secret document proving that Killians were British double agents during the Revolutionary War," Sean suggested, a wicked light in his eyes.

"Gentlemen!" Nora groaned. "Please. Not another Killian curse."

Jack reached across the table and took her hand.

"Don't worry, sweetheart," he said. "We've got what it takes to get rid of any curse that comes our way."

"Oh, yeah?" She smiled at him. He loved that about her. Whenever he touched her, she smiled, as if it were not a choice but a reflex. "And what exactly do we have that is so powerful?"

He brought her palm to his lips and kissed it.

"We have each other."

New York Times *bestselling author
Linda Lael Miller is back with a new romance
featuring the heartwarming McKettrick family
from Silhouette Special Edition.*

*SIERRA'S HOMECOMING
by Linda Lael Miller*

*On sale December 2006,
wherever books are sold.*

Turn the page for a sneak preview!

Soft, smoky music poured into the room.

The next thing she knew, Sierra was in Travis's arms, close against that chest she'd admired earlier, and they were slow dancing.

Why didn't she pull away?

"Relax," he said. His breath was warm in her hair.

She giggled, more nervous than amused. What was the matter with her? She was attracted to Travis, had been from the first, and he was clearly attracted to her. They were both adults. Why not enjoy a little slow dancing in a ranch-house kitchen?

Because slow dancing led to other things. She took a step back and felt the counter flush against her lower back. Travis naturally came with her, since they were holding hands and he had one arm around her waist.

Simple physics.

Then he kissed her.

Physics again—this time, not so simple.

"Yikes," she said, when their mouths parted.

He grinned. "Nobody's ever said that after I kissed them."

She felt the heat and substance of his body pressed against hers. "It's going to happen, isn't it?" she heard herself whisper.

"Yep," Travis answered.

"But not tonight," Sierra said on a sigh.

"Probably not," Travis agreed.

"When, then?"

He chuckled, gave her a slow, nibbling kiss. "Tomorrow morning," he said. "After you drop Liam off at school."

"Isn't that…a little…soon?"

"Not soon enough," Travis answered, his voice husky. "Not nearly soon enough."

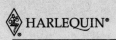

HARLEQUIN®

American **ROMANCE**®

IS PROUD TO PRESENT

COWBOY VET
by Pamela Britton

Jessie Monroe is the last person on earth
Rand Sheppard wants to rely on, but he needs
a veterinary technician—yesterday—and she's the
only one for hire. It turns out the woman who
destroyed his cousin's life isn't who Rand thought
she was. And now she's all he can think about!

"Pamela Britton writes the kind of
wonderfully romantic, sexy, witty romance
that readers dream of discovering
when they go into a bookstore."

—*New York Times* bestselling author
Jayne Ann Krentz

Cowboy Vet *is available from
Harlequin American Romance in December 2006.*

Silhouette
Desire

USA TODAY bestselling author

BARBARA McCAULEY

continues her award-winning series

S E C R E T S !

**A NEW BLACKHAWK FAMILY
HAS BEEN DISCOVERED...
AND THE SCANDALS ARE SET TO FLY!**

She touched him once and now
Alaina Blackhawk is certain horse rancher
DJ Bradshaw will be her first lover. But will
the millionaire Texan allow her to leave
once he makes her his own?

Blackhawk's Bond

On sale December 2006 (SD #1766)

Available at your favorite retail outlet.

HARLEQUIN® *Romance*®

**From the Heart.
For the Heart.**

Get swept away into the Outback
with two of Harlequin Romance's
top authors.

Coming in December...

Claiming the
Cattleman's Heart
BY BARBARA HANNAY

And in January don't miss...

Outback Man Seeks Wife
BY MARGARET WAY